THE DEAD DON'T WAIT

THE DEAD DON'T WAIT

Michael Jecks

CRÈME de la CRIME

This first world edition published 2019
in Great Britain and the USA by
Crème de la Crime an imprint of
SEVERN HOUSE PUBLISHERS LTD of
Eardley House, 4 Uxbridge Street, London W8 7SY.
Trade paperback edition first published
in Great Britain and the USA 2020 by
SEVERN HOUSE PUBLISHERS LTD.

British Library Cataloguing in Publication Data
A CIP catalogue record for this title is available from the British Library.

ISBN-13: 978-1-78029-120-8 (cased)
ISBN-13: 978-1-78029-631-9 (trade paper)
ISBN-13: 978-1-4483-0324-3 (e-book)

All Severn House titles are printed on acid-free paper.

Severn House Publishers support the Forest Stewardship Council™ [FSC™],
the leading international forest certification organisation.
All our titles that are printed on FSC certified paper carry the FSC logo.

MIX
Paper from
responsible sources
FSC® C013056

Typeset by Palimpsest Book Production Ltd.,
Falkirk, Stirlingshire, Scotland.
Printed and bound in Great Britain by
TJ International, Padstow, Cornwall.

This is for Steve Barge with thanks!

ONE

April 1555
London

There are times in a man's life when he has to accept that he might have made an error.

This was one of those times.

If you have ever found yourself staring down the barrel of a pistol, you will know that the thing looks big enough to dive into. This one was enormous – seriously, it looked as though my thumb would slip in without touching the sides, and I was appalled to think what a slug of lead that size might do to me. I had only recently been forced to work with a gun like this, a wheel-lock. Truth be told, I had taken to carrying it around with me – a fellow in my line of work cannot afford to be without a means of protection, after all – and I knew what damage such a gun can do to a man. I was highly unwilling to be exposed to this one.

At that moment, the main thing that took my interest was the gun itself. Everything else around me took second place as far as I was concerned, and when the woman sharing my bed clutched at my arm, I yelped in surprise. I had forgotten she was there. I confess that my first thought, on being reminded, was that I might swing her before me and protect myself – but, slim as she was, she was heavier than I could manage while lying in the bed. It was nothing to do with morals or politeness; I simply didn't think I could wrestle her into the bullet's path from my recumbent position.

Yes, I was in bed. Not my own, I should say. I was in a pleasant chamber in a house in Pope's Lane, having enjoyed a thoroughly pleasant time with this lusty wench in a tavern near St Paul's, which led to her suggesting that we repair to her rooms to complete our evening to mutual satisfaction with a saucy entanglement. I was very content to agree.

'Who the hell are you?' I demanded, trying to feign righteous anger. It made me sound like an adolescent with a broken
voice.

'I am her husband, and you are in my bed!' he snarled.

My day had started to go wrong from the moment I rose
from my bed. I stubbed my toe and was set to hopping about
the bedchamber, clutching my poor foot and swearing at the
excruciating pain. Shortly afterwards, while washing my face,
fate conspired to upset the dish, hurling water all over me and
the floor, the bowl landing on the same injured toe and making
me hop about in agony once more until I tripped over a stool
and fell headlong.

Raphe, my peculiarly incompetent manservant, appeared to
smile at my discomfort as I carefully descended my staircase.
I dislike the fellow, but he was set in my household by my
master, John Blount, and I do not consider it likely that my
dismissing Raphe would be well received. I believe the lad to
be related to Blount, and that he was sent to serve me either
from despair at the fellow's inability to find any suitable
employment of his own, or because he was to spy on me – I
did not know which it was, but I could guess there was a good
admixture of both.

My servant added his own peculiar brand of idiocy that
morning when he managed to spill a cup of wine over my
hosen while I broke my fast at table. I had been about to go
out, and my leggings were particularly fine, setting off my
calves to good effect. They matched my new jacket, which
was green with red piping, and I had a cloak of emerald with
a lining of red silk. Topped with my hat, which had a scarlet
feather in the band, I was a figure of great style. Those who
knew me at the Boar or the Pheasant Without were always
complimenting me on my elegance. In short, I was a man
known for my effortless style. Now my green leggings were
sent a dirgeful brown with the red wine he had sent over me.

I was furious. Raphe received a cuff about the head that
would have rattled his brains, had he possessed any, and I had
to dress again, this time in my second-best hosen and jacket
of a pleasing faun, which once had been first quality, but now

bore the marks of a dozen unfortunate accidents. Still, they were at least dry.

As I walked from my door, I instructed the fool to have my clothing cleaned before I returned, or I would colour my hosen with more red, but this time it would be his gore. He gave me that sneering smile that showed his disdain for me, and I slammed my way to the taverns with my companions.

At noon I was to be found at the Boar, drinking with some pleasant cock-robins at the back. The fellows were all keen to try their luck, and so, after feeding, I and the others made our way to an alehouse nearby, where we were entertained by a series of cock fights. The money flowed from one man to another, and a riotous, fun afternoon was enjoyed by us all. We had a few drinks, and then some more, but at the end of two hours together, many of us had lost the funds we were willing to risk, while others had been tempted by the women offering themselves for a quick alley-fumble and had already departed. I took my leave too, happily enough, but as I was on my way, I happened to meet Arch and Hamon.

These two are well known in certain parts of London. If there is a game of chance, they will be involved, be it dice, cocks, dog fighting, or even betting which rain drop will run fastest down a window pane. And often they will make loans to those who lose, so that they can throw themselves further into the mire. And Arch was particularly keen to extract all his debts in full.

I was walking past them when a hound saw a cat who, deciding that he had already risked too many lives in his time, disappeared like a streak of black-and-white lightning up a nearby tree, from where he hissed and spat at the hound, who stood on his hind legs and barked and snarled for all he was worth.

'That cat would've been eaten alive if 'e'd had to run further,' a voice at my side said.

It was Arch, an unenticing sight at the best of times.

'Yes, very likely,' I said.

'You think I'm wrong?'

'No, not at all.'

'Yes, you do, don't you? You think the cat was fast enough to flee, don't you?'

'I wouldn't know.'

'Well, 'ere's five shillin's says 'e would.'

'I have no need of gambling.'

'You callin' me a liar, then?'

'No!' I protested. 'But I have no money, and I don't wish to gamble with you.'

'I'm not good enough, you mean? 'Ere, 'Am, 'e says I'm not good enough to gamble with!'

A rumble at my side told me that Hamon had joined us. I could have cursed my luck. Hamon had a fearsome habit of getting into fights, his ginger hair a warning about his peppery spirit, while Arch was no less choleric, for all that he smiled all the while.

'I cannot place a wager. I have no money,' I said, thinking that would save me.

Arch's face lit up. 'I can 'elp you there. I'll lend you the stake, and you pay me back when you 'ave the dibs.'

'No, seriously, I . . .'

Of course, it was no good. In a trice, Hamon had reached up and grabbed the cat, throwing him into a sack, while Arch and another fellow threw a coat over the hound and wrestled him away. They held him, still snarling, while Hamon dropped the sack in the road. A hideous shrieking and yowling could be heard. Arch looked over at Hamon, and I saw some silent communication pass between them. Then Hamon released the cat, and as he did so, Arch let slip the hound, who took three bounds, scarcely believing his luck, since the cat was at the moment expounding upon his extreme displeasure at having been bundled into the sack. There was a vicious spitting and then a startled yowl, and a crunch as the hound's jaws snapped over his spine.

'That will be ten shillin's you owe us,' Arch said. And then he said a lot more, all about debts that should be paid as soon as possible. I gave him one of my false names and hurried away.

I was already half seas over after my drinking, but not so far gone that I would give out my real name or address to a fellow such as Arch.

So you can see, when I discovered that a man with the looks and intelligence of a gorilla was pointing a pistol at me for galloping his wife, it seemed to me to be only the capping of my misfortune.

Of course, I was not to know that this was not the cap, but only the beginning.

That evening had begun so pleasantly, too. I had met Mistress Catherine at the Cheshire Cheese. She was sitting in a corner and trying to repel the advances of a pair of swine-drunk oafs.

'Leave us,' I said firmly, crossing to her side.

'Go swive a goat,' one said.

He looked so drunk that he could barely keep both eyes open, so I took the risk of hauling him from his seat by grabbing his ankles and pulling. He was too far gone to defend himself, and slid from the bench, his head bumping on the floor as he went. Once on the floor, he closed his eyes with every sign of comfort and began to snore. His companion took the view that I must be some form of Hercules, and scurried away without a backward glance.

'Thank you, master,' she said nervously, as though she was alarmed as much by me as the two drunks.

'There is only one way to deal with brutes like them. A strong hand and a firm determination,' I said. 'Are you new to London, maid?'

'Yes. I have only been here a few hours,' she said, and there was a faint note of anxiety in her voice. Her accent was plainly not from the city, but from the east, if I was a judge.

'Where are you from?'

She didn't answer that, but looked about the room with trepidation.

Well, when I had been a cut-purse, I had always enjoyed the process of putting my gulls at ease, and with this one it took a little longer, but soon she and I were engaged in wordplay of the most promiscuous kind, Cat complimenting me on my new codpiece, and I staring at the assets that were scarce restrained by the thin material of her blouse. There was not as much as I would usually hope for, but a good handful that would make a reasonable pillow, so I thought. For all her slenderness, she had a wit and ready enthusiasm that was most appealing. Her tongue was by turns sharp and tender, and I was soon given to understand that she would happily consider a bout in the lists of lechery.

It was when Arch and Hamon arrived that I decided it was a good time to leave; I had no wish to be discovered by either so soon after the hound and the cat. I saw them walk through the door and over to a table at the farther side of the chamber. The fact that I owed Arch ten shillings over the 'gambling debt' was potentially enough to make him reach for his dagger rather than his fists. Except it was no gamble. He had rooked me.

Ten bob was a mere trifle to a man like me, of course, with my advantages, but a rich man wouldn't remain rich, were he to give away money unnecessarily. Besides, I had the impression that Cat was in a hurry, and since I was eager as well, leaving suited me fine.

London, so it is said, is a place where a man can never grow bored. I would wholeheartedly agree with that. Tedium was never a part of my life. But I would prefer a little of it, in preference to the regular moments of terror that plagued me. Arch and Hamon were more than capable of making my life very exciting indeed – if only briefly.

I was fortunate, so I thought; neither of the two sons of vixens appeared to notice me, sitting in the farthest corner as I was, so I threw myself over my companion, making her squeak with feigned alarm.

'Fie! You want to cover me here?' she giggled. 'I am not a draggle-tail to be serviced in a tavern. Come, my fellow. You must take me to a bed first. Then we shall see whether you deserve a reward of some sort!'

'To my home? I doubt I can make it that far,' I said with a leer.

'Well, master, if you are so hasty and incapable of staying the distance, perhaps I should find a man with more stamina? A woman like me needs time to be satisfied. I don't want a man who'll be spent in a moment!'

'I'll be happy in your service, maid,' I said with a quick leer.

'So long as your service is matched by your stamina,' she said tartly.

'Come with me and I shall gladly demonstrate,' I said.

I rose, carefully keeping my hat's brim towards Hamon and Arch, leading her behind me, where she would conceal me from their gaze. Although there were many men in the Cheese at that time, we made our way quickly enough from the bar and were soon in the road, where Mistress Cat grappled again, but with little urgency. She was anticipating a wrestle as keenly as I, but she would not agree to a trembler against an alley wall. I had already asked. No, she wanted a warm bed with a lighted fire, so we broke off the engagement and made our way to a house in Pope's Lane, where she had a key.

And all was going swimmingly, until this great brute appeared with his cannon.

You will perhaps understand me when I say that I was rather reluctant at this point to go into details with the man. Truth be told, I was more than a little befuddled from wine, and being interrupted early on in a grapple with a cheerful maid by what looked like a gorilla with a gun was enough to leave me confused.

He was one of those fellows who seem to have been born with too much hair. He had a shaggy brown thatching that ran down the sides of his head and somewhere became a beard. A fringe smothered his brow so heavily that he was forced to keep pushing it from his face, which was fixed into a scowl of such ferocity that it looked as though his brows had been bunched together like a fist of rage.

There was one other aspect that drew my attention, of course, and that was the size and number of muscles that rippled up and down his arms as he looked from me to my bedmate and back. He wore a thin linen tabard without sleeves, and his arms were distinctly impressive in a way that was not appealing at this moment.

'Perhaps I should leave you both. I am sure . . .'

The gun moved back in my direction. I took the hint and was silent, but a doubt was raised in my mind as I stared.

Despairingly, the woman clutched at me. I was irritated

by that. Cat should have been able to appreciate that this
was a rather serious moment in both of our lives, which were
likely, all things considered, to be curtailed. I wasn't ready
for death yet.

'Who are you?' the man demanded. His eye moved to my
jack and clothing, which had been dropped on the floor near
the bed.

'I am called Hugh Somerville,' I said.

He sneered at that. 'What's your real name?'

I quickly ran through some of the alternative names that I
had used in the past, discarding those that had been stained
with arrests or accusations, and returned to one that I felt was
safe enough. 'Peter of Shoreditch.'

'Well, Peter of Shoreditch, you've been swiving my wife,
and you'll have to pay for it.'

'Don't, Henry! He's not worth it! Don't kill us! I'll make
it up to you, honest I will.'

'Too late, slut! You've dragged your backside past a gull
once too often. I knew you were steeped in treachery, but to
take an old fool like this – this is an insult too far. You'll both
die!'

'Old fool?' I repeated with some asperity.

'No, Henry! I won't do it again, Henry,' she protested, and
as he pointed his gun's barrel at her, something clicked in my
head.

You see, before I became a professional assassin – or, at
least, a professional contractor of assassinations – I had a
moderately successful career as a pickpocket. In those happy
days, I lived with other disreputable characters in a number
of properties of greater or lesser elegance, and I had come to
know experts of lock-picking and gambling, and cheats of all
stripes and colours. There were many women who would sell
their bodies, and some who would pretend to, before practising
their best purse-diving and bolting.

'Why should he live? He's taken advantage of my wife!'

'Oh, Henry, please, don't do anything rash!'

'I'll make him pay!'

'Oh, Henry, think of the children!'

And although many of those same women would have

convinced on the stage, this one – well, she was a poor actress.

I pushed Cat gently from me and bent to pull on my hosen, setting my codpiece in place. 'I am sorry, but if I want to watch play-acting, I will go to a good inn and watch it there with a quart of ale in my hand.'

'You think I'm play-acting?' the man said, the barrel turning to me once more.

'No, I don't think it; I know it. In the first place, your wife was too quick, too keen to take advantage of me. And while I know I am better-looking than most, I feel sure that her eyes were more fixed on my purse than my cods,' I said, 'and in the second, your story is not convincing.'

'What?' the man said. His tone was threatening, and the barrel was a hideous sight. I peered at it and then pressed on.

'If you wish to continue with this line of work, I really must recommend that you have your woman instructed in how better to show alarm. Her feigned concern really will not do,' I said.

'What do you mean?' she said, a scowl darkening her pretty features. She pulled away from me, kneeling at my side, long dark hair all awry and not covering her modesty. She was wearing a shift against the chill of the evening, but it was ancient and thin, and I could see the entrancing figure beneath. I tried not to be distracted by it.

'Cat, if you wish to entrap a man, you need to show genuine fear for your own safety, not for his. After all, a jealous husband would be likely to slaughter you both when he found the two of you in his bed, would he not? And for all that your partner here is a strong, bold-looking companion, I can see and hear little of the true rage in his voice that a man would exhibit on finding his wife enwrapped about her swain. My apologies, but a husband in such a moment would be less likely to speak to her and threaten the ravisher, and more likely to slaughter them both. And he would not do it with a firearm, but with a club, knife or anything else that might come to hand speedily and with ease. A man in the throes of jealous, righteous rage doesn't pause to discuss the adulterer's offences, but simply leaps in and punishes both his wife and her love-lad.'

'Damn your eyes!' the man said, and the gun barrel was thrust towards me.

You can believe me or not, but I merely smiled at him.

'Leave it, Henry,' Cat said. She had her head tilted as she surveyed me. 'What should we do, then?'

'You did quite well,' I said. I was pulling my shirt over my head now. 'Your man's apparent rage was well feigned, but slow, and your snaring of your gull was most efficient, but you needs must think of your reaction when your man appears.'

'It worked well enough so far!' she said, and she sounded hurt. 'I got you here, didn't I?'

'Your attractions did,' I said, glancing at the body semi-concealed by her shift. She pulled the edges about her and glared at me. I continued, 'Perhaps you need to think of a new patter. It sounds contrived, Cat. As though you have learned the words, but not the emotion. You need to think up a different line, something that will sound fresh and new.'

Henry was scowling now, but he had the appearance of an offended man rather than an angry one. 'You mean we've wasted all this time and you . . .'

'I am not fearful, no.'

'We could still rob you.'

I stared at him, and for the first time I realized he was a little older than me. Cat was herself about two and twenty, I guessed, the same as me, but he looked to be three years our senior. There was another difference between the two: *she* was delightful.

Her hair was as black as a raven's wing, and now that it was released, it curled about her shoulders like an inky water-fall. It framed an oval face with cheekbones that would have looked good on a Spanish princess. I may, like all natural Englishmen, dislike the Spanish for their arrogance and greed, but no man could deny that their women have great beauty. Cat's own face was so pale that it had an almost transparent quality. Usually, I prefer women who have more colour to them – blondes with skin that has been lightly bronzed, or auburn-haired harpies with freckles and cheeks the colour of damask – but I confess Cat was the sort of woman who could entrance with a glance. Her mouth and eyes were, if not already doing so, always on the verge of smiling. Hers was the sort of face next to which a man could wake up every day for the rest of his life and feel honoured.

Which is why I found it hard to understand what she was doing with the gorilla.

'No,' I said. 'You can't just rob me.' I pulled on my jacket, feeling the comforting weight again.

Henry was a dolt. A clod of the first water. He may have been a quarter of a century in age, but he had the look of an apprentice who had found his vocation by tripping over it, more than by dint of any effort. His dark eyes were suspicious as he stood glaring, his gaze moving from Cat to me and back, with an air of offended pride, like a child who has been thrashed for another's offence, and his mouth moved like a landed fish gasping on the deck. 'What, you think you can protect yourself against this?' he demanded, and thrust the gun at me.

I put my left forefinger on to the very end of the barrel and pushed it aside. He glared at me. When he tried to grab my hand and move it away, I pulled out my own handgun and pushed the barrel into his cheek.

'What are you doing?' he said.

'I am showing you what a real pistol looks like. Because yours is a pale imitation, Henry. It isn't real, and it won't fire. Whereas this thing most certainly will. In other words, step back and don't act like a lunatic, you great lummox.'

'Let it go, Henry,' the woman sighed. 'He's beaten us.'

Henry groaned, and the gun in his hand fell to his side. 'What do you mean, it's not real?' he said in hurt tones. 'I paid good money for that.'

'They saw you coming, then,' I said. I pulled the dog from the wheel to make my gun safe and thrust it into my belt. 'You have a nice idea for a scam; I'll give you both that. All you need to do is make it a little more believable. More panic on your part, Cat, and, Henry, you need to make it sound like you really believe that she's done something. You didn't convince me, and you won't convince others.'

'It'd work with others,' Henry said grumpily.

'Not, I'll wager, in London. Folk are more suspicious here. And now I will be off.'

I stood. Cat was eyeing me suspiciously, head set slightly to one side. I admit, I preferred to see her with the half-smile on her face.

'How do you know so much?' she said.

'I have lived in London most of my life,' I lied. I had only been living here for the last few years. I had been born in Whitstable, and when my mother died, I became lackey and slave to my father, who was more interested in the contents of a cup of ale than me. It was good to come here and be free of him.

'You could teach us a lot.'

'If I wished, no doubt. But I have better things to be doing, I am afraid, Cat. You must shift for yourselves.'

She lithely climbed from the bed and made her way to me, the thin linen of her tunic falling open to show the swelling of her breast. 'I could make you feel it was worthwhile, if you helped us.'

'What? Oh, no. You're not going to lie with him just so he can tell you a load of . . .'

'Henry, be still,' she said. She was standing before me now, her back to Henry, and her eyes delicately dropped to my cods before she looked up again, and now she raised an eyebrow. The offer was clear enough.

'Just to tell you a little about the city?'

'Yes. Just to help us a little.'

I considered. There was no doubt that she was a pretty little piece, and there would be some satisfaction in having my way with her against the will of her own husband. Not that Henry would be difficult as an amorous antagonist; I would surely be able to entice her away from him with my charms and money. Perhaps holding a few little engagements with her, I might be able to get further than I had this evening. If the benighted Henry had only given me another few minutes . . . but there was no point weeping over lost opportunities. Far better to make an assignation for later.

Thus it was that I arranged to see her the following day, at the Cheshire Cheese again, where I hoped to be able to arrange for a quiet, snug little chamber where we might discuss a number of topics and I might give her a practical demonstration of my own qualities.

I was not to know that I would not be able to honour the arrangement.

Leaving the house, I stood a moment or two in the street, reflecting. It was tempting to propose that we might immediately move to discussing their predicament and other possibilities, ideally while sending Henry out on a wild goose chase, but I felt it would be safer to leave the two together, in order that she might persuade him of the merits of learning from me.

I strolled eastwards, along Pope's Lane, past St Agnes, then down past St Vedast to Westcheap, and thence turned towards my own house, which lay just off Alegatestrete. It was a pleasant abode, with a goodly sized hall, parlour, buttery and pantry, a small room upstairs next to my bedchamber, in which I kept my money box, and a kitchen that a cook might make good use of. However, I had no cook. Instead, I relied on the less-than-incompetent servant who stood as butler and cook: Raphe, the whining scoundrel whose sole strengths lay in his ability to throw wine over my best hosen and disappear whenever there was work to be done. I would have to dispose of him somehow. As things stood, his only other skill being an apparently rapacious appetite for my meat and wine, he was costing me too much to justify his lack of effort on my behalf. However, casting him from my door might prove difficult, bearing in mind he was related to my own master. Throwing him out might have complications.

It was while I was considering this that I heard a loud 'Hoi!' from behind me.

This was just as the light had fled the city, and I was startled by the call. After all, a man is always in danger in London, and never more so than at night. I reached under my jacket for my handgun, catching the dog in my shirt as I pulled it free, and I was attempting to extricate myself when the man appeared from the shadows, two others at his side.

'Master Blackjack, I want a word with you.'

'I am otherwise engaged,' I said, with a slight bow to indicate that I was a man of quality, not a mere 'Hey, you!' to be stopped in the street.

'You are now,' the man said, and that was when I noticed his staff of office. 'You are wanted for murder, my bully boy!'

'Murder?'

Now, I have had my fair share of arrests over the years, and generally I have not enjoyed them. Today, after my frustration with Cat, the damage done to my breeches and my gambling losses, I was not in the mood for another. In the past, of course, I would merely have submitted, were there no escape in sight. I was young enough in those days to leap up like a deer and spring into the middle distance before the average tipstaff realized I was gone. I imagine a few of them saw little more than a shimmer in the air, which faded like dissipating mist before their eyes, while I set off at speed.

But that was before I became a man of quality. Now I had a house, good clothes and regular meals. I was not content to be berated by an officer in the street, and I made that clear to him.

'Then you'd best let us inside, hey?'

This was from somewhere near my left ear and was so loud that I felt sure my ear would never stop ringing. I sprang round, clapping a hand over it, and found myself looking up into a beaming, bearded face.

'Who are you?' I asked weakly.

'Me? I'm Sir Richard of Bath, sir,' said the fellow, and I felt myself rocked back on my feet by the blast. His voice was so loud, it was like hearing the crack of doom pronouncing, and it was unpleasant to be only inches from it. When he spoke, birds stopped tweeting, and dogs stopped barking to slouch away, whimpering.

You see, it wasn't just how loud he was; it was the mere fact of his presence. It was like standing before a gale and listening to a message on the wind. He was huge. I swear his chest and belly together were like a barrel, and I had the distinct impression that were I to attempt to punch his stomach, it would hurt as much as striking an oaken stave with my fist.

For all that, he did not look a dangerous man. He had kindly blue eyes that twinkled, more wrinkles than a mastiff, and his beard looked as if it had never come in contact with a comb. It was gingerish, shot through with threads of silver, and hung halfway down his breast in a thoroughly unfashionable manner. He was plainly some yokel knight who had come to the city to see the sights. Still, he was deafening.

'Who?' I said dully.

'The Coroner for this ward. Come, man, let us in and we can tell you what the matter is, without disturbing yer neighbours, hey?'

I felt bewildered, but did as he asked, and when I stood aside to let him pass, he gave a cheery chuckle and waved me in before him, as though I might have bolted, had I the chance. It was damned disrespectful and proved that he was not as dim as most rural knights. I was about to make a pointed comment when I heard a strange sound from inside. It was a dog barking. I don't have a dog.

'Raphe!' I shouted as I entered. 'Bring wine! And what is that noise?'

The boy would usually be sitting in the kitchen with a flagon of my best sitting beside him, if I knew my servant at all, and I knew him all too well now. But what he was doing with a four-legged flea-farm, I had no idea.

His head appeared around the doorway. 'What?'

'What are you doing with a brute? Are you turned dog-muffler?'

But he made no comment as to whether he sought to flay the animal to sell the skin. He took one look at Sir Richard and hurried out of sight.

'Well?' I demanded as I walked into my hall and took my place before the fire, warming my backside. 'What the devil is this about?'

The man who called himself the Coroner, still smiling broadly, walked to my favourite chair and plumped down into it with a sigh such as Bacchus might have given after a gallon of the best. 'Ah, that's good, master. You are, I believe, Master Jack Blackjack?'

'Yes, servant to John Blount and, through him, Sir Thomas Parry. What of it?'

'Ah, you see, there has been a murder, master. Very sad, very sad. And there've been accusations laid at your door.'

'Mine?' I said. 'Who dares accuse me?' In the last months I had been hired as assassin to Master John Blount, a professional position to which I was less than enthusiastic to be wedded, but which had compensations, such as this house, my clothes, my wine and food. It paid very well, as my little strongbox upstairs could attest. In recent weeks I had been commissioned to remove certain two-legged impediments to the plans of Master Parry and Master Blount, and although I had not completed the commissions myself – instead, I had taken the opportunity to subcontract them – still, the knight's announcement shook me. It made me feel weak, and I slumped on to a seat and made a show of clearing my throat. One of my supposed killings had come back to haunt me, clearly. 'Murder?' I tried again. 'Who could you mean? Who has died?'

'The sad truth is he was a priest. Leaves a wife and five children.'

'That is sad . . .' I said no more, but he and I both knew the fact of it. The Queen, God bless her, had decided early on in her reign that the priests who had been forced to give up their Catholic faith under Good King Henry, God bless his memory, and then Edward, his son, had all been told to give up their new faith and return to the fold, as it were. Those who had taken advantage of the new religion to marry the women with whom they had already been sharing their beds, begging forgiveness from God each Sunday, were now told to set the women aside and leave them. The alternative was to keep the women but lose their benefices. And unlike when King Henry had dragged the monks and abbots from their homes so that they could be torn down or sold on, giving them generous pensions in many cases, the Queen had resolved that those who refused her kind offer were to be ejected from their livings. They could keep wife and children or their incomes. Not both. 'What has this dead priest to do with me?'

'His servant said that ye were responsible.'

I gaped. 'Who? Who is this servant? Who is the man who's died?'

'As to that, who d'you think?'

I racked my brains, but I was no closer to a solution. 'I have no idea. I don't know many priests, and none with five children.'

'Hah! That's what they all say. Mind you, the fella shouldn't have had a wife and children if he's still a priest. So either he was a bad priest or he was calling himself "priest" when he wasn't, if ye follow me meaning.'

'It isn't difficult,' I said. 'Who said I was responsible?'

'His servant, a Master Atwood.'

'Atwood?' I yelped, and sprang to my feet.

'What of it?'

I could, of course, have said, 'He's the murderous pickthank, a mischief-maker, who tried to murder me,' or 'He's the unscrupulous bastard who turned his coat three or more times during the Wyatt Rebellion,' or 'He's a man who would open your belly to see what you ate last night,' or any one of the many of the other things that immediately jumped into my mind. Instead, I said calmly, 'He is a fellow who used to work for me here. I was forced to part with his services after I saw the sort of man he was. I kept him as butler, but the damned fellow sold off much of my wine, ate my best meats, and then tried to rape a serving wench from the house next door.' I have always found that, when attempting to give false witness, it is better, if possible, to embellish and leave the listener in no doubt as to your feelings in the matter. 'He was not the sort of man whose word I could trust.'

'Ah. I see.'

The Coroner's eyes were very shrewd. When he set them on me, I felt as if I had been pinned to the wall by a pair of stilettos.

'What?' I said.

'It's just that he said you would say something of that sort.'

'He would, wouldn't he? He knows how badly he served me!'

'Aye, well, I can see that,' the Coroner said thoughtfully.

The tipstaff and his two companions were sulkily listening to us, but their expressions lightened visibly when Raphe suddenly appeared in the doorway, glowering about him like a man who had just been woken from a comfortable doze before the kitchen fire after drinking strong wines. He brought a tray with him, on which were several cups, while a large flagon hung from his hand. It was an enormously heavy flagon when full, I knew, and he handled it with the care of a man to whom a drop of wine spilled was a drop of liquid happiness lost forever. He poured, but was two cups short, which surprised me. He had not seen the two with the tipstaff; even so, the flagon, when full, should have held more than enough to fill all the cups twice over. I reflected that he must have only half filled the flagon. No wonder he could handle it with such ease.

I said, 'Raphe, what are you . . .' but he passed one cup to me, and left to refill the flagon and fetch two more cups.

Manners are important, I have always believed, so I passed my cup to the second man with the tipstaff. The knight, I noticed, had taken a sip of his wine and now smiled broadly.

As soon as Raphe returned, he filled two fresh cups, and when he saw me without a cup, he was flustered. 'Give me the cup, Raphe,' I said sharply. I was growing thirsty. 'What are you doing with a mutt in my house?'

I took a sip while I waited for his response, and all but spat it out. Raphe was carefully avoiding my eye. I had bought a firkin of good Bordeaux only a day or two ago, but if this was Bordeaux, I was a Cardinal. I could feel it strip the flesh from my throat as it passed into my stomach, where it tried to set up a happy conversation with any ulcers it could find. The other man who had been forced to wait for wine had also taken a sip and was surveying the cup with the wide-eyed horror and suspicion of a monarch who believes he has been poisoned.

'Dog, master?' Raphe asked innocently.

There was a scrabbling noise at the kitchen door. A bark soon followed. I eyed Raphe with stern disapproval. 'Well?'

'It was just hungry. I gave it some food,' he said defensively.

'Do you have any comments, Master Blackjack?' Sir Richard said.

Pulling my thoughts back to the issue at hand, I said, 'So you say Atwood has accused me of having something to do with this poor fellow's death?'

'Yes.'

'It's more likely Atwood killed the man. Who was murdered, anyway?'

'Father Peter. He was vicar of St Botolph Without.'

I shook my head. 'Where is *that*?'

'It's east of the city by some few miles. It is a sad story. His woman was in the area, and she stumbled over something when she was in the road. She raised the alarm when she realized it was her husband. Except it wasn't, of course, since they were declared unmarried by the Queen. So she found him, and the hue and cry determined that he had been stabbed in the back, repeatedly.'

'How do you mean, "repeatedly"?'

'Nine times. That's pretty much as repeated as any stabbing I've ever seen.'

'That doesn't sound like him,' I said, musing. 'Atwood is a bold fellow, and I can easily imagine him killing a man, but not like that. He would merely stab the once, then a second time to make sure, and perhaps a third if the first two didn't suffice. But nine times? That sounds more like a frenzy.'

'I agree. That was me own reading. However, he said that you got frenzied when you were in a hot temper.' Sir Richard emptied his cup and sat looking at the jug hopefully. I motioned to Raphe, who reluctantly approached with the flagon. He poured and sidled away in what looked like a hurry. Sir Richard sipped and pulled a face, glaring into his cup. ''S'lids, what is this? Piss water from a privy?'

Raphe's eyes remained fixed on something in the far distance beyond the walls. I stared at him and sniffed my own cup. Sir Richard was right. It did smell of piss.

'Ye need to get rid of that little streak of shit! You have foul luck when it comes to hiring your own people,' Sir Richard said, as I told Raphe to find some decent wine and throw this away. 'First you have this Atwood, who you say drank all your good wine, and now you have this disreputable little squeeze-grab, who seems to want to do the same, and serves you and your guests the foulest wringings of a child's clout!'

He goggled at his cup again and clearly tried to set aside

the thought of what could have been in there. 'If Atwood served anything similar to that, I'm surprised you allowed him to go. He'd have deserved a week in the stocks and then a rope about his throat, rather than dismissal!'

'He undoubtedly deserved it, but I am a man of peace,' I said. It was plainly true.

'My apologies, Master Blackjack. That foul concoction was too much of a shock to me blood for me to be able to contain meself. Looked fine, but damme, they were different as a pea from a bean. Reminds me of the story of the fellow who was talkin' to a friend, and said, "My woman is lovely. Beautiful, affectionate, and ever prepared to go to bed." "Aha!" said the second, "If she had a twin, I could enjoy myself, too." "She does have a twin," said the first. "Can you tell them apart, then?" asked his companion. "Well enough. She has long hair and a figure of perfection," the man said, "and her sibling has a beard!" Eh? See? Her twin was a man, eh? Ha ha ha!'

I tried to smile, both ears ringing.

Sir Richard's mind swiftly turned to important matters. 'Where's your boy? He should be back by now with the wine. We can drink that, and then we must take a walk.'

'At this time of night?'

'Aye, well, the dead don't wait, do they, master?'

Thus it was that a scant few minutes later I found myself bellowing for Raphe, who had finally found a decent wine, which he set about pouring into fresh cups. Sir Richard took up one and sipped it with a black glower fixed to his face, which was suddenly washed away and replaced by a beatific smile. 'Hah! That's more like it, boy! Next time I come, you will make sure that you find that barrel again, won't ye? And next time we come here and find you're serving dregs to your master, I will have you taken to the stocks personally. Understand me, boy?'

'Y–yes,' Raphe said, and I was delighted to hear him stammer. It was the first time in months that I had seen him lost for words or anxious, and it was a salve to my soul.

'The dog,' I said before he could scurry away. 'You will have to put it out. I don't want some mangy cur in my house. It could have rabies, for all you know.'

'Yes, sir.'

That itself was a major success. He tended to avoid calling me 'sir', as if that was to concede that his own position was inferior. I watched him with narrowed eyes. I didn't trust his sudden conversion to politeness.

He walked out carrying the two dirty cups and the empty flagon before I could comment further.

'So you deny knowing this dead man?' Sir Richard said.

'Yes! I don't even know the place you're talking about. I've never been there. I spent all day today here in London.'

'What about yesterday?'

'I was in the Boar most of the afternoon. Why, when was the man killed?'

'He was found earlier this morning, but he was as cold as a tombstone. I suspect he could have died yesterday and—'

There was a flurry of barking, shouting and cursing, and suddenly a disreputable, wiry-haired black dog, with white patches over one eye and his shoulder, burst into the room, barking and trailing drool. He rushed to me and jumped up, making me spill my wine over my jack, and when I roared, he flung himself at the tipstaff, still barking, apparently in joy at meeting so many people. Sir Richard bellowed for Raphe, and the dog ran to him, but without the pleasure he had shown at his first appearance. He crouched lower, and his hackles rose; he stopped barking and showed his teeth, eyes narrowed, like a lion stalking his prey. When Sir Richard stood, the dog backed away, still snarling and growling.

Raphe appeared, apologetically flapping his hands, trying to get a grip on the monster. It evaded him, still glaring at Sir Richard, who eyed it with glowering distaste. I have to confess, I warmed to the mutt. Anything that would dare to stand against the knight was deserving of respect, I felt.

Throwing himself on the dog, Raphe managed to grip it about the belly and throat. He stood, with difficulty, four legs struggling manfully – dogfully? – to escape his grip, but Raphe knew when he had gone too far. Red-faced and bitter, he retreated, while sounds of rage and defiance issued from the hand he had clamped over the animal's mouth.

'Be off with you, then. Ye must have duties to attend to,'

Sir Richard said equably. 'And I would kill that thing. It's clearly dangerous. You don't want to be reported to the City for owning a dangerous dog, do you?' he added, looking at me.

'Yes, sir,' Raphe said.

Sir Richard eyed him benevolently as he scurried away. 'Little urchin! Ye need to keep both eyes on squeakers like him, Master Blackjack. He'll try every trick under the sun to gull you, that one. Keep him under a close observation, and trim his wings every so often, whenever the opportunity allows. Ye'll find it worthwhile to strap him once in a while, too. He'll need it. And make sure you have the brute killed.'

'Yes,' I said, but, truth be told, I felt almost affectionate towards the thing. It had been braver than me when facing Sir Richard.

We walked on towards Aldgate's great . . . well, gate. 'What is that at your belt?' Sir Richard asked as we walked.

'This? A gun. I was given it a little while ago,' I said. It was true enough. I hadn't wanted the thing, but it was foisted on me, and could easily have cost me my life.

He grimaced. 'Don't like the things. They make an ungodly row, and rarely hit what ye want. Knew a man once, fired it, and the thing didn't work. He thought he hadn't put in the powder and ball, so he shoved both in and fired again. Still didn't work, so he tried tipping even more powder down the barrel, and another ball. In the end, he had it loaded four times, and finally put a bigger charge in the pan, only to have the damned thing explode.'

'Did it kill him?'

'No, but it made him much more thoughtful in future. Now he sticks to plain steel, sharpened both sides. After all, at least with a sword or dagger, you know where it's goin'. You push it into a man, you know you hit him. With those things, you can pull the trigger, but it may misfire, and even if it does go off, ye don't know where the slug will fly.'

Just then we reached the city wall, where we found that the gate itself was closed, it being after dark. 'Hoi, Ballock-features,' the knight shouted out.

A warm, orange glow lit a chamber beside the gate, and now a wizened old man peered round the doorway. 'What is it? Who are you?'

'Who d'ye think, Oakley, you scraggy old rat! Me! Sir Richard of Bath. Now open the gate.'

'You? Again?'

'Queen's business, Oakley.'

'If you want something, you'd best keep a civil tongue in your head, you old goat.'

Sir Richard swelled like an inflated bladder. 'You dare call me a goat? I'm a Queen's officer! Open the gate.'

'Swive a goose, you old fool,' the man said. 'You know the City demands that the gates be kept shut from sundown to sunrise.'

Sir Richard's face suddenly darkened. 'What did you say to me, fellow?' he said, and although the first word was at – for him – normal volume, the rest of the sentence grew louder and louder with every syllable. I swear I could feel the ground trembling beneath my feet.

The effect on the gatekeeper was pronounced. He darted into his room and returned with a pike that was almost twice his height. At my side, Sir Richard strode forward, and I saw the keeper point his weapon at the knight with a trembling hand. Gatekeepers are rarely the boldest of guards, and this one was about to meet with divine retribution in the form of Sir Richard of Bath, I was sure. While I dislike the sight of blood, I was interested to see how this bout would go. I scampered after the knight.

'Fellow, did you tell me to go and do something unnatural to a goose?' Sir Richard bawled.

'It's after curfew, ain't it? I'm not allowed to open the gates to anyone. Not even a Queen's officer!'

'Are you a loyal servant to Her Majesty?'

'Of course I am!' the man said shiftily. It was difficult not to look shifty just now, with plots and rebellions on all sides.

'There is a man over the other side of the wall who has been murdered. Do you value your immortal soul?'

'Of course I do!'

'The murdered man was a vicar, Porter. A vicar! Just think

of that, hey? Poor fellow doing his best to look after those in his parish, and someone stabbed him nine times. Someone like that, who can kill a vicar, he doesn't care about your soul, does he? He doesn't care about anybody's soul, not even his own. And he is more than likely a murdering rebel. If he can kill a vicar, then no one in the realm is safe from him, hey? Not even the Queen.' Sir Richard's head had dropped, as had his voice, and he stood sorrowfully shaking his head. Now it snapped up. 'So if you don't let me out there right now, I will have to report you for endangering the Queen. I don't think I need tell you what the penalty would be for treason of that nature.'

'Treason? Wait, you can't tell me that—'

'I am waiting. I expect that gate opened by the count of ten. One.'

The pike was still pointing at Sir Richard, but now it wobbled alarmingly as the porter began to panic. His breathing was coming in shallow rasps, and I feared he might collapse, but then he came to a conclusion, swore a couple of times, span about and darted into his chamber. When he reappeared, he gripped an enormous key, which he thrust into his belt.

We walked to the gate, and the porter slid back bars, shot bolts and generally made a din about trying to open the wicket gate. He tugged hard on a bolt to no effect whatsoever. Eventually, he threw us a disgusted look, before pulling the enormous key from his belt. He shoved the handle over the bolt's handle, and with a heave against the thick barrel of the key, the bolt finally squeaked itself open. The porter threw the door wide with a sour glare, and as soon as we had all traipsed through, he slammed it shut again, and we heard the series of locks and bolts being shoved into place.

'I don't think we'll be getting back in there in a hurry,' I said.

The tipstaff gave a grunt of agreement. 'I hope he knows what he's doing,' he said, nodding towards the figure of the knight, who was trudging off into the gloom.

I have never been superstitious, but I don't believe in taking risks either. I looked at the tipstaff and his two companions.

They were all moderately sized men. Yet somehow they were not as reassuring as the burly figure striding off away from the city walls.

'Oh, 's'blood!' I muttered, and set off after him at a trot.

'Here it is,' Sir Richard said, as we reached a large building some two miles from the city. In the dark, it was hard to make out much about the place, but a steady squeaking when the wind blew spoke of something moving overhead. When I looked up, there was a post with a weather vane that moved sluggishly with the breeze. Above it was a dim shape.

'What is?' I asked. I had never come this way. East of the city there were fields, and I knew of St Botolph's, but when I wanted to go whoring, I would go over the river to Southwark, and if I wanted ale or wine, I would stay within the city. There was nothing out this way for me.

'Haven't you eyes in your head? There! The sign of the crown, isn't it? This must be the inn.'

I stared up, but he must have much better eyes than me, for I could see little of the crown. He began to beat heavily on the door with a fist that made a noise like thunder claps in a heavy, humid summer's evening, while I remained standing and gazing upwards like a philosopher seeking the stars. Not that there were any to be seen. A cloud hung low over the sky, adding to the general gloom.

There was a rattling noise and a weedy voice called out, 'Who is it?'

'I am the Queen's Coroner. You have a stiff. Let me in.'

'I can't do that. You'll have to come back in the morning.'

'You wouldn't want that, my fellow.'

'Why?'

'Because if you send me away now, I will return with the posse of the county, and I will have your miserable inn closed and you and your master taken to Newgate in the morning.'

There was a pause of some moments, and then I heard the slow movement of a bolt, then a second, and a bar being removed. Soon a gingerish thatch of hair appeared, closely followed by a pair of large, anxious blue eyes. Sir Richard thrust at the door with the flat of his hand and the owner of the hair and eyes disappeared with a bleat of alarm. There was a loud clatter.

'What is it, in the name of heaven?' Sir Richard bellowed in what he probably thought was a quiet, sympathetic tone.

I followed him inside. There, on the floor, lay a young ragamuffin clad in scraps of old cloth and bare-footed, a rough three-legged stool at its side. The child was only some ten or eleven years old, and was wiping its nose with a filthy sleeve. Large eyes stared up at us. Sir Richard stood over it – and yes, I did not know whether it was male or female – and cleared his throat. The instant reaction from the child was to draw a breath in terror and try to shuffle backwards, but the stool was in the way.

Sir Richard bent and held out a hand. 'Were you standing on the stool when I pushed the door open? Please accept my apologies, young master. Are your parents here? Let me help you to your feet.'

The child accepted his hand after giving it a reluctant and fearful glance, as though expecting to be roundly thrashed at any moment. Sir Richard stood straight, pulling the – as he assumed – boy to his feet.

As he did so, a fellow walked in and glared at Sir Richard suspiciously. A man of about thirty years, I guessed. A scrawny fellow, with sharp eyes under his thatch of thick, dark hair. He had a stubbled beard that spoke of a shave delayed, and that added to the air of distrust about him. 'Are you well, Ben?'

'I fear I shoved the door a little hard on entering and knocked him from his perch,' Sir Richard said. 'Who are you?'

'I am a friend to this boy and his family. Who are you?'

'I am the Queen's Coroner, here to hold inquest.'

The man's expression altered, but only to harden. It was normal. Coroners had the duty of imposing fines for any infraction of the many rules about finding a dead body, so a coroner's visit was rarely to be celebrated. Anyone hearing of an inquest would show the same enthusiasm as he would on hearing a cut-purse was working in the area.

'Who are you?'

'I am called Roger. My apologies. I saw the door was open and thought some mishap . . .'

'You thought that felons could have broken into the place. You are a brave fellow, master.'

'Are you well, Ben?' the man Roger asked again. The youngster nodded, and moved towards him, I noticed. He plainly trusted this man, although I could not see why. He was clad in ill-fitting clothing that was obviously cut for a much larger man, and he had little to commend him. The fashion of his clothing was not of a standard I would ever consider wearing.

Sir Richard appeared to put him from his mind and walked to the fireplace. There were some wisps of smoke rising from the embers, and he stirred them, blowing gently until a flame appeared. There was a wicker basket with kindling over a damp patch on the stones of the hearth, and he carefully selected a few pieces and set them over the flame, placing logs nearby. 'Where are your parents?'

The boy retreated nearer to Roger and he stood there now, with Roger's hands on his shoulders, staring from one to the other of us. When Sir Richard repeated his question, he shook his head and began to tremble visibly. Sir Richard grunted and rose to his feet, but I held up my hand to stop him.

Walking to the lad, I squatted in front of him so we were on the same level. 'My name is Jack. We don't want to upset you. Do you live here, Ben?'

'Yes, sir.'

'With your parents? Do you know?'

'With my mother, sir. And Master Nyck – he is the host.'

His tone changed subtly as he gave that name. It sounded as if he wanted to spit it.

'Where is Nyck? Or your mother? Do you know?'

'He went to church with my mother.' Suddenly, his eyes filled with tears.

'What of your father?'

The tears could not be stemmed now. Roger gently said, 'He was murdered. He's in the back room.'

Sir Richard and I made our way through to the lean-to chamber at the rear of the inn. It was an old dairy, or so it felt. Cool even now, and growing cooler as the night drew on.

I was reluctant. There was that familiar odour, the smell of death and decay, with the tang of iron. I knew that scent well enough now; I may be a poor assassin, but there are aspects of the job that I have not been able to avoid. No matter how I attempted to evade dead bodies, I had managed to stumble over more than my fair share in recent months.

'I don't need to see this.'

'Hey?' Sir Richard turned and saw my face. 'God's blood, man! It's just a dead fellow. Don't be a mulligrub! No need to be down-spirited. This fellow won't harm ye, will he? Hey? Ha ha!'

He clearly perceived this as the very height of humour and returned to the trestle table which had commanded my attention since we had walked into the room. It held a large figure wrapped in a white winding sheet, and while I doubted the enclosed man would be likely to spring from the table to assault me, it was a daunting sight. Sir Richard went to it and began to remove the linen. 'Whoever thought it would be a good idea to wrap him up like this, hey? There's been no blasted inquest yet! And look! The damn fool's took off his clothes! This is ridiculous!'

As he spoke, I heard footsteps in the parlour. I turned in time to see a woman standing in the gloom. She held a candle, shielded by her left hand, and the light shone pink and orange to outline each finger.

'Who are you?' she demanded shrilly.

'I am the Queen's Coroner. Who are you?' Sir Richard said.

She looked away. 'I was this man's wife.'

That was an interesting way to put it, I thought. Not that she was his widow, but that she had been his wife.

She was a comely enough woman. She had her hair concealed beneath a coif and hat, while her figure was concealed by the heavy travelling cloak she wore, which was muddy and stained. Her face was long, and she had a high brow, with slightly slanted eyes that made her look kind and affectionate. She had that sort of look about her that made me want to take her in my arms and console her. And from the look in her eyes, there was plenty to console her about. They were red with weeping, and tears had left tracks in her cheeks, washing away the dirt from the road. The child from the door was behind her, and I could see others behind him in the passageway.

'Where've you been? Your child had to let us in,' Sir Richard said.

'At church. We wanted to pray for his soul.'

She looked close to tears, but Sir Richard was not a sensitive soul. His tone was brusque and unsympathetic. 'Who cleaned him and took his clothes?'

'I did. He was murdered, and I couldn't leave him in the state he was in.'

'You realize, madam, that you broke the law? He should have been left where he had been found so that I could inspect the body *in situ*. There is likely to be much evidence that has been lost, because you moved him here.'

'I wasn't going to leave him lying in the dirt at the roadside just so that you could study him there. He was my husband. I loved him,' she snapped, and added quietly, glancing down at the man's face, 'There was no need to leave him there. He was my husband, Coroner. My husband. I loved him.'

'You may think so. However, it was not your choice to make, woman. Now we may never know what I could have learned. Where are the clothes he was wearing?'

'I gave them away,' she said with a defiant tilt of her head. 'What, you think I want to be reminded that someone stabbed my poor Peter in the road and left him to bleed to death?'

She looked as though she was close to tears again, her gaze moving from Sir Richard to the pale face on the table.

I put on my best smile. 'Madam, I am very sorry that you have lost your husband.'

'I lost him a long time ago,' she muttered. 'As soon as King Edward died.'

'Eh?'

She looked up again, shaking her head as if bewildered. 'I am sorry. I was thinking out loud. What do you wish to know?'

Sir Richard draped the linen back over the man's face. 'Nothing for now, except to know that you will be here tomorrow for the inquest. I must have the local jury called – all the families who live in the near vicinity. I dare say there won't be many. I will need you to bring all the clothing you still possess, and tell those you gave his other clothes to, to bring them as well. I will hold the inquest at noon sharp.'

'I understand.'

She had a great gift of stillness, which gave her a calm dignity as she stood there, staring down at her husband's body.

'Madam,' Sir Richard said. 'I am very sorry for your loss. However, since this is an inn, is there food for me and my men? And a chamber for us to sleep tonight?'

'I shall see what can be provided.'

When I returned to the parlour to stand before the fireplace, I found that the tipstaff and his men were already halfway to the happiness that can be found at the bottom of a cup or tankard. Roger was standing in the corner, eyeing the men with disfavour. It was like so many local taverns: introduce a stranger, and the peasants would always become silent until they left.

The landlord was a cheerful-looking man of some five-and-thirty summers. 'Sir? What may I fetch you?'

'I'll have a pint of sack,' I said.

He disappeared, soon to return with an earthenware jug. He set it on the table beside me and placed a cup next to it.

'Excellent,' I said, pouring a measure and sipping. It was a great improvement on the foul concoction Raphe had served me earlier. 'This widow – do you know her well?'

His rotund features stiffened. It was like watching a door slam. I could feel the waves of discontent from Roger, and the landlord glanced at him quickly before returning to me. 'I know her.'

'What was her husband like?'

'Father Peter? He was a very capable, pleasant fellow. Everyone liked him.'

I didn't see the point of mentioning that one person clearly didn't like him so much. 'Was he true to the old faith or the new?'

'Well, he held services in the old when he arrived here.'

'Which means little enough.'

'He had been a priest in King Henry's Church.'

'I see. But when Queen Mary decided to change the law, so that the women married to priests must be thrown aside and their marriages declared illegal, he was one who found that easier than keeping hold of her? A shame, I'd have thought. She looks a prime article.'

'She is widowed today, master,' he said shortly. Roger slammed his cup on the bar and walked from the room.

I stared after him a moment before returning to the landlord. 'I know, but . . . anyway, why was she here? The fellow would not have been allowed to keep his concubine with him.'

'He did not live here with her. The Queen's law meant that priests like Peter must move away from their original parish. He came here, leaving his wife and children behind. They were forced to accept poverty as punishment and were not allowed contact with him.'

'So when did they arrive here?'

'Some weeks ago. They have been staying here with me for the last fortnight.'

'Why would she follow him here?'

The landlord didn't meet my eye, which gave him an oddly shifty appearance. 'I wouldn't know.'

'Perhaps she wanted to remind him what he was missing,' I mused. 'A dangerous plan, though. A priest trying to keep his family would lose his benefice. And any discovered cohabiting would be severely punished. I have heard of a priest who was caught carrying his babe in the street. He was known to the officer, and when he was discovered, he was arrested and beaten. Some bishops are not understanding like that.'

'Yes. The stories of how they were beaten, just for taking wives, makes a fellow shrink in horror,' the landlord said.

It was a sad story. Many of the priests were forced to walk as penitents, while senior priests or their bishop lashed them. Personally, I would have kept the woman. After all, most of the poor devils had only married the women who had kept their beds warm before the change in the Church's rules. At least the men had made honest women of them – for a period.

The landlord was keen to be away. I didn't wish to delay him. 'What is your name again?'

'Nyck, sir.' I nodded. The man whose name had made the lad Ben pull a grimace.

'Have you seen a man about here called Dick Atwood?'

'Him?'

If I had held any concerns about my old servant being able to injure me with his allegations of my being involved in a murder here, they were instantly dissipated. The look of disdain on Nyck's face was unmistakeable. If Atwood spoke against me, it would most likely count in my favour with the locals here.

I returned to my pot with a feeling of reassurance.

As I drank, I saw the lad who had opened the door to us. I beckoned him. It was not something Ben had expected, plainly. I saw him glance about him, as though ensuring that no one was watching who might take offence at his communing with me, and then warily approached me.

'Come, fellow,' I said heartily. 'Would you hob or nob?'

Ben shot a look at the jugs. One was standing on the hob, right next the fire, where it was warmed through. The other was on the nob, set away from the fire, remaining cool.

'I can see you feel cold. You would prefer a hob, would you not?' I said heartily. I poured him a small measure, replacing the jug on the hob, and sat back, indicating to him that he should take his seat on a stool nearby. 'Tell me, so you live here?'

'Yes.'

'And a fine place it is for a lad to grow up, too. A good little business. I dare say it grows busy at market time? Travellers on their way to the city, others returning. All with money in their purses, ready to be spent. You must have a lot of stories to tell of the people passing the inn? I used to know a man who lived about here somewhere,' I added, frowning as though with recollection. 'A man called Dick – er – Atwood. I don't suppose you have heard of him, have you?'

'I know him,' the boy said with feeling, and this time his face was sour as a green cherry. 'He beat me, when he thought I was stealing apples from the vicar's orchard. Atwood was his servant.'

'Haha! That's the fellow. He can be a bit hard on a lad, I expect?'

'He said he had been a soldier.'

'Yes. I used to know him then. But he's not a man I would trust much. Would you?'

The boy turned his big, innocent blue eyes on me. 'No.'

'Is he here now?' I asked, feigning lack of interest.

'No. He left this afternoon.'

'Oh?' I sipped my drink, and then a quick, sharp pain caught me as a thought speared my brain. 'Um . . . did he leave just after the body had been found, do you know?'

'Yes. It was just after the alarm was raised. He said he would be back shortly, but he isn't.'

Well, I considered, it would be a wonderful thing if the man had been caught by outlaws and slaughtered at the roadside, just like the unhappy priest Peter.

I did not like Atwood.

Atwood was a man I had met during the short-lived Wyatt Rebellion the year before. Wyatt and a number of others were determined to remove the Queen and replace her with young Lady Jane Grey, or perhaps even Princess Elizabeth, as she then was. Queen Mary, to prove her own legitimacy, had to declare her mother's divorce illegal and baseless. England would not happily accept an illegitimate woman taking the throne, after all. So her repeal of the law stating that her mother's marriage to the King had been illegal for reasons of consanguinity, had the simultaneous effect of declaring Anne Boleyn's marriage to the King to be illegal. If that was illegal, any children from that union were also illegitimate. So in order to save herself embarrassment, Queen Mary willingly imposed the same shame on her half-sister. Elizabeth lost her royal title of 'Princess' and became merely 'Lady'.

That being so, the Lady Elizabeth likely discovered an anger towards her half-sister, an anger that would soon be expressed as jealousy, I suppose. In any case, the Rebellion, so it was said, was launched in order to remove Queen Mary and impose someone else – either Lady Jane or Lady Elizabeth – and I became embroiled. Atwood was a soldier at the time, and I had good cause to distrust him. He was a dangerous man, and held no fond memories of me, I was sure. The last time I saw him, he was employed by my master, and that might mean that he was involved in politicking here. If so, my own life could be in danger.

I resolved to leave the inn and the village at first light.

'Hah! Master Blackjack! Would ye mind if I hobnobbed with you? Eh?' Sir Richard said as he came and sat at my side.

TWO

When I woke, a horrible sense of disaster over-whelmed me.

I have become, as it were, a connoisseur of pain. When I first knew Atwood last year, I suffered several blows to my head. I have been attacked at Woodstock, where the Lady Elizabeth had been staying, and several times in London, both during and after the Wyatt Rebellion. My head, I some-times feel, might have been the favourite camp ball of any number of violent men. It had been buffeted by a lot of blunt weapons and threatened by more not-so-blunt ones.

And yet, even with my exhaustive experience on the quality of pain that can be inflicted by men of all conditions, this was worse. I must have been savagely beaten about the head.

I cautiously felt my brow. There was no injury there. I searched over my scalp, seeking lumps, sorenesses, or crusts of scabbed blood, but could find none. Eventually, I opened one eye to take in my surroundings, and found that I was still in the chair that I had taken the previous evening.

My neck hurt, for the chair had a back that was too low to support my head, and I had slid down in the seat until my rump was hanging part off the edge, my chin uncomfortably pressed down to my chest. My left leg was twisted and caught under me, and as soon as I tried to move it, pins and needles jabbed up and down. I groaned.

'Hah! A good morning, Master Blackjack! I trust you slept well?'

The Coroner sat in front of the fire, beaming at me, while the tipstaff and his men were sprawled on benches and chairs nearer the bar. The man's voice was so loud, I felt it necessary to place a gentle hand on top of my head to stop it flying loose.

I was still in the bar!

The smell of sour wine and spilled ale was prominent in

the room, and I could almost taste both. My mouth was like one of the city's sewers, and I did not wish to investigate what was lying on my tongue. It felt like some form of grease or tar. When I opened my other eye, I was forced to close it again quickly. My vision was not helped by trying to focus with both at the same time. It seemed to send the room spinning about me.

I burped, and immediately feared for my teeth. The acid from my belly tasted so concentrated that it was a miracle my breath didn't dissolve them. I groaned again.

'Hey! Master Blackjack! You slept well. Hardly a mumble from you. Do ye want some eggs and bacon? I asked for some kidneys and a pot of pease pottage, too; they don't have any, but there's some blood pudding and we can fetch you a quart of ale or cup of wine?'

There was a sizzling, and my nostrils flared at the odour of cooking bacon fat. The thought of that, or any of his other offerings, was enough to make the acid in my stomach begin to roil. The bile rose, bubbling, and seared my throat.

Making my excuses, I hurriedly left the room. I could not bear the smell any longer. Out in the rear yard there was a privy, and I sat inside it, trying to ignore the foul emanations that rose from the pit below, and voiding my bowels as best I might. With my hosen drawn up once more, my codpiece in place, I walked about the yard for some while, trying to get rid of the shivering that shook my entire frame like the ague.

What had happened to me? I recalled some little drinking, and then Sir Richard had suggested a game or two – only simple jests, in truth, which involved minor forfeits for those who failed. I was sure I was no more prone to failure than the tipstaff – or Sir Richard himself, come to that. Yet my head felt as if it had been battered and misused from the inside as well as out. If I had been told that Sir Richard had opened my skull and scooped out my brains with a spoon, I would have believed it. I was glad that the weather was cool and overcast, because bright sunshine would have been reason enough to pluck out my eyes. The pain would have been intolerable.

And then the realization hit me. The sun was out. Daybreak had been some little while ago, and I had intended to flee before Sir Richard had woken. I vaguely recalled thinking to myself that this would be an easy task: I would simply make the old knight drink himself to oblivion, and then I would wake early in the morning and be off before he could raise himself from his slumbers. That had been my plan, and it had seemed perfectly workable, but something had gone seriously wrong: my plan had gone awry, and I was caught here on a dagger point of my own making.

I could hurry away now, though. Perhaps there was a horse I could hire or borrow? Surely an inn this close to London must have the means of providing some form of travel? Although just now, the way my stomach and head felt, it would be a miracle if I could ride ten yards without falling from the beast.

'I heard you were here, Jack. It's good to see you again.'

Hearing the suave tones, I felt my back clench as though in preparation for a thrown dagger, or perhaps a crossbow bolt.

I turned. 'Good morning, Dick. I hadn't expected to see you here today.'

Which was true. I had expected to be many miles away before he appeared.

Dick Atwood smiled. I didn't.

'It's good to see you again,' he said.

I glared.

'My friend, what is the matter?' he said.

'I am here because, I understand, you accused me of murdering a priest. That, to me, does not seem like cause for celebration!'

'Ah, but you will not mind when you hear why,' he said.

'I don't think I can guarantee that.'

He grinned. 'Would you like me to fetch you an ale while we chat?'

There was a volcano in my stomach at the mere thought, but I did not think that anything could make my life appreciably more miserable. I nodded. 'Yes.'

I have often heard it said that a little of the drink that caused offence is the shortest route to a cure for the worst symptoms of excess, and so it seemed today. I forced down a quarter of a pint of ale and closed my eyes, fully prepared for the most unpleasant possible results, but, to my surprise, the monster in my belly appeared to be appeased by the arrival of a fresh onslaught. I sank another quarter pint, and then topped up my pot from the jug and sat on a bench, my back against the wall. Suddenly, the world seemed a great deal more pleasant. Well, bearable, at least.

'Why did you accuse me of murder?'

'It was an excellent way of distracting people from me.'

I eyed him grimly. He wore a repellent grin, as though this was all a wonderful game. Dick Atwood was the sort of man who could see pleasure and enjoyment in the midst of a battle. I was all for pleasure and enjoyment, but I preferred to take both at moments of peace. Besides, Atwood had tried to murder me. 'It was not an excellent way for *me*, was it?'

'Oh, I knew you would be fine when you realized how important this opportunity was. You will have your own alibi, I am sure, and you can always blame a terrible form of London servant, so useless that I had to be thrown from your door and told never to return.' He grinned.

'What opportunity?'

Atwood leaned closer. 'You know this priest was murdered in the road?'

'I had heard.'

'Did you wonder why a man would murder a priest?'

'No,' I said simply.

He rolled his eyes. 'What if the priest had a box of gold that he took from an abbey before King Henry's men arrived to take command? What if he was so revered by the abbot that he took the box for safekeeping, but the abbot is dead now, and the priest decided to sell the box to support his poor wife and five children? What if that gold was not on him when he was murdered, so the gold is still somewhere about here? What if you and I could be partners looking for the box, and share the winnings equally?'

'A box of gold?'

'Yes.'

His eyes had lit up, and I could see the terrible greed in them. Not that it was a problem for me. I was sure that my own eyes had begun to gleam in exactly the same way. The thought of gold is a wonderful cure for all ills.

'Where is it?'

'Oh,' he said, and pulled a grimace. 'That's the one thing I don't know yet.'

'What do you mean, you *don't know*? You accuse me of murder, drag me across London in the company of this drunken Coroner, and all that just to tell me that you don't know where the treasure lies? What sort of foolishness is this?'

'Hear me out, Jack, before you do yourself an injury. Too much choler in you, you know. You should take some medication to soothe your temper.'

'Don't tell me I need to calm myself!'

'I am sorry that I mentioned you, Jack, but it was important to keep that damned Coroner away from me. I thought if I sent him to find you, he would leave me alone.'

'Why, what were you doing?'

'I was hunting through the man's belongings and his boxes in the church, of course. I've spent the whole of the last day doing that, but there's no sign of any gold.'

'Wonderful. So you have forced me to become involved for no reason, and all I can do is hope that the same good Coroner will not decide to accuse me of taking part in this murder?'

'You will have a series of alibis, I am sure. Where were you the day before yesterday in the early afternoon? That's when he was killed.'

I turned my mind back. Recollections of Arch and Hamon, of the dog and the cat, seeing them in the Cheshire Cheese . . . and suddenly, an entrancing vision came into my mind: Cat the delectable, sitting close beside me, while the gorilla pointed his firearm at me.

My face fell. I was supposed to be entertaining her, teaching her some of the more efficient ways of persuading men to give up their money, while also receiving payment of a different sort. She would be there waiting for me, and here I was, bound by an inquest, whether I liked it or not.

'See?' he said. 'You have witnesses already to speak for you, so you have no need to worry, and I shouldn't concern yourself with this Coroner. He's only a country yokel, and it won't be difficult to pull the wool over his eyes.'

'You think?' I said. I was doubtful, it has to be said. The Coroner sounded very loud and rough, but there was a shrewd glint in his eye that made me unwilling to cross him.

'Of course he is! Listen to his voice. All he knows is how to bellow at hounds. A hunt wouldn't need a whipper-in or blasts on the horn. Anyone would hear his whispers from the far hills! Besides, if you wanted to feel secure, all you need do is run. The man wouldn't survive a chase of more than two tens of feet!'

'How do you know of the priest's box of gold, in any case?' I said.

'Ah!' Dick Atwood laid a finger aside his nose. 'I have friends everywhere, as you know. One fellow was the door-keeper to the abbey at Ilford when it was sold off, and he saw the box himself. He told me it was worth a fortune, that it contained a valuable treasure.'

'He said it held gold?'

Atwood waved a hand airily. 'He didn't say it held three bars or four, or whether it was full of coin, but the man didn't need to. When you see the glitter in a fellow's eyes, when you see how he turns his gaze inwards . . . well, avarice is a terrible thing, but it's understandable. Confront a man with a box of gold, and he will dream!'

'Wouldn't a fortune in gold be missed? All the cathedrals had records of their valuables.'

'My doorman told me that the King's auditors were late to the abbey, and when they arrived, much was already gone that they missed. My confederate wondered later where the treasure had gone, and then he remembered that Father Peter had visited the day before, and the truth came to him: the priest had taken the box.'

'Where is Ilford?'

'Some distance away.'

'Where is this doorkeeper?'

'Alas, he suffered an accident and died.'

'What sort of accident?' I asked sourly. 'A fatal dose of steel in the heart?'

Atwood looked hurt. 'You're not suggesting that I would do such a thing?'

I looked at him, but as usual his features gave little away. 'Who was this priest, then, in Ilford?'

'Try to keep up with me here,' Dick said in his most condescending tone of voice. 'There *was* a priest at Ilford, who was young and married a woman from the area. The abbey was ordered to be dissolved some fifteen years ago. Are you with me? And then, recently, when our glorious Queen decided to reverse the direction of our English Church and return to Romanism, she decided that priests should set aside their women. Yes? You're keeping up with me? And the priests were sent to new parishes – note that, Jack – where they must once more adhere to the rules of celibacy. The fellow who was sent here – guess where he came from?'

'Ilford?'

He slapped his thigh. 'You see? I knew you would understand! There is a valuable hoard somewhere around here.'

'Except that the priest himself died. Clearly, there is a contagion that affects those who hear of this treasure. Those who get too close might all suffer from the same fate.'

'Jack, I was trying to help you. Wouldn't a share of untold wealth be good?'

The idea of a box of gold was most appealing, it was true. 'An equal share?'

'We can discuss that.'

'So you decided to accuse me purely so that you could save yourself from being arrested? How will that help you? As soon as the Coroner sees I have a perfectly good alibi, he will be on to you again.'

'Oh, yes, but that isn't the main point. The key here is that there is a delectable young widow who has lost her husband, and who may well know his favourite places of concealment. And since she is young, impressionable, attractive and lonely, she might well respond well to a young man whose legs look good in tight hosen.'

'What, you want me to seduce the man's widow? He's not even cold yet!'

'I'm sure he is. He's been out there overnight. Besides, warm or cold, he's no good to her now, is he?'

The inquest began just as a light drizzle began to fall.

I took my place standing beneath an elm, from where I could see and hear the whole meeting while remaining moderately dry. Sir Richard stood before his jury, a group of sixteen sulky, solemn or stupid-looking boys and men. One in particular had the wide-eyed, slack-jawed appearance of the village idiot . . . although he still looked a lot brighter, naturally, than Raphe.

They were all gathered about the figure of Father Peter, whom Sir Richard had ordered to be brought out and laid on some planks on trestles, to stop the linen becoming muddied. Not that it would matter. The winding sheet would soon be thrown into the mud at the church, after all. The men of the jury shrugged deeper into their jackets and hats against the rain, but they were all peasants and used to whatever the weather threw at them. Two or three began chatting, and I noticed one pair casting looks of disgust at the sky, but more than one threw similar looks at the widow. That was a bit callous, I thought. It was hardly her fault that we were all standing there, unless they suspected her of killing her husband, of course.

Sir Richard stood before the jury, the tipstaff and his men ranged behind him, while at his side sat a clerk at a little rough table upon which he had set out his inks and reeds. The jury was asked if all who should be present were gathered, and only one man was absent, Saul Miller.

The clerk began to write as Sir Richard pushed his hands into his belt and glared around at the jury, his gaze finally coming to rest on the clerk himself. 'Are you makin' a good note for the record?'

'Yes, Sir Richard. I have to—'

'You will pardon me, fellow, but the first thing *you* have to do is pray and ask God's direction in this matter!' Sir Richard boomed. I was quite surprised to see that his amiable demeanour was turned so swiftly to anger, but the clerk hurriedly rose to his feet and mumbled some incomprehensible Latin, which could easily have been a curse on all coroners, for all I knew. Sir Richard's ire left him, and soon the knight was his usual affable self. He took a deep breath and addressed the jury.

'Is the whole jury present?'

'The miller is away in London, but everyone else is here,' a man said. He had been elected their mouthpiece, no doubt.

'Very well. We are here to hold inquest into the murder of the priest, Father Peter of St Botolph's. You will listen to the evidence carefully, and when I am done, you will give me your veredictum. If you have any questions, speak up, but if you waste my time or try to confuse the inquest, I will have you arrested and taken to Newgate gaol. You will not like it there!'

He stared about him with a glare that could have fried eggs. 'Now, where is the First Finder?'

Peter's widow held her hand up and, on being beckoned, stepped forward. 'I found him.'

'Give your name.'

'I am Dorothy. I was married to Peter.'

There was a hiss at that, and when I cast about, I saw a prosperous-looking yeoman standing behind the jury near the inn's door. A ruddy-faced fellow, he was very sure of his own status, standing with his thumbs hooked in his belt for all the world like a bishop's steward. As Dorothy spoke, I saw his eyes glitter with contempt.

'Where did you find him?'

'He lay in the roadway some few hundred paces from here, eastwards.' She was not alone. About her were five figures. Clinging to her skirts were three small children, of whom the eldest was Ben. He stared at the figure on the trestles with such unconcealed grief that it quite touched me. The two oldest stood at either side of her. One was perhaps twelve, the other fourteen, I would guess, with the height of a man, but gangling. He had the look of a fellow who had suddenly grown tall, but without the food to support his new size. Mind you, I think most boys of that age look like that. Both these boys were staring at the jury as if daring the men to say anything to the detriment of their mother.

'It was in the morning, very early,' she continued. 'I was out at the Ladywell, filling buckets, when I saw him. He passed by in the road, and I called out to him, but then he disappeared into the mist.'

'It was foggy?'

'A ground mist. We have them here sometimes.'

Sir Richard nodded to himself. 'And this was at what hour of the day?'

'Only a little after dawn, sir.'

'Was it full daylight?'

'Not yet, no.'

'What did you do then?'

She looked down at Ben and her two younger children as though steeling herself. 'I left my buckets and ran after him.'

'Why? You knew that your marriage had been annulled. The Queen's law—'

'No law can change my feelings for my husband!' she declared sharply, fists clenched as though preparing to fight the Coroner himself. 'I made my vow before God – as did he! A law cannot change my oath, nor his!'

The Coroner frowned at her tone, but he appeared to feel that there was little point in pursuing her at this point. 'Tell us what you found.'

'As I said, I ran after him. It could only have been a few moments, but he had disappeared into the mists. And then I saw him, and knew at once it was him.'

'How could you know?'

'Who else could it have been? There are not two priests in the village!'

'The body has been washed and cleaned, his clothes removed, and he has been laid out for his grave. Did you do that? Did you wash all the blood from his wounds?'

'Yes – well, no.'

'Which is it?'

'I did remove his clothes and tidy him and wash him ready for his burial, but there was little blood on him.'

'The fellow was stabbed. There would have been blood all over his back. Perhaps his shirt would have absorbed some, but it would have been all over his back.'

'There was little enough when I laid him out,' she said doggedly.

'I see. Who can confirm that?'

'I can, sir.'

It was Roger of Ilford, our fellow from the inn the previous evening. He looked concerned, but most men would when confronted by a speaking mountain like Sir Richard. The ruddy-faced yeoman cast a glance at him with his lip curled in disdain, I saw.

'State your name for the clerk,' Sir Richard said.

'I am Roger of Ilford, Sir Coroner. I used to work with Father Peter, before he came here. I heard poor Mistress Dorothy scream and went to her aid. The body was that of her husband, but she is right. There was no blood about him.'

I peered at him with interest. No, not because of his evidence: but if he knew Peter before he arrived at St Botolph's, it occurred to me that he might have been the priest's companion for some time. He would be worth getting to know, in case he knew of a box of gold.

'There would have been a lot of blood, surely,' Atwood commented. 'Even if it had not spread over the roadway, it would have beslubbered his back and clothing.'

'Yes, thank you, Master Sexton,' the Coroner said with heavy sarcasm. 'When I require your aid, I will be sure to ask for it! You, Roger, you are sure of this?'

'Yes.'

'You used to work for the priest? How so?'

'I was his sexton, sir.'

'Here at St Botolph's?'

'No. Before that.'

'Where was that?'

'St Mary's at Ilford, sir.'

Aha, I thought. So he had known Peter for some little while.

'You must have got to know him well at Ilford.'

'Yes, sir. He was a good master.'

'And you got to know his wife as well, hey?' Sir Richard asked, and the sexton flinched as though he had been struck.

Sir Richard stood silently for a space before nodding to himself. 'When did you leave that place and come here?'

'When Peter's wife decided to come to speak with her husband.'

'But he had left her because of the law?'

'Our sovereign Queen has returned the priesthood to the Catholic faith, yes, sir.'

'You are not convinced about such a return?'

Roger of Ilford's head had dropped, and he looked about like a cornered rat seeking escape. 'No.'

'You wished to remain within the Church of England?'

'I did. I felt I had taken vows in good faith and in earnest. I didn't see that I could change like that,' he said, snapping his fingers.

'I see. So you decided to walk here with this priest's widow?'

'It would have been dangerous for her on the road alone.'

Sir Richard studied the collection of children about Dorothy. 'I can see that,' he said drily.

'I thought it my duty to protect her,' Roger burst out. Even I could hear the desperation in his voice.

Sir Richard studied the man for some little while. Then, 'Where are you living?'

'I have been allowed to sleep in the hayloft at the inn here.'

'Not at the church?'

'Father Peter had a sexton already. The man Atwood.'

'Did he resent you coming here with the woman who had been his wife?'

'Why would he?'

'He might well wonder why you had sought to take on the protection of his illegitimate family. No matter. How was the body when you found it?'

Roger looked close to tears. He had to struggle to control his feelings. 'Peter was lying on his belly with an arm outflung, as though he was reaching for something or someone. He was at the edge of the roadway, as if he'd been pushed there, or knocked there by a cart.'

'What did you do?'

'I rolled him over, pulled out my dagger and held it over his mouth to see if he was breathing, but there was no misting of my blade; then I listened for a heartbeat, but I couldn't hear anything. I was sure he was dead, as Mistress Dorothy said.'

'She said he was alive a few moments beforehand. Did you see him?'

'No,' Roger said, throwing a quick glance at her.

'And she said he was cold. Was he?'

'Yes.'

'What then?'

'I . . . I was distraught. He was an old friend. I knelt and prayed for him, and I confess that I wept. Mistress Dorothy was there, and we consoled each other for some little time, until a carter arrived. He agreed to raise the hue and cry, and soon others came to help us.'

Yes, I thought, I wouldn't have minded consoling her either.

'Who moved the body from where it was found?'

'I did,' Roger said firmly. 'No one helped me.'

I could have groaned as Sir Richard chuckled. The fool thought he was being honourable, but every eye in the place could see that this fellow, with his narrow frame, could not have moved a dead cat. Every man there knew Dorothy had helped him. He could not have moved the body on his own. Any punishment for interfering with the Coroner's inquest must be inflicted on both.

Sir Richard continued his inquest with the carter and some locals who helped pick up the body, and then he called for the sexton to come and be questioned.

Atwood had that casually negligent attitude I remembered so well. He stood next to Dorothy and smiled at the company all about.

'You are the sexton to the dead priest?'

'Yes.'

'So you can identify him?'

'Yes, the dead man was Father Peter,' Atwood said, peering at the corpse.

'When did you last see him?'

'The previous day, at Vespers. We completed the service, and then Father Peter left me while I tidied the church. I left there, oh, some while later.'

'Where did he go?'

'I don't know. I know he had many calls to make most evenings. He liked to go and comfort the women who were deserving.'

'What does that mean?'

Atwood shrugged. 'Only what I say. He was a good man and a better priest.'

'Do you know of any man who would want to harm him, injure or kill him?'

'Why, no. Everybody respected the good father.'

'One man didn't. Or woman,' Sir Richard observed frostily. Then, 'You told me that your old master, Master Blackjack here, might have killed him.'

'Oh, I think you misunderstood me. I said, "No one could have wanted to hurt him. Only Master Blackjack in a rage would have attacked him." You see, I was showing that only a man in a terrible rage could have wanted to hurt him. I didn't mean my Master Blackjack actually *had* harmed him – how could he? I doubt Master Blackjack even knew of the good priest!'

Sir Richard glared at him and was plainly preparing to blast Atwood, but Atwood had set his head to one side and now thoughtfully considered the body again, saying, 'Of course there was one man. I saw him in the shadows as Father Peter set off from the church. He was in the little copse at the other side of the roadway, and I could have sworn that once Father Peter walked past, the fellow moved after him.'

He stopped and turned to face the knight with a quizzical look in his eye.

'Did you see the man clearly?' Sir Richard said.

'No, I fear not,' Atwood said thoughtfully. 'I wouldn't want to try to describe him.'

'Very well. That was the night before his body was discovered?'

'Yes.'

'And we have heard that the body was cold the following morning. It could have lain there half the night.'

'I suppose so.'

Sir Richard remained fixed, and his eyes gradually turned down to the figure on the trestles. 'But no one saw him until Mistress Dorothy happened upon him.'

Atwood gave a lazy grin. 'As you know, Sir Coroner, many people will accidentally fail to notice a body at the roadside, since discovering a body and reporting it will mean a man can be amerced. No one wishes to be fined just for discovering a man's murder. But I dare suggest that the man's widow' – and here he bowed slightly to Dorothy – 'would have more honesty than other passers-by.'

'You have little faith in your fellow man,' Sir Richard observed coldly.

'Oh, I think I have plenty of faith in others. But, like you, I have experience of what others can do and try to do. We both know how evil men can be, I suppose.'

'I suppose,' Sir Richard said. 'So, although you accused this man, Master Jack Blackjack, you now say you retract your accusation?'

'As I said, with apologies, I did not mean to let you think that I accused Master Jack. I was making an observation about men generally.' He smiled at me, and I felt it curdle my blood. 'My dear master wouldn't hurt anyone, I am sure. Not for love nor money.'

It was a little while afterwards that we began the revolting task of viewing the body. I could see that the clerk helping the knight found that part as distasteful as I did myself. I have never been keen on the sight of a dead man, and to see a fellow stripped naked – his pathetic organs on display for all the world to mock, the sad flabbiness of his flesh now that all life and vigour has fled – is always indescribably sad.

Then again, it was necessary to view the man and confirm who he was and how he had died.

As to who he was, that was clear enough. He was a tall man with broad shoulders, and had the look of a man with whom it would be worth avoiding any disputes. I could easily imagine his fists being clenched, and the thought of them striking me was enough to make me wince and draw away. One thing was painfully obvious, and that was that the weedy Roger could never have picked up Peter's body and carried him back to the village alone.

I was intrigued when Peter was hauled over to lie on his belly, and the extent of the wounds on his back became visible for the first time. While Dorothy wept silently, her smallest children clutched to her thighs, the jury leaned forward with eager interest, and I confess I did lean a little myself. The drizzle had stopped now, and a weak, pathetic sun was fighting through the clouds overhead.

'I can count nine stab wounds on this man's back,' Sir Richard declared in a quiet tone that set the bells in St Paul's ringing gently in London. He was at the trestle table now, studying and probing with his fingers. 'One at the top, just to the left of his spine. It is inside the shoulder blade, between the second and third ribs. There are three others on the left of the spine – one that lodged in the spine itself, and two more to the right. Two final wounds are low down, at the line of the top of a man's belt,' he added thoughtfully, his hands reaching about his own back and measuring where the same wounds would have struck him. 'The wounds are an inch in breadth, so the blade of the weapon must have been one inch broad. The depth' – here he prodded with a forefinger, pulling it out and wiping the blood from it on the winding sheet – 'the depth goes in deeper than my finger can reach, so it's more than three and a half inches. It doesn't reach through the man's ribcage to the front of his chest, so less than eight inches, I would guess. The blows were struck quickly, I think it is safe to say.'

'Sir Richard,' Dick Atwood called. He was peering at the body closely. 'There is a bruise on that wound,' he said, pointing.

The Coroner peered, and the jury, as one, craned their necks.

'Yes, Master Atwood. Let it be recorded that the killer struck with full force. The weapon's hilt has bruised the flesh. That indicates that the killer thrust as hard as possible, which means the blade struck as deeply as possible.'

'Perhaps we should ask everyone here to show their daggers?'

'Aye, perhaps we should,' Sir Richard said, but he didn't give the instruction. Rather, he stood contemplatively eyeing Dick Atwood, with what I could only consider was a measuring, doubtful expression. Dick did not appear concerned about enduring that serious stare, and just as I was convinced the Coroner was about to accuse him of participating in the murder, Sir Richard shook his head. 'Any murderer will have disposed of his weapon, or at the least cleaned it, without doubt. No.'

He turned away from Dick and beckoned me.

'Master Blackjack. I came to arrest you last evening and brought you here, because that man Atwood claimed he used to work for you. Is that so?'

'Yes. Although a more slovenly, useless—'

Another man might have permitted a little asperity into his tone, but the Coroner was not so subtle. His bellow was like a gale. 'Stick to the question! Never mind that! Stick to answering me! He alleged you knew this priest. Did you?'

'No. I've never seen him before,' I said heatedly. 'I have not spoken to him or met him.'

'What of the suggestion that you might have killed him?'

'It is nonsense. Why should I do that?'

'There are always many reasons. Perhaps you wanted his wife for yourself, or you fancied that he had insulted you, or you took a dislike to a man who would consider returning to the Catholic Church rather than honouring the newer English Church? There are many reasons why a man might turn to murder.'

'Well, I did not. I was busy yesterday and the day before, and I can prove it. I didn't know this priest and had no reason to wish him harm.'

'I see. Do you know the widow there?'

'You know I do. We spoke to her last night.'

Sir Richard rolled his eyes heavenwards. 'I meant – and I think you must know this – did you know the woman before last night?'

'No. I had never seen her before last evening.'

This time it was me who was treated to the judicial frown of suspicion. I was relieved when a man appeared in the doorway and hurried to the Coroner. 'Sir? Is this what you wanted?'

I recognized him as one of the tipstaff's men. He held in his hand a bundle of dark material, wrapped up tightly like a travelling man's pack, and as soon as he reached the Coroner, he passed it over.

The knight took the pack to the table where the clerk had been scribbling. The clerk was finished for the moment and watched as Sir Richard unwrapped a jacket of dark material. 'I have here the coat that the unfortunate fellow was wearing when he was slain,' Sir Richard said. He held it up. 'It was given away to a passing traveller, apparently, by Dorothy, the fellow's widow. Luckily, the transaction was witnessed by Master Jonathan Harknet, who advised me this morning.'

'It is not his jacket,' Dorothy cried out. She looked appalled to see the coat appear. I wondered why she should care so much.

'It's easy to test,' Sir Richard said. He lifted it up. 'There is a series of stabs through the cloth.' He took it to the body and laid it over the man's back. 'I can see that the wounds match . . . Wait! All bar one. That one is a stab wound on the left side of his back, which I think might well have punctured his heart.'

He left the coat draped over the body and walked pensively back to the clerk. Standing there, Sir Richard cast a glance about the men standing in front of him, before his eye came to rest on the woman and her children once more. 'Madam, I am deeply sorry to have to ask this, but I must do so. Do you know how he might have been stabbed without his coat, and then his coat arranged over his body, before he was stabbed again?'

'I know nothing of this,' she said, and I swear I thought she might topple. She looked so enfeebled at this news, although whether it was the sight of his bloody garment or the question, I couldn't tell. Her denial that it could be her husband's was transparently false, however. It only served to make her look guilty.

It was then that Sir Richard held up the shirt. 'You will see that there are only eight holes in this, too,' he said, holding it up for the jury. 'It is plain to me that the man was stabbed once through the heart while he was not wearing his shirt. That, to me, suggests that he was either undressed or wearing something else when he was slain. Later, he was dressed in his shirt and jacket, and stabbed eight more times to make it appear that he was killed on the roadway.'

'How can you tell that?' Roger blustered. 'It's impossible to guess all that from a shirt and a jacket!'

Sir Richard turned to him and studied him. There was a sudden rainfall, and in the silence, all I could hear was the light rain pattering loudly on sodden hats and coats or cloaks. I took two breaths before Sir Richard spoke again, surprisingly softly. 'The first wound killed him. Someone cleaned his body after that, and there is little blood on the shirt as a result. The other wounds passed through shirt and coat, and there was some little bleeding shown on his garments, but only a small amount. If he had been alive, as my good friend Master Atwood pointed out, there would have been much blood. If he had been wearing clothes, they would have been heavily soiled. These were not, so he was already dead.' He turned back to Dorothy. 'Are you sure that there is nothing else you would like to tell me about your husband's death?'

The Coroner spent some time after that talking to the clerk, remarking on the quality of the garments and how much they were worth, the value of the weapon used to murder the priest, and the total of the fines he would have to impose for this appalling infringement of the Queen's Peace. I have often thought that the sole purpose of the Coroner was, in the main, to squeeze the poor folk who discovered a dead body and make sure that next time a body turned up, they would walk on by, or, as so often happened, give the corpse a ride to the next parish, and leave others to bear the costs.

While Sir Richard loudly discussed the fines, and the jury stood shuffling unhappily from foot to foot as they listened to the mounting costs of Peter's death, the yeoman stood watching matters with a sort of smug anger, like a man who has predicted disaster and now sees his forecast come true to his own cost as much as to that of others. He threw an occasional glare in the direction of Dorothy, who stood as though rooted to the spot. It was plain enough that the poor woman was holding her tears at bay with the greatest of difficulty. Her oldest boy had gone to her now and thrown his arms about her; the fellow was almost a man, and plainly took his position as head of the household seriously. I noticed that she glanced at him and then averted her head. He looked at her with a hurt expression.

I was intrigued by the yeoman. When the Coroner had mentioned the name Jonathan Harknet, the fellow had preened like a peacock, and I guessed that he was the owner of the name. Yet for all his personal pride, he was not popular with the others of the village. He stood alone, away from the other men. When the landlord of the inn came out with trays of ale, I noticed that he walked away from Harknet and instead made his way straight to the Coroner first, delivering a pair of pots to Sir Richard and his clerk, and then moved to Dorothy, giving her a pot of her own and one each to her boys. He deposited a jug on the floor for the family, and passed another to Roger of Ilford. A good, supportive host, I thought. I cleared my throat, but he appeared not to hear me.

Harknet was trying to attract his attention all the while, but Master Nyck appeared not to notice him either, and disappeared inside once more.

I wandered over to Harknet. 'Good day, master. A sad tale, this, isn't it?'

'A rogue and scoundrel has died? You think that a disaster?' he spat.

I was surprised to hear the dead man so roundly criticized. 'You say Father Peter was a scallywag?'

'Not only a scallywag! He was a foul influence on our village. Priest, indeed! My sow would be more honourable! She has more decorum and feeling for her brood than that man lying there. Look at all the unlawful pups he fathered with that poor dupe of a woman, and God alone knows how many other squalling brats he sired up and down the country. It is one thing for a priest to be confused about the rightness of the liturgy, when the King declares this and then the Queen declares thus. But a man in Holy Orders who fathers so many children, and who still feels the need to father more, is a man who is unsuited to his calling.'

'He had many women calling on him to visit them? You saw this?'

He looked away, and I wondered. If he had been convinced of the truth of his words, he would have held my gaze. Yet some men will not. Perhaps this was one of the fellows who felt intimidated by another. Naturally, a man of his class would feel threatened by a man such as me. I was of a different level, as would be entirely clear from my clothing. To put him at his ease, I said, 'Of course, a priest will naturally be asked to help many women with their prayers, or to intercede for them, when something—'

'*Intercede?*' he sneered. 'Oh, yes, he would *intercede*, I have no doubt! You have no idea what sort of a man he was! He would *intercede* with any woman when she was on her knees before him, I've no doubt! He was nothing more than a lecher and a molester of women.'

'You saw this?'

'I don't need to see the sun to feel its warmth, just as I don't need to see the water to know when I've fallen in a river, and don't need to look to see when I've stepped in ox shit – the smell's enough! I have eyes to see, and . . . and, anyway, just look at the poor drab over there with all her squalling brats! She had nothing to hope for from him, did she? He gave her that litter and didn't even attempt to protect or help them; he dropped them all and scuttled over here to a new benefice. That tells you all you need to know about *him*.'

'She must have felt something for him to have travelled all the way here. And the man Roger, too.'

'They were both probably trying to demand money from him after his behaviour before. She was desperate for money. That's why she sold his coat.'

'You saw his coat being sold by his wife?'

'She was flagrant about it! As soon as she could, she was bundling the clothes up and giving them to a passing tranter. I made sure that the good Coroner was fully aware of it, too. The priest may have been a dreadful influence on the community, but that is no reason for his wife to become a drain on our parish. And as for her thinking she can do away with him with impunity – where would we be, if women were able to do away with their husbands for any imagined slight?'

'Where indeed?' I agreed. It struck me that a coat with eight or nine stab-slashes in the back would be worth little enough. But it did make me wonder what would have tempted the woman to dispose of coat and shirt.

I gave him a smile. 'Women with any cause to dislike their menfolk, whether they had been bullied or beaten, might decide to take revenge, and then where would their tormentors be?'

He gave me an odd look at that and soon sidled away, muttering under his breath about city folk with no knowledge of real life, or somesuch. I didn't feel he liked me. It was mutual.

Seeing the innkeeper return with a full tray, I beckoned him and took a good cup of ale. The earlier one with Dick Atwood was beginning to lose its beneficial influence, and my head was hurting again – although a large part of that could have been due to the voice and volume of the Coroner. He really was an appallingly loud man.

'That fellow Harknet,' I said to the innkeeper, 'seems to have very set views about your dead priest.'

'He is a whore's son and never happy unless he's making others miserable.'

'He said a lot about Father Peter being less than strict in his relations with women about the place.'

'He said what?'

I sought a polite phrase for such a delicate matter. It wasn't easy. I was the son of a leather worker, not a master of philosophy from a university. 'He implied that the good father was rather incontinent in his relations,' I said, ending on a higher note.

The innkeeper was also not from a university. 'Eh?'

'He said the priest was groping and swiving women who went to him.'

'Oh!' Nyck's face cleared as he absorbed the explanation, and then he pulled a grimace and glanced about him quickly. 'You know why that is? Harknet is a vicious little churl – and unmarried. I dare guess that he is as jealous as a fool can be. Father Peter was a good man, I'd swear. He was kind and always had a listening ear for those with troubles or fears. Harknet would like to believe poor Father Peter was some kind of sinner because it fits with his view of the world. Look, Harknet is a devoted Catholic – now. When King Henry created his own Church, Harknet was terrified of upsetting people and enthusiastically turned to the new order. He was vocal about moving and promoted the English Church like one of King Henry's courtiers. Well, everyone did. No one's going to *obviously* argue with the King or Queen, are they? We like our ears in place. But Harknet took things too far, thinking King Edward would be on the throne for years and see him out. The fool tried to press anyone he suspected of being Catholic into declaring their devotion to the new Church. That made him enemies. So now that the Queen has tacked to a new course, he is in a difficult predicament. He finds he must woo those he was persecuting.'

'That will make him a cheerful companion.'

'No one trusts him. So now he seeks to curry favour with those who trust him least, and his erstwhile friends – those he supported when he was a committed member of the new Church? None of them will speak to him either. I suppose for him this is an ideal matter. Peter's death gives Harknet a new reason to speak with the Catholics. Many of them will believe his poison, although most will want to have nothing to do with him. They remember how he persecuted them during King Edward's reign.'

'So you don't think he's right about the good Father Peter? About the women, I mean?'

He gave me a curious look. 'No. Not at all. Look at her, his widow! Her misery is unfeigned, isn't it? Do you think she would look like that if she had any doubts about his behaviour?'

I couldn't help but think, as Nyck wandered off to serve more customers, that she would also look like that if, say, she had murdered her husband in his bed, clothed him and dumped him in the road, only to realize that the coat and shirt would incriminate her.

But then I have spent too long in London. I tend to think the worst of people.

When the inquest was finally done in the hour before noon, I managed to find a seat near the inn's fire. I was well into my fourth cup of ale, and the world was feeling a great deal more comfortable. My bowels had settled to a general rumbling discontent, but there was no immediate threat of spewing, even as more and more members of the jury arrived, bringing with them the odour of the cowshed, piggery and their own unwashed bodies. After the drizzle, the inn had an over-whelming scent of wet sheep, too. The number of men wearing woollen clothing meant that the room became filled with a misty fug as all the wool gave up the moisture from the rain.

In short, although I felt that I was not going to be sick from the drinks of the night before, I was less convinced that I would not throw up as a result of the lack of cleanliness of the people in the room with me. I began to long for the streets of London, the fellows I knew in the drinking clubs, the whole-some taverns and alehouses, the gambling dens, the women who would negotiate by the hour . . . And that brought me to thinking about Cat. She was a wrigglesome little wench, and I was very keen to renew my acquaintanceship with her. Ideally, without Henry at her side.

The thought was most appealing, and I was lost in a reverie when a shadow was suddenly cast over me.

'Ha! Thought you would be here!'

The Coroner turned and pushed me along my bench by the simple expedient of squashing his arse into the gap between me and the fireplace. It was as if the fire had been dowsed with water. I could feel no heat at all. Grumpily, I thought about complaining, and then thought better of it and moodily sipped at my ale.

'A hard morning's work,' the Coroner said with a grunt.

'You are going to fine this parish how much?'

He shrugged. 'The final sum will be a lot, especially when the Church gets involved. They will be looking for compensa-tion for the death of their man, and no doubt will want the parish to pay for the hearse, the wax for the candles, and all the usual charges.' He sighed. 'The lot of the peasantry is not a happy one. These poor fellows fight every year against the elements, against diseases, against predators trying to kill their animals, against deer eating their crops, against the uncaring powerful people who own the land they live on, the houses they live in, and often every other aspect of their lives. Ye know, I feel more fellow-feeling with folk like these peasants than I do with me companions in London.'

'Would you swap your place with them?'

He turned and stared at me with horror. If I was a demon that had materialized beside him, he could not have looked more appalled. 'Me? Become a peasant? What are ye talking about? 'S'bones, are ye mad? Now, this matter about the accusation against you – I would like to say that you can go, if you want. I don't think you had any part in this matter. It's plain to me that the man Atwood was accusing you to divert attention from himself.'

An expression of acute suspicion flitted across his face as he said this, and I wondered why. I had not expected that he would show such feelings for others. Coroners tended to be rough and ready men, used to the sight of death, often caused by violence and cruelty. They rarely showed sympathy for the victims. Sir Richard in particular seemed a rough, hardy fellow with all the sensitivity of a bull.

'Yes, well, I am glad to hear it. He was ever an unreliable, mendacious fellow,' I added. One good accusation deserves a damaged character, after all.

'A strange matter, this,' Sir Richard muttered.

'In what way?'

'His wife said that she saw her man up ahead of her. D'you believe in ghosts?'

'Of course I do.'

'Hmm. It would be a strange ghost, wouldn't it, to appear in daylight, in a roadway, just to torment his widow.'

'Why do you say that?'

'Because she and Roger, that fool of a sexton, both say that the body was cold. If he had been walking in front of her only moments before, he would have been warm still, and there would have been blood all about him. As it is, the man was clearly not killed there. Someone put him there to conceal where he died.'

'I see,' I said. 'You need to find where he was killed.'

'I am glad you are so quick to understand.'

'Not only that, I am quick to move, too. If I am swift now, I should be able to reach the City's gate before curfew,' I said.

He cocked an eyebrow at me. 'So you'll leave?'

'As soon as I can.'

'Aye, I suppose I cannot keep you here,' he said, frowning, deep in thought. He stretched his legs out before him, groaning like an old man, and bellowed for fresh ale. Sitting there, scowling at the floor before him, he looked like a man who had been presented with a puzzle and was unsure how to deal with it.

Seeing him relax, I was tempted to ask, 'What will you do with Atwood?'

'Him? I'll threaten him with a fine, if I can. I'm not sure that he hasn't already disappeared, though. I was looking for him just now, and he is not here. Perhaps he has gone to the church – but I would not be surprised if he has left the village. He is not the sort of man to wish to wait while men like me suspect him.'

I didn't care. Visions of Cat rose in my mind. As far as I was concerned, Atwood could find someone else to seduce the man's widow. Cat was an altogether easier prospect, I thought.

The return from St Botolph's took little time, and I was back at my house within the span of three hours, glad to find that Raphe had not completely emptied my stores of wine. I had walked with the tipstaff and his men, who were no longer needed, Sir Richard said. They were happy enough to be away from the town.

'All I want,' the tipstaff said as we trudged on, 'is a hot ale, a bowl of pottage with a hot sausage boiled in it, and a saucy maid to sit on my lap afterwards. A pox on villages and peasants!'

It was a relief to be rid of them when I left them at the gate to the City, and I made my way homewards with a feeling of joy to be back in my natural environment again. There were few things that the tipstaff and I would agree on, but the obvious superiority of London as a place to live was not an issue we would debate.

At my house I was almost tripped as soon as I opened the door. 'What is that thing doing here still?' I demanded, as the dog rushed up to me, barking and throwing himself at my waist. He bounded about me, yapping excitedly. He looked like a slavering brute with rabies.

Raphe gave me a glowering welcome. 'You didn't say *when* I had to get rid of him. I thought having him help me guard the house would be a good idea.'

'He'll have to go,' I said.

'Why?'

I was about to reply that because this was my house, I could choose who lived within its walls, but even as I opened my mouth to speak, the dog threw himself upwards once more, and I accidentally caught him. The brute licked at my chin and cheek in an ecstasy of adoration. 'He is affectionate,' I said.

'And quick to learn. He'll make a good guard. There are so many stories of people being robbed in their homes. A dog is the best protection for a man like you,' the devious little cully added.

Could Raphe be right about keeping him? I began to have second thoughts. After all, London could be dangerous. A dog to guard the house might be a good idea.

Raphe had succeeded. The mutt was granted a stay of execution. 'Very well, the brute can stay for now. But the first time I see him piss in the house, he's out.'

Raphe nodded while I went upstairs to my bedchamber and changed into my suit. The wine had stained it, but the material did not show it badly – it was already dark enough. I went to my strongroom and checked that my money box was safe and locked, and took some coins for the day's expenses. The rattle of change in my purse put me in a cheerful frame of mind as I strode out of the door a little while later. It was at the doorway that I remembered I had left my handgun in the house, but I decided that there was no need to return to fetch it. I had left

it on the table in my parlour, I thought, and as long as Raphe
didn't play with it, all would be well. And if he did pick it
up, in all likelihood he would only injure himself. That thought
was enough to improve my mood still further.

I had arranged to see Cat at the Cheshire Cheese, but we
had agreed to meet at noon. It was unlikely that she would
still be there, waiting hopefully for me. However, she might
well have been there in order to view the lawyers and
merchants, and decide which might succumb to her charms,
and she could still be there now, waiting to see which man
would be her best target.

It was worth going to look, I reasoned, and I bent my steps
towards the tavern.

The Cheese was a raucous, low alehouse. I passed up the
alleyway and in through the main door, slipping aside to allow
a man to totter out, and he smiled at me charmingly, until a
look of uncertainty splashed across his face and he darted from
me to the far side of the alley, where he bent over and spewed
copiously. He rose, blinking, wiped his face and, smiling once
more, returned inside.

He had taken a turn to the right. I took a different path,
leftwards, and walked through the various chambers. There
were many rooms here, all smelling of the effects of drinking.
The rushes hadn't been changed in a year or more, from the
odour of sour wine and beer. But as I moved through the place,
the warm fug of men drinking, laughing, telling ribald jokes,
haggling with the tarts for their attentions, soon got to me.
Before long I had forgotten the odour of ancient drinking and
could concentrate on the faces, hoping against hope that I
would see Cat. Even seeing Henry would be good, bearing in
mind he was a convenient conduit to Cat herself.

It was my enthusiasm that was my undoing. I was pushing
past a table of gamblers when I caught a glimpse of a woman
with a less-than-perfectly filled bodice at the farther side of
the room. It was hard to tell, because the fire had been smoking,
and there was a thicker atmosphere than usual, but I felt almost
certain that it was Cat. I barged through the crowds, my eyes
fixed on her, in case she might disappear from sight and I
would lose her again. The men were squeezed into a small

space, and for much of the way I was forced to barge past men who were happily chatting. Several passed comment on my parentage as I knocked into them, but by issuing profuse apologies for every yard I passed, I successfully avoided altercations. In fact, the disaster was not my finding an opponent who wished to quarrel with me, but two men I had not noticed because I was concentrating on Cat so firmly.

I was close to her, and fitted a broad smile to my face. Calling, 'Cat! I am so sorry!' I was about to hurry to her side when something caught my shin, and I tumbled to the floor.

It was such a surprise – for I had seen no impediment to my progress – that I fell badly and was winded. Something smelled very rank, and I realized that the owner of the boots to my left had stood in a dog's turd, and I was just rising to my elbows and starting to climb to my feet, when I saw what had tripped me.

''Allo, Peter,' Arch said. 'You fell over my boot. Look, you've scratched the leather.'

'He has, Arch, hasn't he?' Hamon said.

This is what passed for wit between them.

'Excuse me, but I must—'

'We won't mention the damage to my boot leather, though, will we, 'Amon?'

'No, Arch. Not if he sees his way to buying us a quart of ale each.'

'I . . .' I stood and stared about me. There were many men there, and all appeared to be laughing at me, but of Cat there was not a sign. She had disappeared through a door in the farther wall.

I turned to Arch and gave him a sickly grin.

Arch sat back and studied me as I stood. 'So, friend Peter, where 'ave ye been? Strange, but you know I haven't seen you since we had that little bet the other day.'

'Shall I go and buy you your drinks, then?' I said.

'No 'urry. One of the girls'll be here soon, I 'ave no doubt. No, what we were wondering was, when you were plannin' on paying me back my money what you owe. Only, you see, it's a guinea now.'

'What? A *guinea*? It was ten bob!'

'Well, it's like this, Peter,' Hamon said. 'You get to owe Arch money, and he has to go to all the trouble of making sure you're safe to pay it. Now, what that means is, he has to buy in snippers and things so that if you was to forget you owed him money, he had a way of remindin' you. Such as, say, taking the snippers to your little finger, or your nose, or your ears, or maybe something you'd miss even more,' he added, staring at my codpiece. 'Snip, snip, snip.'

I felt a cold trickle move down my spine.

Arch shook his head. 'It's not just the snippers, you understand,' he said. 'I 'ave other people who want to borrow money from me, and if it's all out with you, I can't take their money from them, can I? It's simple, this. I lend money, people pay me back. If some thieving scrote keeps 'old of my money, I can't lend it out, can I? So the thieving bastard 'as to pay me more, to compensate me for the money I can't earn from other people. Oh, an' to stop me getting interested in 'im and 'ow his cods are attached, and whether I can remove 'em to make sure 'e remembers in future.' He gave me a broad grin. 'And that way, everyone's 'appy, aren't they? So it *was* ten bob, but now it's a guinea.'

Have you ever had the sort of sinking feeling in the belly that paralyses you? Usually, with most men who wanted to investigate the inner workings of my body, I could be on my feet and away in moments. Fear provokes responses of varying types in different characters. I have known men who, at the first sign of a problem, would swallow their terror and run towards the danger. That is always good to see, because it tends to mean that the enemy is busy watching them, and paying less attention to someone like me, who was quietly sidling away in the background. Not that I'm lacking in courage, you understand. It's only that I never saw the point in getting involved in unnecessary fights. Or fights I would lose. In other words, usually fear was a wonderful motivator for me to practise my sprinting skills.

Not today. The sight of these two smiling at me was enough to send all the right signals to my spine, and thence to my feet, but the degree of horror and panic was enough to confuse.

And even if I were to issue definite instructions to my legs, the simple fact is that there was not enough space in that room for me to have any certainty of escape. There were too many obstacles in the form of benches, tables, and men.

'I am sure that I can pay you back tomorrow,' I said with an anxious smile.

'Ah, he says tomorrow,' Hamon said to Arch.

Arch nodded sadly. 'Tomorrow is such a long time away, ain't it, Peter? You might forget by then. And that would be dreadfully sad, wouldn't it, 'Amon?'

'It would, Arch. It would.'

'Because we'd 'ave to give him something to remember us by, wouldn't we, 'Amon?'

'We would.'

'Some people, you know, Peter, have this way of remembering. They tie a knot in an 'an'kerchief. Then, when they need to blow their bugle, they see the knot, and they think, "Why'd I go an' tie a knot in my 'an'kerchief?" and then, they think, "Oh, yes, it was to go and pay Arch that money what I owe him," as it might be. And that is all right and good. Do you have an 'an'kerchief about you, Peter?'

'No.'

'Oh, dear. Oh, dear, that is a shame. You see, you could 'ave tried to tie a knot in it, and then we'd think you'd be likely to remember that you owed me one guinea and fifteen shillings.'

'Fifteen? You said it was—'

'Ah, but you're making me explain things. You wouldn't expect to get all my advice for free, would you? Naturally, you'd expect to pay for good advice, just as you would if you went to a lawyer or a medic. So the price has gone up, but we need to make sure you remember, don't we? So, 'Amon will need to introduce you to his snippers, is what I'm thinking.'

'No, there's no need, I swear.'

'Yes, well, you swore to pay me the next day, didn't you?' Arch said nastily. He leaned forward, head jutting like an angry lizard. There was something reptilian in his eyes as he held my gaze. 'That's today. So if you don't bring me two guineas tomorrow, 'Amon will put a knot in your tarse that'll make your ballocks wish they'd been cut off. And if you still don't bring me my money, 'e'll grant their wish. Do you understand me?'

'Yes.'

'Good. Now disappear, Peter. You're blocking my view.'

You can imagine that it was a thoughtful, anxious Jack Blackjack who left them hurriedly, trying not to stumble over any other men as he bolted from the tavern.

There was no sign of Cat or Henry. At the farther doorway, I stood and stared into a new room. A man was enjoying a woman against the wall, and she peered at me over his shoulder, making the requisite moans and groans to hurry his inevitable end, while no doubt reminding herself that she needed to purchase milk on her way home, or eggs, or some other comestibles. I recognized her vaguely, and she acknowledged me with a quick smile and a wink, before returning to her shopping cogitations.

Beyond her there was another doorway. I walked through the room and came to a staircase that led down. Following this, I came across the tavern's cellars. There were more people down there in the gloom and damp, but my main thought was that Arch and Hamon weren't, and I darted from one chamber to another, trying to find my way back to the daylight.

Two guineas! It was a shocking sum of money, especially since the two had fixed the gamble. Hamon had released the hound so soon after Arch let the cat from the sack that the cat could make only a quick dash of five paces, turn, give a mew that, to me, sounded like ''S'wounds!' before the hound was on it. And now I was learning that I would have to pay still more the following day, and more each day after that, because kindly Arch was helping me maintain my honour by lending me the money I needed to pay him back for a gambling debt I never wished for in the first place.

It was enough to make my head spin.

However, I was determined that I would not pay Arch and Hamon. They could keep increasing the amount of the debt all they wanted, but I was not going to pay it. I had the money in my strongbox back at home, but that was for me to use, not for those two. They could threaten me all they liked, but I knew something that they didn't: my name wasn't Peter, and they didn't know where I lived.

At the far end of the cellars there was a set of stone steps leading up to the dim alleyway, and I took these, hoping to find the fair air of London again.

I had not even managed to find a quart or two of ale. Although the entrance to the tavern was only a short way back up the alleyway, I chose to walk back down to the road. I felt safer there, with more people milling about, the constant shouting of the hawkers, the hurdy-gurdies playing where buskers were pestering the public, demanding money by menacing them with music, and the occasional dog barking and snarling. I had no enthusiasm for dogs just at this moment.

There was a tavern called the Sign of the Fox a short way up towards the Fleet prison, a foul building that held some three hundred miserable souls. It was a debtor's prison, and the victims were held inside with their families, unless they could afford to pay the keeper and take lodgings outside. The other denizens were often to be seen at the grilles in the doors, begging for any coins that passers-by could spare. The thought of being locked up and having to pay for every meal, for the removal of irons, for – well, for everything – was hideous in the extreme. I stood outside and stared at the place for some little while.

Money and debts were lying heavily on my mind.

At the Fox, I soon found myself comfortably ensconced before a roaring fire, a pot of warm ale in my hand, and feeling considerably more cheerful as the level in my cup went down. After all, Arch and Hamon would be unlikely to find me, and if they did, as long as I kept to busier thoroughfares, I would be secure enough. I had a reputation, after all. As long as I kept my pistol close by, I should be safe.

I ordered a pie and ate it thoughtfully. There was, after all, one other consideration, which was that story of Atwood's. Was it really possible that he was telling the truth? It seemed barely credible. I hoped that he would have been arrested by now, anyway, and with luck he would be held for a good long time. I didn't think he was a murderer of wayward priests, but I knew that he was capable of killing other men without a qualm, and I had no desire to be his latest victim. And if he was telling the truth about the gold, it could be quite profitable for me if Atwood was held in Newgate or somewhere similar. I could find the gold and keep it all.

Cat was nowhere to be seen now, and searching for one woman with her occupation was unlikely to be productive. London was a seething mass of women who sold themselves on the streets, in brothels, in clubs or taverns. I could hardly run about all the taverns in London. There were twenty or more within the square mile, let alone all the alehouses and drinking chambers without the City walls. It might take me a year or more to find her. The room to which she had taken me the day before was nothing more than a chamber paid for by the hour, I had no doubt. But then . . . well, I had little else to do just now. It would be good to see her. And perhaps, if I couldn't find her, I might make my way back to St Botolph's and enquire of the widow Dorothy about Dick Atwood's story of a box of gold. If I knew Dick Atwood at all – and I knew him alarmingly well – he would be keen to find the gold, but also to keep it entirely for himself. He was not the sort of man to share his good fortune, and no matter what he said, the idea that he might willingly allow me to keep a brass farthing from the box of gold was stretching the imagination. He was not a trustworthy man.

He must know that I wouldn't trust him. So what was his aim in telling me about the box in the first place? Was he being hopeful, thinking that I would drop everything to help him discover it? Surely the man would realize that I would be likely to keep it, were I to find it?

Since he had told me about it, he must have had a feeling that I was more likely to find it than him. Perhaps he believed that I was more honourable than he himself? Well, naturally, I was. Maybe he thought that my natural generosity of spirit and sense of fairness would mean that I would instantly let him know, were I to discover the box? If so, I hoped I might disabuse him of that belief.

Of course, he would know that I had a good opportunity to

find out anything from Dorothy. Better than his own chances. You see, I have a welcoming face – a regular, pleasing face, which women like. They think I am comely and want to coddle me. It is a difficult cross to bear, but bear it I must. I am attractive to all women. Obviously, Atwood knew this. He had known it from the first time he saw me chatting to one of the working women in the street, I have no doubt. I have charms that put other men in the shade.

He realized that I would be able to work my charms on the widow Dorothy. Dick Atwood must have been counting on the fact that I would so entrance the woman that she would tell me all her secrets. He thought that if there was any remote possibility that she knew where the abbot's gold was hidden, she would find it impossible to hide from me.

I took a long draft of ale.

Well, who could say that he was not right? Maybe the woman would succumb to my many advantages. She would not be the first, nor the last. I could inveigle my way into her affections by using Ben or one of her other sons, perhaps.

I would return to St Botolph's, I decided. I'd woo the woman and she would soon tell me all.

And that way I'd evade Arch and Hamon too.

I enjoyed a second quart of ale, and then a pint of wine to wash it down, and then, as the light began to fade, I set off homewards.

The porter at Ludgate was grumpy that evening and glared at me when I gave him a 'Good evening', but I was used to that. The lower classes of servant are often jealous of a man who is as well attired as me. I strolled along happily enough, up past St Paul's, and on.

There was a tavern up near the cross, and I stopped off for a quick refresher and repaired to the main room, taking my seat at a bench not far from the door. I was not known to frequent this place, but I didn't want to take any risks; I would keep a wary eye on the door, in case Arch or Hamon appeared. The keeper was a miserable, black-featured fellow, but I did not require conversation just then, and was glad to receive my quart of ale without having to entertain him.

It was when I lifted the pot for the first mouthful that I almost choked.

There, opposite me, was Cat.

She looked delicious, although a little distressed in some way. Her eyes appeared wider than usual, her cheeks slightly more rosy, and she looked as though she was panting slightly. But much more to the point, she appeared to be alone.

'Hello, young maid,' I said in my smoothest manner. 'May I take a seat with you?'

'Peter!' she said.

I had forgotten she knew me as Peter. It gave me a jolt for a moment, but then I smiled. 'You were at the Cheese earlier. What made you hurry away in such a madcap manner? You disappeared before I could catch you.'

'I am so glad to see you, Peter,' she said, and leaned into me as I sat beside her, her head resting on my shoulder.

Her hair smelled of hay and freshness and all that was good and wholesome, and the warmth of her beside me was enough to stir the blood. I remembered my plans for her earlier today. Looking down now at her blouse, I came to the conclusion that her figure was more than adequate.

'Where were you? I was at the Cheese when we agreed, but you never arrived. I thought you must have been injured or killed,' she said, and there was a marvellously broken quality to her voice that thrilled my blood, and other organs besides.

'I was held up, maid. I had to go to a Coroner's inquest east of the City, and the damn thing kept me occupied until the afternoon. I was desperate to get back to you, but the Crowner wouldn't let me go. Officious fool that he is.'

'Why? Were you accused of murder?' she asked, sitting up, her eyes round as pennies.

'Me? Hah! No! Well, sort of. A malcontent fool chose to deflect suspicion from himself on to me. Me! I ask you! Who could accuse me of something like that?'

She nodded, but there was a faintly anxious look in her eyes still.

'What is it?' I asked.

'What happened?'

'There was no suggestion from the Coroner that I was involved,' I hastened to reassure her. 'It was just something dreamed up by a man who was once my servant. Nothing more than that. He wished to clear his own name by muddying another's. That's all, maid.'

'Where was this?'

'A little village near St Botolph's. The local vicar was murdered.'

'That's terrible! Who would kill a vicar?' she said. She had snuggled up to me again, her thigh wondrously warm on mine, and her low voice was breathy in my ear.

'Ah, well, you see, there are always men who can be jealous of a vicar. Someone who sees a man who had been a devoted member of the new Church, and who now throws over his old life in order to embrace the old Church – it can make some men angry. The vicar concerned had suddenly decided to give up his wife and children, and return to Holy Orders in the Catholic faith, rather than keep to his family. A sad case, no doubt, but the fellow has paid for his inconstancy.'

'Who killed him? Did the Coroner arrest your servant, if he was so obvious?'

'He may have done by now. There was little evidence as to who might be guilty, but Atwood would deserve a few weeks waiting at Newgate. No doubt they will find the culprit before long, and if not, perhaps he will be taken.'

'But the priest. What sort of person could kill a man of God?'

I didn't want to say that if I was to bet, a troublesome, murdering bastard like Atwood would spring to mind quite easily. Instead, I sighed and looked doleful. 'There are some men in the world who have no conception of the depths of their depravity. You should be careful. The streets are full of dangerous men.'

'I am safe with you, though. I always feel safe with you.'

There was a little wriggle then of her bottom, bringing her thigh into still more glorious contact. Her breast was on my upper arm, and I dared not move in case she pulled away. 'Of course you are,' I said suavely. 'You will always be safe with me, Cat. But heavens, look at the light outside! Even I need

daylight to be able to see dangers. Cat,' I said with great
seriousness. 'You should not be out at this time of day on
your own. I have to return to my house, but I cannot leave
you to fend for yourself. Would you come with me, so I can
guard you on the streets?'

She looked up at me, coy and slanted-eyed, as though she
did not quite trust me.

''S'blood, Cat,' I said. 'I hope you don't mistrust me? On
my honour, I only seek to protect you.'

She nodded, but there was a shadow on her face.

'What is it, Cat?' I asked earnestly. 'I only want to protect
you.'

'Are you sure you intend to be honourable?'

I gazed down at her, and my eyes could not escape the
glorious sight of her apple dumplings, scarcely constrained by
the tight bodice. 'To the extent that I can be, maid.'

'What does that mean?'

I gave her a wolfish grin. 'Whatever you want it to!'

A short while later, we left and walked up Westchepe, heading
for my house.

I was feeling distinctly cheery with the maid on my arm.
She was an attractive little bundle, and as lecherous as any of
the strumpets in the Cardinal's Hat, the brothel south of the
river where my friend Piers worked. He was doorman, hair
butcher and servant of all work. Cat had been an enthusiastic
galloper last evening, before her damned pimp Henry appeared.
He had savaged the atmosphere when he turned up.

That gave me pause for thought. I hadn't seen him in the
tavern, but that meant little enough. I hadn't been looking for
him. 'Your young friend, Henry. Where is he tonight?'

'I don't know. That's why I was nervous in the tavern. He
said he had to go and see to some business, but he shouldn't
have taken so long about it.'

'What, he left you alone in the Cheese?'

'Yes, and then a horrible man came and made me a most
improper proposition.'

She went on to describe Arch, and I felt myself thrill to a
feeling that was quite novel to me. I mean to say, usually when

I think of Arch or Hamon, it's with revulsion mingled with a healthy portion of concern. If I did not regularly feel concern, my self-preservation would not be so assured. Men of their type are best avoided, after all. A man can only afford so many enemies in a city, and with men of Hamon and Arch's form, it's best to keep as far away as possible. Arch was the sort of man who would order another fellow's death without any compunction. He could command a murder in the blink of an eye while in bed with his woman. Hamon could not spell the word 'compunction'. He would agree to kill someone because he enjoyed it. The man was one of those who would break a leg purely from a scientific interest. He would want to see what sort of noise the bone made, or what noise the victim made. Neither was the sort of man to trouble himself over another human's feelings. Especially if there was money involved.

'Are you all right?' she asked. 'You've gone quite green.'

'Not green. Only horny, Cat. I can't wait to get you home.'

'You said I'd be safe, Peter.'

'As safe as you want to be,' I leered.

'I don't know—'

'Let's get to my house and open a barrel of something decent,' I said.

I held her about the waist. She was a taut little temptress. Her thigh bumped mine as we walked, a pleasant sensation; meanwhile, my hand had rested on her hip, and now it slipped and came to rest on her buttock. It was a firm, round handhold, and I squeezed it until she meaningfully grabbed my wrist and pulled it northwards. I allowed my hand to remain there, in the curve between rib and hip, before trying the same manoeuvre, and this time she tutted and sighed, but left it there.

For some reason, my mind returned to the inquest, to the gold Atwood had spoken of – and to Dorothy. She would not be so easy a bedmate to persuade, I felt. Still, it would be a simple enough task for me to win her over. She would never have experienced seduction of the sort I could offer her. And she would be unable to refuse me, naturally.

It was while I was enumerating her many attractions, and

looking forward to meeting her again, that I reached my door. Standing on the uppermost step, I brought Cat to the door and then, placing both hands on her hips, I pulled her to me. She was nothing loath, and her lips met mine in a long, lingering kiss. I pressed her back so that she was leaning against the door itself, and our tongues played tickle-the-tonsil until we both had to come up for air.

'Let's get inside,' she breathed. Her lips were flushed, as were her cheeks. I smiled my manly smile and rapped with the brass knocker. It gave a good, loud sound, and then there was a furious barking that filled the house with noise.

When the door opened, my hand was still gripping the ring, and the movement almost pulled me in to fall flat on my face. 'What do you mean by opening the door like that? I nearly fell, Raphe,' I said, and then giggled.

'Peter!' Cat cried, and helped me to my feet.

My giggle stopped as I looked up into the impassive features of Sir Richard of Bath.

'Hello, *Peter*,' he said.

To be fair to the Coroner, he did not take my sudden nervous laughter as a reflection of my feelings towards him. Rather, he seemed to realize in an instant that I had been enjoying several pots of the good stuff, and he smiled broadly to see Cat. He looked like a man who was inclined to join me, rather than denigrate my behaviour. He was effusive in his welcome to her, holding her hand as though to prevent her running away. With an ogre-like build and face like a bearded accident, I imagine that any time he wanted to satisfy his natural carnal desires, grabbing hold of a woman and not releasing her would be the only way he would succeed.

'I thought . . . thought you were out at St Botolph's still,' I said, while Cat tried to straighten her clothing one-handed. My wandering hands had somehow disarrayed her bodice and chemise.

'I was,' Sir Richard said. 'But the matter is recorded. The peasants know what their fines must be, and the Rolls are deposited safely. RAPHE!'

The sudden stentorian bellow made me spring briefly into

the air. Cat gave a short scream. I felt my heart thudding painfully. 'What do you shout for?'

'Wine,' he explained as if surprised that I had not realized. 'I thought you would like a little, too.'

'Yes, a good idea,' Cat said.

'Sensible woman,' Sir Richard said, eyeing her appreciatively. I stepped between them to give her some privacy. Some men don't know when to show a woman a little respect. 'Maid, you are most attractive. You seem familiar. Have we met?'

Possibly, I felt, the very worst approach to a woman I had ever heard. Still, she giggled and simpered a little as she took her hand back.

Raphe appeared and stood gaping with apparent admiration at Cat. The barking was muffled by several doors, from the sound of it, and I guessed that he had locked the patched brute in the small yard beside the house. On being given his instructions, Raphe departed, slouching away grimly with a glower. I guessed that the idea of sharing my wine with anyone other than himself was painful. Before he left, he gave a very hard glare to Sir Richard, but the Coroner ignored Raphe, having given him his orders. The knight was concentrating on Cat.

Before long, a large tray appeared with Raphe almost hidden behind it. He had filled it with wine in my flagon, cups, a joint of beef, some bread and half a chicken carcass. These he deposited on my table, and then turned sorrowfully, seeing how we were to become so steeped in gluttony, and left us to it. I had no doubt he was in a hurry to become reacquainted with the barrel in the buttery. He could not, however, refrain from turning and staring open-mouthed at Cat in the doorway.

'Close the door behind you,' I said.

'It was a sad case, that,' Sir Richard said, pulling the chicken's leg from the bird and then, recalling his manners, offering it to Cat. She smilingly refused, and Sir Richard took a bite, adding, 'Seeing a poor priest slaughtered in the street is hard. He was a kindly man.'

'I was told he was a womanizing lecher.'

Sir Richard shot me a black look. 'What?'

'I know,' I said. 'Shouldn't speak ill of the dead and all that, but it would explain things, wouldn't it? Perhaps a jealous woman, or a jealous husband? Someone slew him and then went home again, leaving his body in the road.'

'You should keep thoughts like that to yourself. Hardly respectful to the dead, especially a priest. In any case, his behaviour is no one else's business,' Sir Richard said. 'Still, the clothing was the oddity. Why would someone kill him, then dress him and stab him another few times?'

'If he was rutting on another man's wife, and the husband found him there, he might stab the priest. Maybe he only discovered what he had done later, and realized that he must cover up his crime. He dressed the priest, took him out to the road and stabbed him again to make it look as though it was the random act of outlaws,' I suggested, and belched behind my hand.

The Coroner pulled a face, but nodded. 'So you think he was committing adultery, found pinning the cuckold's horns on the husband, and the husband in a mad rage slaughtered him with a single blow? It is possible. It would explain the lack of blood about Peter's body, too. The blood, if there was much, would have been left in the bed.'

I studied the beef and cut off a segment, while Cat took the chicken's remaining leg. I said, 'Or perhaps his wife was jealous? She was his wife before, and now she comes into his chamber to discover him giving another woman lessons in the amorous arts. Dorothy was his wife, but he had set her and their children aside, just so that he could remain in Holy Orders. She would be furious to discover that he was enjoying the favours of some other woman, while she was destitute and hungry, desperate to feed her children. Five of them. So she stabbed him in the back as he lay on top of his lover.'

'What would his lover do?'

'She would scream and cry, so perhaps Dorothy killed her, too.'

'There is no body.'

'It hasn't been found yet,' I said. I ate a little more. 'That explains things neatly, I think. She walked in on him, murdered him, and then the woman, too. She would be stuck, after all. She wouldn't be able to leap to her feet to escape, not with Peter lying on top of her, dead.'

'That is a very interesting theory. But surely other aspects make it unlikely.'

'Such as what?'

Sir Richard peered at me. There was a benevolent look in his eye. 'The fact that the poor priest was very much in love with his wife, was not a womanizer, and was invariably shy and quiet in the presence of women.'

I confess, I scoffed at that. 'Really? And who told you this? One of the women in the village, I suppose. What else would they say to you, Coroner, but something to deflect attention from them and their amorous adventures with the wily priest?'

'No, it was not them. Dorothy has told me so, and I know that her husband was no libertine.'

'How would you know that?'

Sir Richard sighed. 'Because Peter was my brother.'

There are times, even when I have drunk significantly more than usual, when suddenly clarity springs itself upon my mind, like a steel trap closing over a man's ankle. This was one of those moments.

'Oh,' I said. And then, thinking this was perhaps not quite enough, '*Oh!*'

Cat put her hand on his. 'I am sorry,' she said softly.

'Aye, well, nothing to do with you, madam, is it?' Sir Richard said gruffly. I swear that these were the first words he had spoken that didn't rattle the windows or cause the walls to creak.

'It must be horrible. Was he older or younger than you?'

'Oh, he was younger. Always the tearaway when we were young, Peter was. But kind, ever kind. He was ideally suited to the priesthood. Whenever someone was unwell in the village, or when one of the animals was found to have been suffering, he would be the first to go and comfort them. He had a soft heart.'

'But he left his wife and family behind when he was given the chance to return to the Catholic Church?'

'Many priests did that,' Cat observed, pouring herself more wine.

'Of course they did,' Sir Richard agreed. 'They had little

choice. What, starve with their families, or win a chance to
retrieve something from their situation? It was the only sensible
thing to do.'

'Except it meant leaving their wives and children in poverty,'
I pointed out. 'If he was as soft-hearted as you say, why didn't
he stay with his children and protect them? He could have
found a new job, surely? Coroners always need clerks, don't
they?'

He shot me a black look. 'I had a clerk already. Damn me
eyes, if I could have offered him something, I would have.
But I had nothing at the time. I know he knew that. But it
didn't make it any easier to accept. As soon as I heard he was
being forced to leave his old parish and come to St Botolph's,
I knew he would have a hard time of it.'

'Why?'

'They're more keen on the Catholic faith in that village.
Surely you will have noticed that grasping fellow, Harknet?
He was always very keen to show himself devoted to whatever
the latest fad might be. When the old King ruled that the new
Church would take priority, Harknet was the keenest proponent,
and could not help but report those who tried to maintain their
old faith. But then, as soon as Queen Mary decreed that the
Roman Church was to return, Harknet was the most enthusiastic persecutor of those who would not change. Now he has
no friends. No one will trust him. Certainly not me. The man
is steeped in iniquity. He has no feeling for anyone excepting
himself.'

'What of the other villagers?' I said.

'They don't like 'im either.'

'No, I meant how are they about the Roman religion?'

'They'll stick it – those who were never keen to change.
Others, well, they'll pay lip service, I suppose.'

'What did they think of your brother?'

'They mostly liked him, I think. If anyone knew some fact
about his death that could help find the murderer, I'm sure
that they would tell me. None of them wants to let the man
responsible go free.'

'Of course not. It reflects badly on their village if they allow
too many murderers to walk the streets,' I said.

He gave me a cold look. 'And it reflects badly on them if they allow a priest in the Queen's favourite religion to be murdered.'

'Do you think it was Harknet?'

'Him? I doubt he would know how to hold a knife without cutting himself,' Sir Richard said scathingly.

'But whether you like him or not, could he have wielded the weapon?'

'I suppose so.'

There was one thing that disturbed me. 'Your sister-in-law – she did not seem to recognize you.'

'Why should she? We never met.'

'What?'

He sighed. 'Peter decided to marry Dorothy when he met her, and . . . well, I was of the old school. I didn't believe that a priest could be a husband and father. I refused to see him from that day. I've had no contact with him until a few weeks ago, when I learned he was right next door to the City, out in Middlesex. He did try to meet with me, but . . . well, he was not only married, but the fool had so many children it would be hard to count them! And now, I fear, it's too late. So I intend to make things good with him. Even if I can't help him, I can find his murderer.'

'And help his widow.'

'Hmph. Perhaps. Except, in the eyes of God, I doubt she has such a status.'

At that, I almost spilled my ale down my lap, for a sudden thought had gloriously entranced me. I sat with my eyes wide, staring at the fire, my mouth dropping wide.

'What is it, man? Ye're goggling like a frog!'

'I feel so sorry for the widow. I shall help you. Tomorrow I will go back there and see what I can learn.'

'You? Have you ever had experience of such matters? Are you qualified as an inquisitor? It takes a certain skill to learn what people know when they are trying to avoid telling you.'

'I have been useful in other murder enquiries,' I said stiffly, refraining from pointing out that they tended to be murders in which I had been implicated as the protagonist.

Cat yawned, and I hastened to try to evict Sir Richard

from my door. I attempted the subtle approach at first, yawning myself, trying to clear up the food dishes, noting loudly, 'Ah, we have finished the wine!' and giving other obvious hints.

'Oh, ye're tired,' Sir Richard said. He glanced about him. 'Aye, it's been a long day. Well, perhaps we should get our heads down. Where's me room?'

'Your room?'

'Aye. Ye can't expect a man to go walking the streets at this time of night.'

'I only have the one bed, I am afraid.'

'Oh.' His face went blank as he looked at me, and then over at Cat, who had taken her seat on an old chair and whose head was nodding. 'Oh, I see. Well, you and I will be fine down here, eh? Poor woman had best have your bed.'

THREE

There are mornings on which the sun shines, the sparrows chitter happily, the hawkers in the streets call cheerfully to each other, and on which the world seems a good, wholesome place.

This was not one of those mornings.

I awoke on a bench, and as I tried to sit up, something hit me square on the forehead and knocked me back down. It was the heavy atmosphere in the chamber. I groaned, I think, or it might have been a muttered prayer. My head felt as though someone had been hacking at the inner surfaces of my skull with a blunt chisel, and all the chippings of bone had fallen on to my tongue. It was dry and rasped when it moved over my palate. My lips were sticky and reluctant to open, and when I cautiously cracked one eye, it was too painful to keep it open. The hazy view it afforded was thick with smoke from the fire (I need to have the chimney cleaned), but I caught sight of cups, two flagons and a bottle of sack. The sweet, strong wine smelled so potent that my stomach rebelled, and I was forced to turn away and pretend I could not detect its odour any longer.

Gradually, my memory brought back a raucously hilarious Sir Richard, who, once he had stopped singing, proceeded to entertain me by telling the filthiest bawdy jokes I had ever heard. I confess, he was exceedingly amusing company, with a fund of humorous tales that I would have blushed to tell Piers at the brothel. They certainly made Raphe's mouth fall to the floor when he was bellowed at to bring another flagon. I recalled it as a very pleasant evening. However, now my head was repaying the debt in full for my pleasure and drinking.

Gingerly, I swung myself to the vertical, eyes tight shut, and ventured to take in my surroundings. Once more I was forced to hurriedly close my eyes as shafts of sunlight stabbed at them like lances. 'Raphe!' I called, and hesitated while waiting for the top of my skull to return. It appeared to have flown off towards the ceiling with my call, and the whole of my head was opened to a searing pain. But I had no choice. I must make my way to my privy.

'You were loud last night,' Raphe said in a peevish tone.

'Please do not shout – and stop that accursed dog from barking or I will kill it myself!'

'I suppose your head's not good.'

'There are times when you can be highly observant,' I said. It was meant to sting. It probably didn't. Raphe was never strong on sarcasm.

'What do you want?'

'A pot of ale, or watered wine. A pint of it.'

'I don't know what—'

'Get it now, or you can leave my service this morning,' I snarled.

When I opened my eyes, there was no sign of him. That was good news. However, there was also a lack of Sir Richard. While that was also good news, it was more than a little shocking that he had obviously risen and left the room while I was yet asleep. The man must have the constitution of an elephant. Still, at least it was peaceful without his bellowing.

I went out to the privy, and, returning, found a jug of wine and a cup on the table. I drank off some of it in a hurry, and my throat felt like a drain as the liquid gurgled into my stomach. A second cup, sipped more slowly, soon followed the first, and by the time I had drunk half of the third, the world was looking considerably happier. I even managed to refrain from shouting too loudly at Raphe as he moved about the room – I won't say he 'bustled', since that implies more energy than he possesses, but he sort of moped around and gave the impression of restrained energy. The dog, meanwhile, came in, took one look at me, and decided that suicide was not on his list of things to do today. He curled up with his nose under his tail before the fire.

Raphe had fetched me a fresh loaf from the baker's, and I was about to get stuck into it when I was struck by a sudden thought. 'Raphe, is there no sign of Mistress Cat?'

'She was gone before Sir Richard,' he said, and there

was a slight sneer, as though he always thought her too good
for me.

'Did she leave me a message?'

'No. Nothing.'

I sent him away with a lash from my tongue that almost
severed my skull from my body. If Sir *blasted* Richard had
not appeared last night, I would have been woken this morning
by the sight of that beautiful young woman at my side in my
bed. And now, instead, she had slipped away and I had missed
my opportunity. Who could tell how long it would be before
I could find her again, and next time her shadow Henry would
no doubt be at her side once more. He would not be conducive
to lengthy fraternizing. His presence would be obstructive to
my lecherous intentions, I was sure. It was deeply annoying.

Setting to with the bread, I made as good a breakfast as I
could under the circumstances. My belly recoiled from the
sight of the beef, the fat white and glistening, and the cold
pork was no more appealing. Finally, I stuck to a little cheese
and the bread. A fourth cup of wine helped rekindle my appetite, and I ate a slice or two of the beef, and it was as I was
sitting back that the front door slammed, and a bawled
'RAPHE! *Bring me wine!*' rattled the floorboards and brought
down a fine scattering of dust. The dog sprang to his feet and
began a high-pitched barking. Simultaneously, someone shoved
a fine-bladed stiletto into the base of my skull – well, it felt
like it, anyway.

'Morning! Ye slept well, Master Blackjack. Or should I say,
Master Peter?'

I gave him a sour look. 'There were good reasons why I
had to use a different name when I saw her first.'

'Aye, such as hiding from her.'

'If I was hiding, I would hardly bring her to my own home.
It wasn't concealing myself from her, but from . . . certain men.'

'You make a habit of meeting such men, do ye?' He turned.
'*Raphe!* Can you not make that brute belt up?'

I clung to my pate to hold it in place. It felt like a dish
walloped by a club and was apparently trying to flee the scene.

He continued in only slightly more moderate tones, 'That
brute still here? I thought I told your boy to kill the thing!'

I was in a bad enough temper already. Kicking the mutt, I said, 'Yes, well, we have decided to keep him.'

'Ha! Really? I daresay he'll have his uses! Broken yer fast, have ye? Good! Much to do today. Oh, and did ye hear the story about King Arthur? Hey? No? He was off to the war, ye see, and he leaves Sir Lancelot to guard Camelot and his queen, and tells Lancelot, "Look here, Lance, my wife is the most beautiful woman in the land. She'd tempt Saint Peter, if he saw her. So to make sure she's safe and unsullied, I have set a chastity belt about her. She's the most precious thing in the land, and her virtue is more important to me than anything. Here's the key. Ye're the only man I trust with her." And with that, he rides off with his army. But he's only ridden twenty miles when Lancelot appears on his fleetest mount. King Arthur is told, and Lancelot is allowed into his presence. "What is the reason for your leaving Camelot without a knight? Why have you left me wife alone?" "Sire," says Sir Lancelot, "I am sorry, but you have left me the wrong key." Hey? You understand? Eh? Haha ha! Let's be off, then.'

'Eh?' His gales of laughter had shredded what remained of my brain.

'Have ye forgotten? We're riding to St Botolph's this morning. Ye're helping me discover who killed me brother.'

Seeing the village again did not inspire feelings of joy. After yesterday's rain, the place had that grey, filthy appearance that you see all over the countryside when raindrops have splashed and besmirched everything with mud.

The cottages and inn were spattered, the limewash covered with smudges like little streams of mud. The road itself was sodden, and as we rode along – for Sir Richard had hired us a pair of mounts – I could feel the moisture at my shins, ankles and feet. My boots were sponging up all the moisture they could, making my toes feel the chill. As it was, a brief downpour had soaked into my jack and cloak, and both were sodden. Every breeze that whirled about us sent icy chills into my bones, which only seemed to add to the grim, plodding misery of my headache.

In short, I was not happy.

Sir Richard, for much of the earlier part of the journey, was strangely quiet, as though he was mulling over a question of great importance. It was a relief. His voice was so loud it felt like a mallet pounding at my head, and in my present condition that was undesirable: his jokes were invariably hurled at a man with the force of a maul, and his laughter afterwards was so painful that I could have preferred being flayed alive. Perhaps he was silent because he was reviewing his treatment of his brother. It would be natural after deserting the fellow long enough to give him the opportunity to raise five children. It must be hard, after all, for Sir Richard to reflect that when his younger brother needed him, he had done nothing. Purely because he had rejected Peter's decision to marry.

Mind you, if I were him, I would be considering carefully what sort of creature my brother truly was. I was unconvinced of the saintly character of the man. I held strong views about men who left their women and children and ran. I had seen a number of men who had taken that exact route, and had taken a shine to a new woman and fled their family. I suppose it is not uncommon in any life that a man might grow to find living with only one woman boring. I have always been fortunate that my good looks have earned me more than my fair share of bed-warmers, of course. Other men are less lucky. They find that they cannot entice many lovers, and so fall prey to the first woman who bats her eyelashes. And later, they feel they were ensnared, not realizing that they would never have found other women to take them. But by then there are children, and responsibilities, and they feel more pressure . . . and thus have more inclination to run and find others.

I had seen it often enough, yes. Some left their families, while others found their families left them, like poor Piers at the Cardinal's Hat. He had, early in life, developed a keen interest in beers and wines of all sorts. He would drink away the day, every day, until his business was ruined and his wife took the children away with her. I suppose, in a way, for Piers the route to escape was the drink. Other men sought a new woman as their means of escape. They would search for another as though she would give them some validation for their lives.

What they rarely seemed to appreciate was either what they

already had, which was often better than others could hope
for, or that the problem they were trying to run away from
was not the family and their wife, but the loss of their youth.
Sometimes, I have noticed, men of a certain age realize that
their remaining years are to be filled with spectating other
men's lives. Their own is already losing savour as they grow
old, and so they reach a certain age and suddenly understand
that their life is almost over. They rush headlong into an affair
which soon absorbs them. They lose the love of their wife,
the affectionate trust of their children, and when their purse
has run dry, the companionship of the harlot who ensnared
them. The problem, as it were, was always inside them. They
could run from one woman to another, but they still carried
their issues in their breasts.

Or somewhere.

'Ye know, I don't like this place,' Sir Richard said as we
entered the village again.

'Why not?' I said. Just then, there was a cold sweat running
down my spine and I could feel the clamminess at armpit and
groin that spoke of the amount I had drunk the previous
evening. Just at that moment, all I was thinking of was the
idea of a large cup of wine at the inn.

'The place has a run-down look about it.' He was silent for
a few moments. 'Y'know, I knew poor Peter wasn't happy
here, but I didn't do anything to help him.'

'Why?'

Sir Richard was quiet for a moment or two. 'I suppose it
was the way he left his family. You are right. It was not a
good act, not the behaviour of an honourable man. I should
have come and tried to help Dorothy. She didn't deserve to
be left alone to cope with Peter's leaving her and everything.
But I still had the feeling that the woman shouldn't have been
his wife in the first place. I have a stiff neck, I suppose. I
don't like to bend.'

'She gave little enough indication that she knew of you,' I
said. It was something that had been concerning me during
the journey here. 'I am surprised that your brother did not tell
her about you. Surely he would have known that you were
the Coroner, yet neither when we arrived here nor during the

inquest did she make the slightest sign that she realized you were her brother-in-law.'

'Aye, well, ye see, I rather expect that me brother would have kept that from her. Why should she know who I am? I was just a Coroner yesterday, for all she knew, and would Peter have told her about me being a Crowner? I don't expect so. Why should they even talk about me?'

'I suppose so,' I said.

'Besides, it was better that she didn't know who I was yesterday. I didn't want her to realize.'

'Why?' I was bemused by this, but his next words explained much.

'Why do you reckon?' he growled. 'D'ye think with your ballocks only, man? How would the people in the village respond to my inquest if they knew me own brother was lying on the table before them? People react badly to learning that the man judging them is acquainted closely with the victim.'

'Oh, I see.'

'Yes. It was necessary to keep our relationship secret. And it still is,' he added, glancing at me with a frown. 'I don't want people to know Peter was my brother, because that would only confuse 'em.'

I could understand what he meant. If people knew that he was Peter's brother, it was likely that many would be reluctant to tell him anything. They may well expect that a knight who had been deprived of his brother might become very focused on punishing someone – and in those uncertain times, 'someone' could mean 'anyone'.

Besides, his problems were not my concern. I was content in that I had twofold interests in being here: the location of the box of gold that Peter had concealed somewhere, and the fact that, while I was here, I was not in London and near to Arch and Hamon. The poor fools, I thought. They might be hunting for me with diligence and care, and all the while here I was, secure from them.

Of course, there was going to be a reckoning at some point, but right now that didn't concern me. I was sure that I would be able to work out a means of avoiding paying them, and in the meantime I was determined to enjoy my time here. I tried not to think of snippers and my ballocks.

It felt safe and well here, but the thought of those snippers sent a shiver down my spine.

I had taken the sensible precaution of bringing my wheel-lock pistol with me again. It was heavy and cumbersome, and it was irritating to have to carry the balls and powder, but at least if someone was to try to knock me on the head, he would be likely to receive an unpleasant surprise. Meanwhile, for all that it was a heavy burden, it was also comforting. I was tempted to pull it out and aim at trees as we passed them, but a glance at Sir Richard's face persuaded me that he would be unlikely to find it amusing.

As we rode past the entrance to the church, I glanced around and was surprised to see Roger sweeping leaves from the pathway. A little farther on, in the cemetery, I could see a mound of freshly dug soil. No doubt either Dick Atwood or Roger had provided a grave ready for Peter. Roger stopped and stared at us as we passed with a blank expression.

We took the horses to the stables at the back and walked past the trestles, which still stood in the mud of the yard, and entered the inn. At the door, Sir Richard roared out in his usual fashion to ask for someone to come and serve him. It felt as if my head was suddenly slammed into an apple press and the infernal screw was applied instantly. I winced and put a hand to my head.

'Eh? Somethin' wrong?' Sir Richard asked, all concern.

'I am feeling a little under the weather at this moment, and I would appreciate you moderating your volume!'

'I only called for a maid,' he said, apparently offended, and then he grinned. 'Don't tell me you're still suffering from last night, man? It was only a small drink or two! You mean to say that made your head as rough as a bear's?'

It was a relief to see Dorothy appear, wiping her hands on her apron. Her face fell on seeing Sir Richard.

'Two quarts of ale,' he said without preamble. 'We'll take 'em in here.'

'Yes, sir.'

'And food. Do you have any pottage or stew? Some pies?

I'm hungry enough to eat an entire deer and come back for the hounds that caught it, eh? Haha!'

'Yes, sir.'

I could see that his voice was causing her as much pain as it did me. I spoke gently. 'If you could bring them to the fire, Dorothy, we'll be sitting near it.'

She disappeared, and Sir Richard gazed after her, then back at me. 'Eh? What?'

'Try, I beg, to moderate your voice! From the look on her face, you are giving her a headache to match mine.'

'You think so?' he said, and for once his voice was pleasantly quiet. 'I was wonderin' if she was worried to see me back. As if she might herself have had something to do with Peter's death.'

I left him there and walked out to the yard, where the privy stood.

Fortunately, now that we had arrived, the rain had stopped. I could not help but cast a glance of disdain at the clouds overhead. It seemed distinctly unreasonable that they should have opened over our heads in so incontinent a manner, only to stop as soon as we arrived.

The privy was quite civilized for an inn in the countryside, with a plank set over the pit. There were two holes in it, so it was designed to be a sociable latrine, but just now all I wanted was a place to sit and find peace. It seemed obvious to me that I would find none at all in the presence of Sir Richard. The man could destroy the peace in a convent with his brash, country manner and loud voice. He was utterly without self-awareness, and although that fact did lend him a certain charm, it also had negative aspects. It seemed impossible for him to talk to women without terrifying them – apart from Cat, who almost welcomed him, if last evening was anything to go by.

Unbuckling my belt, I was fortunate not to make an expensive error. I had forgotten that the pistol was hooked into it, and as the buckle released, the gun slid away from me. It was only by quickly setting my foot upon it that I saved it from a far worse than merely watery end. I carefully set it on a plank some two feet from the latrine itself and settled myself on the seat.

When I was done, and feeling slightly better for it, I chose not to walk straight back to the inn. Instead, I buckled my belt, set the gun into it, made sure that my dagger was still there and had not itself tumbled into the pit, and finally kicked the door open and made my way to the garden behind the inn, hoping to find somewhere that was not too sodden where I might sit for a while. I could hear the horses bickering and wickering in their stables, contentedly munching, no doubt, and my own belly was grumbling a little from emptiness, but I did not want food at that moment. I craved some silence.

I had an eerie sense that someone was watching me. When I glanced all about, I could see no one, but that did not ease my conviction. You know that feeling when a shiver runs through your spine, and it is said that someone has walked over your grave? I had just that feeling. It was enough to make me leave the place in a hurry – even if the odour itself had not done so.

There was a small orchard beyond the garden, and as I stood surveying the view, I caught sight of a figure moving in the branches. Immediately, I felt my heart pound . . . and then, peering, I made out the tousled head of Ben, my friend from the day we first arrived. I walked over to him with considerable relief.

'Good morrow, my fine friend,' I called. 'How are you this damp morning?'

He had not heard my approach and was startled sufficiently to almost fall from his perch.

'Careful, Master Ben,' I said, and stood beneath him. There was a cracking noise, a squeak, and suddenly I had my arms full of anxious young boy.

'What are you doing?' an angry voice called, and when I glanced over my shoulder, I saw the innkeeper in the garden. Nyck looked like a man who had been watering his greens, and as I turned, he was pulling his codpiece back into position.

'You little . . .!' he shouted and stomped towards us. 'Ben, if I've told you once, I've told you a dozen times to keep out of those trees, you little fagger! I said that next time I found you in them, you'd feel my belt on your back, you – hey, come back here!'

Ben, noticing the innkeeper had begun to undo his belt, had taken the sensible option. As I deposited him on the ground, he started up and pelted away, as fast as a hare seeing the greyhound. I watched with a mixture of surprise and envy. Once, I know, I had been able to make similar speed when there was the threat of a thrashing. That was some time ago, although I still had an impressive turn of speed when necessary.

'The little . . .'

'You called him a "fagger". What did you mean by that?'

'You misheard me.'

'No, I didn't. You called him a fagger. That's a boy who's let in through a small window to burgle a house or to let in his accomplices.'

'It's just a word I use instead of "bastard", that's all.'

'He displeases you?'

'Regularly. I wanted to help the family, but the little . . . anyway, he won't do as he's told. I have tried to make him earn his living, but will he listen to me? No! Instead, he comes out here and climbs my apple trees, damaging the branches. I'll be lucky to see any cider next year, if the little . . . anyway, I'll lash him for this. And if he won't come back, he can stay out. His mother has my sympathy, and I've been kind enough to allow her to stay in the house, but if that little son of the devil doesn't start helping about the place and stop trashing my trees, he'll be out, and the rest of his family with him! I can't keep on helping and feeding them if he's going to—'

'Yes, I see,' I said. 'It was good of you to put them up.'

'Someone had to. Their father refused even to speak with poor Dorothy when they got here.'

'When they got here?'

'They had been living with him at Ilford, and when he left them to come here, they were destitute. He's been here almost a year now, and they arrived two weeks ago. I'm not sure how they learned he was here, but they just turned up one day – she starved, and her children little better. She had tried to speak to Father Peter to get him to help them with a little of his money, as a priest should, but he spurned them.'

'You don't sound as though you were entirely impressed with him and his attitude.'

He looked at me as though I was mad. 'His wife and five children came and he couldn't even find the courage to face them, man! As it was, I had to take them in and protect them. How would you feel if you were to do something like that, and the man wouldn't even give his wife a "good morning"? I call it shameful. He was no priest, to my way of thinking.'

He took off his apron, which was a linen sheet tucked under his belt, screwed it up, and stormed back indoors.

I was left feeling bemused. The man was clearly a good fellow, willing to help those in distress, but there was something that left me feeling a little uneasy about him. Perhaps it was the way he spoke of the boy. It was rare to call a lad a *fagger*, after all. That was a special term for a thieving scrote from London, I always thought – but no doubt the man had only known of it as a pejorative, the same as others would call a man a 'bastard' or a 'son of a whore'. It was just a phrase, nothing more.

There was a low whistle from behind me, and when I peered out over the orchard, I saw a small cap of tousled hair and an earnest, anxious face underneath it. Well, I thought, the little devil won't come back here in a hurry after the threat of a damn good thrashing from the innkeeper. Accordingly, I bent my steps to the far end of the orchard where the lad was peering over a small gorse bush in a hedge to the pasture beyond.

'You put on a good turn of speed,' I said admiringly.

'He wasn't going to catch me.'

'He is keen to take his belt to you.'

'If he tries, I'll *kill* him!'

'I would be careful about how often you say things like that,' I said. 'People can take such words seriously.'

'I am serious. I hate him.'

'Why? He's putting you up here, isn't he?'

'Only because he wants my mother.'

'Eh?'

'He's swiving her in return for letting us stay here.'

I blinked. His language left little to the imagination, after all. 'Perhaps your mother needed the affection. After all, your father didn't do anything to help you, did he?'

'He tried. He couldn't do it obviously. The people in church would have beaten him if they learned he had a wife and family.'

'What people in the church?'

'All of them. He told—'

He clapped a hand over his mouth and turned a face of such despair to me that I couldn't help but smile.

'Don't worry,' I said. 'I won't tell.'

'You promise?'

I put a hand to my heart. 'I swear it.'

'Thank you.'

'So you saw him?'

'Yes. I was in the churchyard, watching, and he saw me and took me inside. He hugged me.'

The little brute looked as though he had been given the keys to heaven, from the way he smiled at the memory. I suddenly had a memory of when I was young. My mother died when I was little, so my old man told me – I always suspected that she grew bored with his beatings and cursing, and left to find a new life. My father was a bully and brute who counted the day lost when he hadn't thrashed me for one thing or another. It was because of him that I had myself fled from home when I was only a lad still, and made my way by degrees to London, where I expected to make myself rich. But London wasn't as easy as people had said, and . . . well, that's another story. My point is that I knew what it was like to go through life without a hug or any affection being given. This little boy touched something in me.

I stepped towards him, ready to give him a hug of my own, but he gave me a look of disgust. 'Hey, what are you doing?'

'Nothing,' I said quickly. 'I was just thinking. What did your father say to you?'

'He said that he couldn't see me and the others in public, but he hoped he would be able to arrange something soon, so

that we could all be together again, somehow. He was going
to arrange things, he said.'

'How?'

Ben shook his head. 'I don't know.'

'Did he mention money? Gold? Something he could use to
provide for you all?'

The boy looked up at me with the sort of look that a physician would give a patient who said he could hear voices.
'What gold would *he* have?'

'Oh, nothing. I just wondered whether he had mentioned
anything like that.'

'No, he didn't. He just said that he had been lucky.'

Being given a box full of gold would be considered fairly
lucky, I considered. But that gold would have been with him
for fifteen years, if Dick Atwood was to be believed. I was
struck with a sudden doubt. Could the priest have kept such
wealth a secret from his wife for fifteen years? Could he have
kept such a treasure and not spent it? 'Do you remember,
when you were a boy, back at your last home, did your father
have a box? A heavy box?'

'Yes. A great chest. It's in the church now.'

I felt a thump as this news hit my breast. My heart was
racing like a horse in a race. 'Oh? In the church now, is it?'

I was fearful only that someone else might discover the box.
While a man is alive, there are dangers inherent in looking
into his belongings, but once the fellow has died, people might
feel it their duty to investigate, and I did not want someone
else opening the chest's lid and finding it full of gold. Having
ascertained that his father's box was a chest about a foot and
a half high, two feet wide, and a foot and a half deep, I left
the boy and made my way to the church.

It felt as if I was walking on air, as though I was inebriated.
Certainly, my head felt fine for the first time that day. My
stomach was unworried and my feet scarcely touched the
ground. My whole body seemed no more substantial than a
feather. The wind might have borne me along the road without
effort. As it was, I hurried along the roadway in the direction
of St Botolph's.

It stood on a prominent lump of ground. I wouldn't call it a hill; it was nothing more than a mound of earth, but it was enough to give the church a good view all around.

Pushing open the door, and ignoring the protesting screech of rusted hinges, I found myself in a pleasant little country church. Dust moved about, and although the sunlight filtering through the clouds was dull, it was enough to create shafts of light in the gloom. There was glass in the windows, and one had been set with colours, depicting a saint – perhaps St Botolph himself. I didn't pay attention to that, because on the left of the nave stood a large box, just as Ben had described.

I couldn't move. It was so enticing and so close. I stood as my heart made an attempt to gallop from my chest, and just stared. The box looked solid, as if it was made from oak. It was set about with iron bands, and there was a large padlock in the front. Someone must have the key to that, I thought. There was a creak from overhead as the wind picked up and moved the shingles of the roof. It sounded like the gusts were trying to pull each shingle from its moorings, one after another.

Going down on one knee quickly, I made the sign of the cross, with my eyes fixed on the altar, but my gaze had moved to the chest before I was fully upright again. There was a fresh sound from above, which made me look up. Two doves were sidling along a rafter overhead. I chuckled – I had thought it was a falling spar or shingles – and made my way to the box.

I tried to lift it, and immediately had to give up. It was an immense weight. That itself made my heart race. Everyone knows that gold is heavy. Very heavy. If there was a lot of gold in here, I wouldn't be able to move it, obviously. For some reason, I had a ridiculous grin fitted to my face, and I had to deliberately wipe it away. This was a serious matter.

The padlock was solid. The hasp itself was a half-inch thick, and the body of the lock was very substantial. But I wondered whether the furniture of the box, and especially the metal ring through which the hasp passed to secure the lid, might be attacked. I pulled and jerked at the padlock, but it appeared immovable. I needed a long pole to use as a lever. I began to search around, but I knew there was little chance of finding something of that nature in a church. Was there a smith in the village? I hadn't seen one. If not, perhaps a shovel would suffice.

There was another coo and a scuffling overhead, but I ignored it. If two doves wanted to get friendly, that was fine. I was content to leave them to it, as long as they didn't aim droppings at me. I was too involved in studying the locks on the box to pay them much notice.

Nor, sadly, did I pay much attention to other sounds, as I discovered when Dorothy said sharply, 'What are you doing there?'

I stared up at the doves accusingly. Their noises and merry-making had distracted me enough to ensure that I could not hear Dorothy's soft steps. Of course, if I had closed the door after me, it might have helped. Someone opening the door, with the resulting complaint of unoiled hinges, would have alerted me to their presence, but because I had left the door open, she had been able to surprise me.

Turning, with an innocent expression carefully crafted on my face, I smiled at her. 'Mistress Dorothy. How are you?'

'Never mind me, what are you doing with that chest?'

Her tone was sharp. It could not fail to impress upon me that she was highly protective of this box. She must know that it contained something valuable.

'Nothing. I merely wondered why it should be locked. A church's valuables are usually kept securely in the priest's chamber. What could be inside this, I wonder?'

'Whatever is inside it is for the new priest to discover,' she said, with a deal of emphasis, I thought.

'Yes, I suppose so,' I agreed, and moved away. I didn't want her to get the impression that I was particularly fascinated by this one box. 'I am so sorry about your husband.'

'Did you know him?'

'No, but—'

'So you have no reason to be sorry. Unless you stabbed him.'

'Eh? No, of course not.'

'Then you are making meaningless comments about a man you know nothing about.'

'I know a little.'

'Such as?'

'He was a good man, loved by many, who served his congregation with honour—'

'He was a dog's turd who left his wife and children with no money and no means of support, who came all the way here to find a new life, and spent not a moment thinking of the destitute conditions in which he left all of us. Why should he care? The Queen had decided he was worthy of his benefice, and he could do what he wanted, and that included pretending that he had no family, no children!'

For some reason, the woman suddenly burst into tears, sobbing most violently. I went to her and put a comforting arm about her, but she shrugged me off with an aggressive jerk of her shoulder. 'Get away from me!'

I drew my hand away swiftly. There was an unconcealed menace in her voice that could not be ignored. She most certainly was a strange woman. 'Did he give you no warning that he was going to desert you?'

'What do you think? No! None! He seemed so happy with me. A devoted husband, a keen father. He was always affectionate with the boys. And then, one day, he told me he had to leave, and I would have to fend for myself.'

'That was it?'

'He said that there were good reasons, that he and I had grown apart, that he needed a new life. Some other guff. It came down to him being bored with me, and there was this new opportunity for him, so he could run away from us. After fourteen years, he chose to leave us and seek a new life, free of the cost of supporting us. What did he expect me to do? Sell the boys into work? Did he think I could sell my body on the streets? That would hardly earn enough to feed all of us for a week!'

I demurred, and she shot me a furious look. 'Don't be ridiculous! No one would pay me to service them. I'm an old maid now. And while we starved, he was here living in luxury. So I decided I would come and demand that he help us.'

To say that she was doing herself down was on the tip of my tongue. She was, at worst, a perfectly accommodating woman, from the look of her, and I was sure that Piers would be able to win her an introduction at the Cardinal's Hat, but on reflection I felt she might deprecate my comments. Instead, I said, 'How did you know where he was living?'

She gave a twisted smile. 'The new rector was most helpful. He was appalled at how I had been treated, because he had himself been forced to go to Ilford and leave his own wife. But he had made arrangements for her to receive half his stipend while he was rector. That was the decent way to behave, naturally. He was thoroughly sympathetic to my plight, and told me where Peter was living now. As soon as he told me, I thought I could come here and demand that he help us. But I couldn't leave the children behind, and it was a long way, so I didn't think I could. Then Roger offered to come with us, and, well . . . It made sense to bring the youngest with me. I wanted to remind Peter of his responsibilities. We left the very next day, and walked all the way. As soon as we arrived, a fortnight ago, I went to the church and asked for his help.'

'How did he react to that?'

She looked at me, and the tears began to well again. 'He went mad with rage! If I had come here and tried to rob him, he could not have been more angry. No, he was worse than that: if I had said to him that I had told the Lord Chancellor I was still living with him, he could not have shown me such contempt and anger! I was scared, he was so angry. He raised his hand as though to strike me, which he never did before, calling me a whore and a thieving witch, a harpy who demanded all and was never satisfied. Oh! It was terrible! I've never seen him so furious.'

'There, there,' I said.

Her hand slapped mine away, and she stood before me with real rage in her eyes. 'Don't say "There, there" as if this is all a silly maid making a fuss! My husband of fourteen years rejected me and my children!' Then she collapsed, sobbing, to sit on the chest. 'How could he do that? I gave him every-thing, and after all those years he threw me over!'

Having endured the lash of her tongue and a slap from her hand already, I made no comment. It seemed safer.

She rubbed her eyes with both hands viciously as if she could rub away her hurt. 'So then I came back here and wondered what I could do.'

'Not easy, I suppose; not in a small village like this,' I said.

'I am not without ability!' she declared hotly.

'No! I didn't mean to say . . . that is, I—'

'I saw the inn, and thought to myself that I could work there. The innkeeper has no wife, and I thought I could at least wash, cook, serve . . . do anything he wanted.'

She looked away then, and it was clear enough to me that her responsibilities probably did not end when the last customer was thrown from the door. I felt an instinctive sympathy for her. She had been forced to accept that, with no husband or means of her own, she must accept any offer. While she was not forced to offer herself to all the customers at the inn, she was still thrown into the humiliation of giving herself to the innkeeper in return for board and lodging for herself and her children.

'Are you content there?'

'It is better than living on the streets or in the woods,' she said boldly, but there was a slight tremble to her bottom lip as she said it.

'Do you have any idea why your husband would have turned against you like that?'

'He was thinking of himself and didn't pause to consider me or the boys. That is all there is to it,' she said firmly.

'Why did you come here today?'

'To pray for him,' she said coldly. A fresh tear sprang from her eye and began to move down her cheek. 'I hate what he did to us, but he was my husband for fourteen years . . . the boys' father. I cannot just hate him and curse him after all that time together, although God knows that I would like to. But He will forgive me that, I am sure. So I come here every day to pray for him, to beg forgiveness for the anger I feel for him, and to ask that his soul be allowed to enter heaven.'

She looked along the aisle towards the cross on the altar. 'Although if he was still alive and I found him in here, I would beat the life from him, and enjoy it!'

*   *   *

I remained there as she genuflected to the altar, and a short while later she walked out.

It was a relief. She was a fiery wench, but one with an exciting gleam in her eye, it had to be admitted. She was old, of course, but, you know, that only means more experience. I felt that she warmed to me, but there was no need to think of seduction. I already knew where the priest's chest was. Now all I had to do was open it.

I considered the thing doubtfully. The locks and padlock looked robust; the oaken staves were as solid as oak tends to be. When I studied the hinges, it took little time to realize that they would not submit to a knock with a hammer either. This was a job for a competent locksmith, not me. I knew of only one man who would be able to open this box.

Now, there was one thing that suddenly struck me as I stood gazing at it. It was this: since Atwood was supposed to be the priest's servant, surely he should have known of the presence of this chest. But perhaps it was simply proof that the fool did not have eyes in his head, or that he did not bother to come into the church to clean. I had no doubt that, as a servant, he would be high-handed and incompetent. No, this must be the chest. There were no others in the church.

Where was he, though? Atwood had been here as servant to the priest, and yet he was nowhere to be seen now. In fact, no one had seen him since the inquest. He had made his demand that I should seduce Dorothy, attended the inquest, and then disappeared.

That thought brought me back to the widow. Dorothy was a strange woman. Plainly, she was still in love with Peter: although she had enough rage built up inside her to fuel a hundred wars, yet she still felt affection for the man. I could not understand how a woman could feel so – what, affectionate, loyal? – towards a man who had treated her with such callous disregard. She was rather like the hound who would still defend his master, even after being whipped and kicked and abused most abominably.

I left the church, ducking and making the sign of the cross as I had been taught, and stood outside. The weather was trying to improve. The clouds scudding past were growing more and more translucent, and patches of blue sky appeared every so often. Just then the sun burst through and lit the area, and it was surprising how much better the village looked under the bright glare. Suddenly, the trees looked greener, the road less dull, the houses brighter and cleaner. Water gleamed and sparkled like diamonds sprinkled all over the landscape. I could almost like the place. And then the gap was closed. Clouds covered it up, and the village became the grim, grey, soulless picture that it had presented before.

'A handsome prospect, isn't it?' a voice said close by my ear, and I leapt like a cut-purse who's touched on the shoulder while engaged in removing the latest victim's worldly wealth. It is not too much to say that my heart was pounding fit to escape the confines of my breast.

''S'bones!' I shouted, spinning about.

It was the fool, Roger of Ilford, who stood behind me. 'Master, I apologize, I meant not to give you a shock!'

I could only stare at him for a while, waiting for my heart to stop trying to leap from my throat as the easiest escape. 'What do you mean by walking up on a man when he's not expecting it?' I demanded. ''S'blood, I could have cut you down in an instant!'

He looked at me in a rather perplexed manner. 'Are you quite well?'

I could feel my racing heart slowing and took a deep breath. 'You were the second person to find Peter's body, weren't you?'

'I was there, yes.'

'Are you here to pray? I saw you sweeping earlier. Hard to keep a sexton from his duties, eh?'

'The man Atwood appears to have been derelict in his duty. There is much to be done here, but he is off out and about. I have been cleaning the place and preparing Peter's grave. Poor Peter.'

He looked quite relaxed about losing a man he had known for some years. Anyway, it was rare that the First Finder of a body would be quite so calm. After all, the Coroner had his details, and the man would be called to give an account when the Queen's Justices came on their next tourn, whenever that would be. And Roger here would have to have paid his surety to prove he would be there, and no doubt he would be fined for moving the body.

'Out and about? Shouldn't he be here, helping prepare for the funeral?'

Roger's face stiffened like boiled leather. 'He appears to care little for his job, but instead wanders about the village when he ought to be working. Why does he follow you?'

'Eh?'

'I have seen him wandering after you a few times now. He seems to want to watch you.'

It was only by exercising all my will that I stopped myself turning to look for him.

'Why did you say that about carrying the body?'

'What?' He looked bemused.

'That you alone moved the body and brought it back to the inn?'

He gave a slow smile. 'Who else was there to help me?'

'She's an attractive woman.'

A scowl passed across his face. 'Don't you say anything about her like that! She's a poor, desolate woman since Peter left her, and it's outrageous that she should be maligned by such as you! Leave her alone! She deserves far better after the way Peter treated her.'

'Why? How did he treat her?' I said, expecting to be told some juicy stories of how he would beat her, or share her with friends, perhaps. Oh, Reader, don't look at me like that! Priests enjoy their fun just like the next man. And so I prepared to take a stern tone with the fool. Instead, he began a maundering, daft speech about how she was glorious, and didn't deserve to be deserted like a dirty glove, dropped at the roadside.

'So, you think that I'm an idiot? She was deserted, yes, but it's clear that you adore her. So you took the blame for moving the body, when it was her, wasn't it?'

'No.'

'It was her and her boys, then. Come along, someone else was involved. You couldn't have moved the man on your own.

Excuse me for pointing it out, but you aren't strong enough. He was a hulking great brute, wasn't he?'

He was staring at me with a rather wild expression on his face, but said nothing.

'Did you actually like him? Or was it the fact that you liked her that made you come here?'

'That is outrageous!'

'Really? I think it's quite understandable. She is a striking woman, and you came here with her, knowing that her man had left her, so she would be grateful for your support, eh?'

'Wipe that lecherous leer off your face before I do it for you!' he snarled.

I was shocked. It was like putting my hand down to a winsome little kitten, only to have the thing bite me. He wasn't a great, strong man, but he could clearly strike like a cat pouncing. I took a step away, just to be sure. 'So you weren't after a . . . er . . . reward for your care of her?'

'That may be the way *your* mind works, but it most certainly is not how mine does,' he said firmly. 'I have nothing but the very highest regard for her. Dorothy is kind, gentle, loving – everything a woman should be.' His face reddened, and I was sure I smelled a whiff of hypocrisy. 'But I would not touch her. She is too fine.'

'Yes. Right,' I said, but I was thinking it wouldn't stop him dreaming of it. 'Still, you helped carry the body. Or she and the boys carried him on their own.'

'I was there. I was the adult man, so I took responsibility. We couldn't leave him there, in the road. It may be the law, but the law's silly. We took him inside so he would be safe. Dogs, foxes, pigs – all kinds of things will scavenge a dead body.'

'And once inside, what then?'

'What do you mean?'

There it was again, the aggressive tone. 'What do you think I mean? Someone stripped the body, cleaned him up and placed him in a shroud. Did you help with that as well?'

'Yes.'

'And then Dorothy went back to Nyck?'

'Don't malign her!' he shouted, fists clenching.

Rather than push him, I shrugged. 'What happened to the old priest, when Peter came here?'

He took a deep breath, calming himself. 'He was moved to a different congregation. That is how it is done. One priest is moved on, a second takes his place, a third takes the place of the second, and so on. All those churches where the priests had married, either the priest gave up his woman and moved to a new area, or he kept their wife and lost his position.'

'And the one who was here was moved to another. I wonder whether he had a woman here.'

'Does it matter?'

'No. When you were at the inquest, you mentioned that the dead man's arm was outflung. How did you mean?'

He demonstrated, bending his head and swinging his right arm over the side of his face, so that he looked rather like a man swimming in a pond. 'I've never seen a man lying like that, alive or dead,' he said.

'I have,' I said. A scene came back to me, the London Bridge, flames gushing as cannon fired at us, shot slamming into boards and rubble set to defend us, and the bodies of men lying all about. Others moving about them, picking them up and staggering away with them. 'He was carried here on another man's back.'

I walked back to the inn. Sir Richard's voice came clearly to me, and I winced at the sound, but my head had recovered sufficiently for me to think that my brain would not shatter like glass hit by a hammer, were I to return to the room with him.

At the door to the inn, I stood a moment, listening to the gales of laughter from Sir Richard as he spoke to the innkeeper. The two were in the parlour to the right, and as I stood in the doorway, I could see through the screens passage to the yard. In the passageway itself was a figure who listened intently, or so it seemed, to the Coroner and the innkeeper.

I am known for many qualities, and one of these is my courage. I am never one to hang back, unless the odds look too heavily weighed against me. No, I have a willingness to press ahead when there is a matter to be debated. From the clothing and the man's manner, it was obvious to me that this was Harknet. I was content that he was not as strong as me. Accordingly, I strode along the narrow way and tapped him on the shoulder.

If I had wanted a sharp reaction, I could not have sought a better. Harknet jerked around, his face a picture of horror, even as he leapt into the air. I swear, his feet must have cleared at least six inches, and that from a crouch. 'What in the name of—'

'No, master, no need to take the Lord's name in vain,' I remonstrated. 'I would like a word or two with you.'

'What? Why?'

'For one, why are you standing here at the doorway and listening to other men's conversations like some intelligencer from Spain, and for another, what was your real reason for disliking Father Peter quite so strongly?'

'I don't know what you mean.'

'Oh, in that case we might as well go and speak to the Coroner directly. You can explain it – and your interest in his conversation – to his face.'

'No, please, I beg,' he said with great agitation. 'I will tell you all, but not in there.'

I allowed him to lead me to a small parlour on the opposite side of the corridor. The fire was not lit, and the room was chill, but Harknet knew where there was a barrel of ale to be broached, and soon we were sitting comfortably on a bench with large earthenware pots of ale.

'Well?' I said. 'Why were you listening at the door?'

'I wanted to learn if the Coroner had any idea who had killed Peter. That is all.'

'Why?'

'There was no suggestion yesterday at the inquest. We were all left with the understanding that it was likely an attack by a stranger or outlaw. Someone unknown to the village must have killed him.'

'But you think differently.'

'I don't know what you—'

'Perhaps the killer was a jealous husband or lover?'

'Lover? Husband? What do you mean?'

His frown was almost convincing. I decided to string this

out a little. 'I don't know, Master Harknet. Maybe someone who was jealous of the man, who thought he didn't deserve the praise and support he was winning? It would be galling for many to learn that their new priest was a man who had embraced the Protestant faith and renounced the Roman. Some would find it difficult to consider him a real priest, after all. Especially if he had been married.'

'He should never have been sent here to see to our souls. What, a man who had been involved with a woman, who had five children? Argumentative, cruel, rude—'

'You said all this only yesterday,' I said, and yawned.

'Then consider this,' he snapped irritably, 'only a day before his death, he was having a loud row with one of his sons, the older boy. How could a man like that be thought suitable for a God-fearing parish like ours? He was a self-righteous bastard as well! He must bring dishonour to us here – that was obvious. But the Church sends its priests where it will, and calls it God's will, or something. God wouldn't have sent him here! That's probably why He saw to it that Peter died.'

'What would you have done with him? Instead of sending him here, I mean?'

'The Queen has already suggested a remedy. Men like him, who held concubines while they were priests, should be thrown from the Church. They are heretics. This Peter, in particular, was a shameless womanizer. You only had to look at him to see that. The women would flock to him.'

'Young women?'

'Yes.'

'And they would go to him and flaunt themselves?'

'Yes.'

'And offer their bodies to him?'

'Yes, that's right!'

'I suppose they would have done this in the church itself?'

'Yes, I think so.'

'Who?'

'What?'

'Who were these incontinent women who threw themselves at the poor priest?'

He stuttered for a few moments. 'I can't say that!'

'Because there were none?'

'No, I . . .' Inspiration struck. 'I don't want to get them into trouble.'

'Really? I think it is a little late for that,' I said. 'Surely they have done that themselves already?'

He looked miserable. 'No, surely not all.'

'You mean you didn't see all of them lying with him in his bed? That is good. Just tell me the names of those you did see.'

'It would hardly be fair to hold them up for condemnation,' he said, wriggling a bit, but this was one little worm I had hooked well and truly.

'You already have, by bringing them up,' I said. I was enjoying the sight of his discomfort. 'Come now, their names, if you please.'

'I . . . I cannot. The man behaved dishonourably towards them. What, should that make *them* guilty? Would you accuse the victim of a rape attack? Would you say she was guilty of lewd behaviour just because she was assaulted? I am surprised at you!'

I was surprised at him. Most men would consider that a raped woman had dressed lewdly and deserved what happened, while the man was tempted just too far and couldn't resist. I hadn't thought Harknet would be so forgiving.

'Did you see him with any of these women? Did you see him swiving them, lying with them in his or their beds? Or is all this mere villeiny-saying and gossip?'

'Anyone who saw him would be able to tell!'

'Tell what? That he was a kind priest who listened to the problems of his congregation?' I drained my cup and rose. 'I think you should ask for forgiveness. Spreading malicious tales about a dead priest will win you few friends, and will jeopardize your own soul.'

'Damn you! Speak to the miller's daughter; see what she reckons.'

'Who?'

'Jen. She's the same as him, mind you. Lusting after every passing trader, opening her legs for them. It's no surprise she allowed Father Peter to lie with her as well!'

'You saw her with men?'

'Everyone knew what she was like!'

And he stood and, with a last filthy glare at me, stalked from the room.

I remained there on my seat, considering, for some time after Harknet had gone. My belt was uncomfortable, and I hoisted it up. The weight of the wheel-lock was dragging the leather south, making it dig into my buttock, and I pulled the pistol from its rest and set it on the bench before pulling up my belt once more and tightening it. I replaced the gun and tugged my jack about my shoulders more tightly. What with the weather and no fire, the chamber felt very chilly.

There were footsteps, and when I glanced towards the door, I saw Dorothy, who stood there for a moment like a ghost. She looked at me with a mixture of annoyance and embarrassment, so it seemed, before she carried on past the doorway and into the kitchen.

Harknet had made it clear that I should speak to the miller's daughter. I had no particular desire to speak to anyone about Sir Richard's brother and his death, but, on the other hand, I was supposed to be helping with the investigation. It would look better, were I to go and seek information. Not that interrupting a miller in his work or making accusations to a man who was likely built like an ox, and had a temperament to match, was appealing. Still, his daughter might be a comely little wench. I had the impression from Harknet that she was not a child of some six or seven summers – his words gave me to understand that she was of an age to interest passers-by as well as a priest.

When I asked, I was told that the mill was out to the north of the village, and I did not bother to fetch my horse, but set off on foot. Anything to escape the accusatory stares of Dorothy and Harknet – and the loud voice of Sir Richard.

I walked up the road, trying to avoid the worst of the potholes. I can remember hearing once about a man who was walking on a road near an abbey, which had the duty to maintain the roads in its area, when he came across a hat. It looked to be of good quality, so he picked it up, only to find that the owner was still wearing it. 'Please keep the hat,' the fellow said, 'but first, I beg, help me out of this pothole!'

It is said that the abbeys and monasteries used to be very lax and often neglected their duties when it came to maintaining the roads and lands under their control. As long as the religious folk kept up their standard of living, they didn't care about the others who depended on them, so I kept clear of potential potholes, which meant avoiding all the puddles.

The mill was down a narrow lane upstream of the village, its path heavily wooded on both sides, with trees and bushes that encroached on the roadway, and branches that met over-head, blotting out any view of the clouds. What with the lack of sun and the shadow of the branches, it was a gloomy walk. I began to feel that there were eyes in the woods, watching me. As the trees blocked out more and more of the sky, I grew aware of a tingling at my scalp. My heart began to beat a little faster, and it was not the exercise. I heard a strange noise, a dull thud, as if a man had slammed into a tree, and span around, to see – nothing. I stood, staring about me with the expectation of . . . something. I didn't know what: a ghost, an outlaw, a sudden slamming agony from an arrow, *anything*! More likely, I told myself, it was just Ben once more. But then there was another crackle, as of a stick breaking underfoot – yet I could see no one. It made my hackles rise, as if there was in truth a ghost stalking me.

Eventually, I gave up and walked on down the lane. But even as I continued, the sense of lingering danger remained with me. Stories of old witches who lived in the woods came to my mind, and when there was another snap, as of a step breaking a stick, I felt the sweat burst out at brow and armpits. It was a struggle not to dash down the path in a panic. I cast glances over my shoulder every few paces, and at one point I thought I saw a figure moving amidst the trees.

However, I am nothing if not bold. I stiffened my back, and if I happened to walk a little more swiftly, well, I have often heard that a trot is a most restful and effective means of travel.

Nonetheless, by the time I reached the miller's house, I was a nervous wreck, clutching the grip of my gun in one hand like a talisman, while my left had a solid grasp of my dagger.

My hands felt incapable of releasing them, they were clenched so tightly.

The mill was a tall building, with two storeys. To reach it I had to cross a small bridge over the leat, and then walk down to the door. The wheel was still just now, the leat almost empty.

When I knocked, the place rang hollow. You know how a building that is empty can sound like a box with nothing inside? I have often noticed that a house with people inside sounds full of life, like a drum or cymbal, somehow, but the same home with everyone dead or fled sounds utterly different, as though everything has been sucked from it and all that remains is an echoing shell. I tried again after a few minutes, but there was no response. Setting my hand to the latch, I pushed, and the door slowly swung wide.

'Hello?' I called, and even to my own ear I sounded nervous. Still, it was better to be inside than out, with that feeling of being pursued by an invisible wraith of some sort, and I slipped inside in a hurry.

The place was like most mills of my acquaintance. It smelled damp and slightly of mould. There was a hollow, empty feeling about the place, and the strange noises that a mill will often contain: creakings and groanings from timbers under stress.

'Hello?' I called again, but I knew there would be no answer. The place was deserted.

Reluctantly, I stepped inside. The boards of the floor had not been swept since the last milling. That was dangerous. Even I knew that the dust from milling could grow explosive. If a man lit a candle, the whole place could go up like a tub of gunpowder. That was why millers tended to be careful, thoughtful men, who were keen to sweep the floors regularly, often with a bucket of water first. It was surprising to see that this miller had left his place in such a mess.

There was a short step up to a platform on the right, and over that a ladder up to the next floor, where the grain would be dropped into the hoppers. On the platform I could see the grinding wheels, and the chute down which the flour would fall. When I went to it, the little floury deposits which lay in the channel were damp to the touch. With the moisture all about, that was hardly surprising, but it showed that the mill had not been in use for a little while. The miller would have swept this of all damp, old flour regularly, so that no damp entered his sacks of fresh flour. A little damp flour could easily turn a sack rancid. If the flour had been left in the chutes long enough to get damp, the mill could not have been used for several days.

At the other side of the room there was a bedchamber, separated from the rest of the space by a thick curtain. The miller had obviously created a chamber in the drier part of the room for himself and his wife to sleep in. Many peasants had such rooms, often built in the eaves, made from simple planks on which a palliasse could be rested, up away from rats and other pests.

I walked about the mill, but there was no sign of any occupants. I went outside and looked at the mechanism of the wheel, then at the leat itself. I had heard from a friend once that the commonest way for a miller to die was by falling into his own machinery or drowning in his leat, but there were no bodies here.

Inside once more, I glanced at the bedchamber's curtain. It was the only place where I had not looked so far. Reluctantly, I set my hand to the fabric and pulled it aside until I could peer into the gloom of the bedchamber. With relief, I saw that there was no dead body inside, only a mess of bedding.

And then I almost bolted from the place when my nose discerned the horrible metallic odour of blood.

Sir Richard stood by the curtain and grunted. It was dark inside, with the growing twilight, but no one was of a mind to strike a light with all the flour dust around. He reached inside and grabbed the blankets, throwing them out. Then he pulled the palliasse out, too. To my delight, the first blanket completely enveloped Harknet, who happened to be standing nearest to the bedchamber.

'Ugh!' someone exclaimed, seeing the state of the blanket.

Harknet gradually reappeared. I enjoyed his look of restrained fury as he pulled the last fold from his head and retrieved his cap from the depths of it. Only then did he see what everyone else had already noticed: the blood.

'Ye can all see this, hey?' Sir Richard demanded, staring about him. There was a freezing anger about him as he spoke. I got the impression that if I were to touch his skin, I would stick to it like flesh to frozen metal.

He picked up the palliasse and led the way outside with it, where there was a little light remaining. He rested it against a litter of logs so all could see. 'See here? Blood all about the top half of the bedding. It is clotted. Probably a few days old. Some of you may be thinking this could be a woman's monthly bleed. All I can say is, if she bled this much, she would still be in her bed.'

Beckoning me, he bade me hold the mattress up so that the others could see it, and then took the blankets from Harknet and two others and held them up. 'This one, you will see, has had a similar effusion of blood. And in the midst of the blood,' he added, thrusting a finger through the material, 'is a knife hole. Do you see that? It looks to me as though whoever was lying in this bed was stabbed through the blanket. We know that the priest was struck with one blow separate from all the others. This could well explain that. He was here, lying in a bed, and someone stabbed him. They dressed him, stabbed him another eight times through his clothes, and carried him to the road where he was left.'

The villagers were a sullen lot, but all nodded as Sir Richard spoke.

'The man who lived here. He was married?'

'No. The miller lost his Katherine years ago. He had a daughter, though – young Jen.'

'Where is she? Has anyone seen her?'

'Not since three days ago,' Harknet responded.

'What of the miller? Who saw him last?'

There was a muttered dispute at this, until one elderly fellow, with the build of a starved lurcher and balding pate, tentatively lifted his hand. 'I saw him four day ago. He were in the cart, goin' off to town to fetch grain, so he told me.'

'That would have been the day before the body was found,' Sir Richard said.

He continued in a similar vein for some little while. I meanwhile took the time to think that four days ago was the day before Sir Richard bounded into my life, so the day that the priest was actually murdered. If Father Peter had been here, enjoying himself with the miller's daughter, then it was possible that the miller had returned to find Peter's backside hammering his little princess, and had been angry. Angry enough to stab the man through the heart, and then try to cover up his crime by carrying the body in his cart out to the road-side, and dumping the priest there? Very likely. Millers were solitary folks, and often held in low regard, because they tended to take a share of whatever flour was milled. Many peasants viewed them as little better than thieves. There was a certain logic to that, I had to admit. As a result, millers often had short tempers.

But what happened to his daughter?

Sir Richard was holding up other blankets for the peasants' scrutiny, and I gazed about us at the men crowded in the mill. There were more in the doorway, and women behind them.

'Where's the daughter?' I said.

'Eh?'

'Where is the man's daughter? She should be somewhere. Didn't she come and tell anyone that she had seen her father kill a man?'

Harknet sneered nastily. 'You think the maid would come and seek help, when she'd been on her back with a priest in here? Her father may have killed the man, but it was her fault. You think she'd want to come and admit she'd been involved in lewd and lascivious acts with the vicar? It was she who brought the vicar's fate upon him! She was the temptress, she was the whore who—'

'I'll have no more of that language,' Sir Richard boomed, and although Harknet opened his mouth to speak again, Sir Richard bent towards him, a finger pointing very firmly. It stubbed into Harknet's breast, and I could hear the thud as it connected, pushing Harknet back a pace. Sir Richard said, very low and quiet, 'If I hear anything more from you, you will regret it swiftly.'

Harknet looked up into Sir Richard's eyes and found that, yes, he probably would. His mouth closed firmly.

'Now! Did no one see her on that day or the day after? Has

no one seen her or her father? Come along, someone must
have seen them?'

There was no comment, only a general shrugging of shoulders and reluctant muttering. Sir Richard shook his head,
walking about the outside of the mill. On his order, two men
bundled the blankets together with a bloodied scrap of cloth,
and tied them securely. There was a soft murmuring as the jury
shuffled from foot to foot, some few of them glancing out to
see where the sun was. They all had work to be getting on
with, they were muttering. What was the point of remaining
here at the mill?

Sir Richard glanced about him, and told the peasants that
they could leave. I was relieved to hear it. After handling the
bloodied palliasse, I was keen to be away and drink a good
quantity of ale or wine. Anything to take away the memory
of the blood. It left a taste in my mouth that I could not get
rid of. I began to move towards the door.

'Wait with me, Jack,' Sir Richard called. He looked down
at the pile of bedding and palliasse, then back to the door to
the mill. 'If the man killed poor Peter, then where is he? And
where is his daughter?'

I submitted to the knight's suggestion that we should take a
look about the mill and surrounding area, and I walked about
the place with some resentment. After all, when you've seen
one muddy pool, you really don't feel the need to stare into
many others. And I wasn't sure what the Coroner was hoping
to find.

To be fair, for the most part he seemed to be interested in
staring at the ground near his feet as he stomped across the
pathways.

There was a second bridge a little farther down from the
mill itself, and here we could look across to the mill pond. It
was a pretty scene, with rushes thrusting their heads above the
water, some ducks dabbling and bickering, and an occasional
splash as something appeared from below and disappeared
again. Trees surrounded the pool, some of them running right
to the waterside.

'Not here,' I heard Sir Richard saying to himself. He had,

at last, discovered how to speak with moderation. His words didn't deafen me.

'What isn't here?' I asked.

He looked at me. 'Me first thought is for the daughter. A man ran in there, went to the bedchamber and stabbed a fellow. Someone who would do that is a man who feels the pressure of honour. A man like that is the sort who could think the woman is also defiled; a man like that, whose blood is already up, could well decide to kill her as well. Perhaps he thought she had betrayed him, betrayed his trust, his honour, his home?'

'So you think the miller did this? That was my thought, too,' I lied.

'We don't know what sort of man he is, but a miller would find it easy to pick up a man like poor Peter and throw him over his shoulder to take him to the roadside. Any man used to handling sacks of grain and flour could grab a man like Peter with ease. But what did he do with his daughter?'

I glanced about us. 'Surely you don't think he just stabbed her as well? Could a man do that to his own daughter?'

The Coroner gave me a long, considering look. 'When ye've been a coroner for as long as I have, you come to realize that there is nothing that a man with fire in his blood won't do. Think! The fellow was here for some years with his daughter. He didn't have a wife, he didn't have a woman staying here. And he shared his bed with his daughter, from the look of it. There was only the one bed roll in the chamber. So he looked on her as his own property, mayhap his lover. How would he react when he came home to find his daughter opening her legs to another man? He would react the same as many would on finding their wife acting the slut. It's very likely he killed her, I think.'

'If he could pick up your brother, how much easier to pick up his own daughter! But why didn't he leave her in an easy place? He was happy enough to leave your brother at the roadside. Why not her, too?'

'She was his flesh and blood. Perhaps he decided to give her a decent burial?'

'Is that what you are seeking now?'

'Yes. Her body must be around here somewhere. I would wager that she is buried as well as the miller could manage.'

'And what of him?'

'His cart isn't here. I would think he's most likely in London. Any murderer can hide in a cancerous hellhole like the city. It's easy. There are so many dives and whorehouses where a man with no qualms could hide himself. He might have friends, of course. Men he knows from the market where he buys grain, or drinking companions from one of the alehouses near the market. And then there is his cart. He'll have had to find somewhere to lodge that, and his horse.'

He was frowning now as he walked. For my part, I was content to let him consider the options. It was really none of my business, but I didn't want to leave the knight there while I hurried back to the inn, thence to collect my pony so I could get to the city before nightfall and curfew. No, I was happy to remain with Sir Richard, even if it meant another night in this foul little village. The alternative was to walk alone up that lane through the woods. A glimpse of a figure through the trees came back to me. Of course, I am not superstitious, but in case there was something in there that I should be concerned about, I would prefer to have the company of Sir Richard on that walk.

So I stumbled along in his wake as he strolled about the place, seeking for a body or the disturbed soil of a fresh grave.

I was relieved that we failed.

We returned to the inn as the light was fading. I was happy just to get in front of the fire, but Sir Richard was still wearing a pensive expression as we entered and took our seats on a bench near the fire.

There was a good crowd of local folk in there. Men who had been working stood in huddles and spoke in their slow, almost incomprehensible local dialect. These fellows from east of London were so backward it was almost sad. Harknet was in the corner, but as we entered, he took up his pot and left. Others were of a happier bent, and Sir Richard seemed already to have made his mark with them. As we walked in, three or four called to him, asking if he would give them a song or a joke. Sir Richard smiled faintly, but shook his head. At the bar, I saw Roger drinking a pot of ale and talking with great earnestness to Dorothy. Nyck appeared in the doorway, and Roger was suddenly still. He nodded to Dorothy, and then seemed to catch sight of Sir Richard. He crossed the floor to join the knight and was soon discussing the funeral arrangements for Peter.

After that, Roger walked out. Nyck was at the bar, and I felt sure that Roger would prefer not to speak to him. I went out to the privy a while later and was surprised to see Roger chatting with Dorothy at the back door. Both fell silent as I passed, and when I returned, they were gone.

Sir Richard was not good company. He remained deep in thought after speaking to Roger, staring into the fire's flames as though he would get the truth of his brother's death from them. Personally, I was happy enough to join the locals, but first I was keen to get some food inside me. The innkeeper said that Dorothy had cooked a pottage and bread, and soon I was eating a thick pease pudding with hunks of bread that were more crust than anything else. Trying to get a decent piece of bread outside London is next to impossible. Still, it was filling, and I ate the pease pudding with relish. Obviously, it was poor fare compared with what I was used to, but it did at least remind me of some meals when I was young, when I would occasionally be fed by one of the young mothers in the area after my mother's death.

While I sat there, sipping ale and letting the solids sink down, I listened to the conversations going on around me.

As usual, most of the chatter was about matters that affected the community: whose sheep had strayed, whose cow had stood on old Harold's dog, the cost of buying good flour, the dreadful prices for produce, how hard it was to make a living – you know the sort of thing. I was listening without much interest, until I suddenly heard someone mention Harknet. There was not much to that, perhaps, but then someone else mentioned 'Sarah', and my ears pricked.

You see, they were talking about this Sarah as though Harknet was keen to be knotted to her. The idea of any poor woman wanting to get spliced with such a sour-minded old devil was hard to conceive of, but according to the fellows at the bar, she was ideal for him, being such a mild-mannered wench. This was received with raucous amusement. Someone said that she would make a man of him at last, to general delight once more, and another said that she was as constant as he, and the couple would do well as parents, for their children would twist and turn with every changing breeze, as effective as a weather vane in telling how the wind blew.

I was confused by this at first, but stood and took my ale to them. 'Gentlemen, would you accept an ale from a stranger?'

There was no holding them back after that, although many of them were drinking cider rather than ale.

'I couldn't help but overhear your comments about goodman Harknet,' I said. 'He seems a man who can be trusted to know how the land lies.'

There was some hesitation at first. These local types don't like to involve foreigners in their personal prejudices, but they began to open up after a few more promptings.

One, a lean fellow with skin like old leather, said, 'Harknet will always be on the side of Harknet.'

A younger man with a face as round as a cherub's nodded. 'Aye, he'd declare himself a Jew if the Queen said she esteemed them!'

'He's a man of changing views, then?' I said.

'A papist, then a Church of England man, and now a papist again. He reported two Catholics to the sergeant when King Edward was on the throne, God bless his memory,' said the first one, 'but as soon as our Queen decided to return to the Catholic Church, he became the most devoted papist in the whole of Middlesex.'

'And now he's found a woman,' said the round-faced fellow. 'Poor Sarah Comely doesn't deserve him. Trouble has followed her for years, but having Harknet pulling at her skirts will be the worst of all.'

There was much sage nodding of heads at that.

The lean fellow sniggered. 'Aye, but mayhap she'll teach him a trick or two before they're handfast.'

'You daft beggars don't know what you're talking about,' a third man said. He had a wall-eye and an evil glitter in the good one. 'She's too bright to get herself wed to him. I'll take my oath she'd sooner wed a hog.'

'True enough,' Round Face agreed, but the others nodded grimly when he continued, 'but she's a solitary maid, when all is said. How long can she stay alone, eh? The women all think she's halfway to being a whore as it is. None of them are keen on having a woman like her about the place.'

'What sort of woman is this Sarah?' I asked. 'Why do you say "a woman like her"?'

The round-faced fellow made a very distinct shape with his hands and guffawed. 'If you like your woman to have a well-filled bodice, Sarah is the girl for you! She's some two-and-thirty years old, and still has many of her teeth, but she has a manner about her that would scare the rust off a worn axe.'

'Aye,' said the lean man, 'and she's without a man now. She can't live on her own for all time.'

FOUR

We stayed at the inn that night again, but next morning I woke with a head that was significantly less painful. Perhaps it was helped by the fact that I drank only ale, and fell asleep before the fire while Sir Richard was telling one of his disgusting jokes. I don't know, but when I stirred, my head felt clear and fresh, and my belly was content and without the boiling acid feeling that I was coming to know so well.

Sir Richard was already up. I don't know how he could survive on so little sleep and such a quantity of drink. The man must have the stomach of an elephant.

I called for the innkeeper and Dorothy appeared in the doorway. She made no mention of our discussion the previous afternoon, but set about fetching me a small beer.

It was when she set it before me that I saw her eye. 'What happened to you?'

She touched it as though she had forgotten. 'This?'

Her eye was so badly swollen that she could barely open it. 'Who did that, maid?'

'It is nothing. I walked into a door,' she said coldly.

'Seriously, tell me what happened. Who did this?'

'It is nothing to do with you,' she said, and this time there was menace in her voice.

As she spoke, I noticed a shadow in the doorway. Someone was out there listening.

'I think any man who hits a woman is the purest coward on the planet,' I said. 'It doesn't matter whether he's a lord or a peasant. It's the most sure proof of his weakness.'

As I said this, the innkeeper appeared. He wiped his hands on his apron while watching me. When he glanced at Dorothy, there was a look of contrition, I fancied. He looked ashamed, perhaps, or apologetic. I was reminded of the look he sent after young Ben the day before. That had been a look of pure malice, or I'm a Dutchman, but this was more like genuine remorse. He was a man capable of violence, but perhaps it was worse when he was in his cups. I had enough experience of that from my own father. He used to think it great sport to thrash me. Thinking that, I was suddenly alarmed for Ben. If the boy was to get into serious trouble, and this fellow caught him, Ben could be in great danger. The man looked as though he would make no allowances for age when he punished a boy.

'Morning, master,' he said, and then, to Dorothy, 'Why don't you go and rest yourself, Dorothy? You must be tired out.'

'I'll be fine,' she said. There was a note of resolution and determination in her tone. 'It's better if I keep working.'

'Hello,' I said to him, and he at last met my eye. 'A nasty bruise that, isn't it?'

'Yes. Accidents will happen,' Dorothy said quickly.

Nyck and I exchanged a glance. We both knew her injury was no accident. Nyck hovered around her like a wasp about a honey-pot, ignoring me as best he could.

I was not to have an opportunity to speak to Dorothy again, clearly. 'I shall be leaving the village this morning. I have business in London.'

'I'll see your mount is ready for you.'

'Thank you.' I hesitated. 'Do you know where Dick Atwood has gone? I have not seen the devil since the inquest.'

'No. He should be at the church, but I don't think Dick does much work up there. He used to spend all his time wandering about the village, but I haven't seen him either.'

'Beware of him, then,' I said. 'He delights in punching people. There are many feeble-minded . . .'

Dorothy span to me, her face a mask of rage and fear. 'Don't speak of things you know nothing about! I have told you what happened, and now leave me in peace!'

Drinking the beer, I left the inn a little later – and I won't deny it, I felt very sorry for the woman. She was not really my type, and she had a hard mouth on her for a man like me, but her evident grief at losing the man she had married, even after he had treated her abominably, and her determination to keep her family together made her seem virtuous. She had tried to hold the boys to her even at the expense of submitting to a bully, and I honoured her for that. It made her seem altogether more decent and strong than any woman I had met before.

She was impressive.

Walking from the inn, I stood in the roadway outside and peered about me. I would be happy to return to London and be away from this village, which seemed filled with death and misery.

The woman Sarah interested me, I confess. The man the night before had said that she could take the rust off an ancient axe with her manner, or something to that effect, while someone had mentioned that she had a good top-heavy build – just as I like. But the other comments were about her being alone, and that other women viewed her with suspicion at the least. It sounded as if she had a reputation for negotiable virtue – which would be enough to give many women in a small community, like this village, conniptions. Few wives would want the competition of a free woman who might tempt their husbands unless she was hideously ugly. However, I was surprised that there was so much talk about them both with me, a relative stranger. Harknet himself must have many enemies, since I had heard that he had regularly denounced those who clung to their Roman faith, which must mean he had lost any friends among the Catholic congregation, and now that the Queen had herself returned to the Roman faith, and expected all her subjects to do the same, he would have lost the others, too. He must be an entirely friendless man, and if that was so, they would feel secure enough in denouncing Harknet's flexible attitude towards religions.

On a whim, I went to the stable yard and enquired of a groom. Soon I had directions to Sarah's house. It was a small cottage on the road east, and I ambled over that way with a kind of casual interest, more a wish to see what sort of woman could appeal to Harknet than anything else – although I did wonder what sort of woman could find him appealing, too – if she did.

My path was a well-trodden route, with deep ruts where cartwheels had sliced into the mud and a filthy mess where the horses hooves had churned it afterwards. It took careful work to avoid being befouled by the mire, and several times I was forced to leap over puddles of mud up on to the verge, either to escape the deeper pools, or to avoid riders and carters who seemed to think it was a great sport to smother me in mud – and worse.

When I reached the cottage, it was a surprise. Without a doubt it was the most handsome property in the village, recently lime-washed, with a new thatch of fresh reeds, and a smart little garden of raised beds before it. Garlic, onions and plenty of salads and greens grew there, and I could see not a single weed.

Somehow I had not expected this pleasant scene. I had thought to discover a hovel, something with less than pleasant surroundings, and an emaciated wench with a hunchback – for I was used to the typical style of what the locals termed 'humour' down here in the country. Instead, when she walked from her door, I was struck by a woman of, yes, some two-and-thirty summers, but one with raven-black hair and a ready smile, and who was singing a lewd song about a woman who gave her body to a vintner and was now demanding maintenance for herself and her child.

When I approached, she cast me a measuring glance and stood very still, gazing at me over her shoulder.

'Good morning,' I called.

'God give you joy of it,' she said.

I was about to go to her, when I caught sight of a man in her doorway. It was Sir Richard.

I would have continued onwards to speak to her, but then I caught sight of the expression on Sir Richard's face, and it froze me, he wore such an expression of guilt and shame. I stared for no more than a moment and then turned on my heel and went back to the inn. Whether he was embarrassed to have been found there because he was trying to persuade her into her bed, or because he had learned something shameful about his brother, I did not care.

It was none of my business what Sir Richard got up to, of course, but there was something deeply unnerving about the sight of him in that woman's doorway. He had looked shifty, as though he had some ulterior motive in being there. Well, if his first thought had been to question the woman, the second didn't need much thought. She was a comely wench.

But no matter what I thought, I could not get the idea from my mind that he had looked guilty. It was as if I had caught him just as he was about to commit a crime. He looked ashamed, but not contrite, like a certain felon I had known, who, when caught, was unapologetic and unrepentant about his crimes, and made it clear he had thoroughly enjoyed every penny he had stolen.

But Sir Richard was no thief. Nor was he, from all I had seen of him, a womanizer. At least, not a successful one. Still, he would be busy today, with his brother's funeral.

Glancing at the church, I saw that Roger was clad in religious garb. Clearly, Dick Atwood was still nowhere to be seen, and Roger would be helping with the service.

I walked into the inn.

'Dorothy?' I called at the bar. There was no sign of her or the innkeeper. I called again and walked through to the rear parlour, where I called out once more. Still I had no reply, and I was debating whether to leave at once and allow Sir Richard to pay my bill or whether to wait a little, when Dorothy's older son appeared.

'What?' he snapped.

'I wanted to pay my reckoning,' I said haughtily.

'You'd best wait for Nyck to return, then. He's not here right now.'

The lad had an expression of truculent fury, as though he was ready to explode. It was hardly surprising. The lad had seen his father desert the family, his mother forced to offer her body to the innkeeper, and then seen his mother beaten black and blue. Any fellow of spirit would deprecate the world that permitted such intolerable insults.

'Fetch me an ale, then,' I said, and wandered to a bench.

Since the idea of an angry Sir Richard appearing at my door in London was deeply unappealing – especially since I was sure that if he grew displeased, he could smash me to a thin pulp before I could land a punch on him – it was better, I considered, to remain here and then attend Peter's funeral with him. I settled myself, preparing to wait. Soon I had a large pot of ale and supped it slowly. 'It must have been hard on you to discover your father's body.'

'My mother did.'

'But you were there. You helped bring him back in, didn't you, with Roger of Ilford?'

He shrugged. 'We couldn't leave him there. It wasn't right.'

'What do you think of Roger?'

'He's all right. A bit pathetic, though. He won't stand his ground. People can trample over him.'

'Who?'

'He didn't really want to come here. It was mother who made him. He would have been happier staying in his home, avoiding that journey. But she needed help, she said, and he gave in to her.'

'You think your mother is unreasonable?'

'No! She's just found life tough. Who wouldn't?'

'Have you seen the sexton from the church?'

'Several times. So has Ben. He's always somewhere around, but never at his work.'

Hardly surprising, I thought. Atwood was off out and about looking for a box of gold.

I glanced up to see that the boy was still glowering at me. It was disconcerting. Rather than meet his fierce gaze, I pulled my hat over my face.

What if Sir Richard was merely doing the same as I had intended? Perhaps he was only going to see what the woman might have known of Harknet, of his brother Peter, and possibly the miller and his daughter. For it seemed obvious that the miller must have slain his daughter, Jen, as well as Peter. We only had to find her body. And what would Sarah and Harknet have had to do with that? Beforehand, I had wondered whether Harknet could have killed Peter, but the discovery of the bloodied bedding at the mill spoke against that as a possibility. Why would he have gone to the mill? It was more likely that Harknet was a merely peripheral character, an unpleasant side-road, perhaps, but no more than that. And surely his woman was little more than that herself.

No, the miller was an unpleasant-sounding fellow, who had more than likely been bedding his own daughter, and who would not hesitate to exact punishment when he found the priest making merry with her, too. If Sir Richard wanted to find the murderer of his brother, he would have to seek the miller, and, as we had discussed, that must mean hunting for the fellow in London itself.

Yes. There was no point getting excited about Sarah or Harknet, I thought, and no point worrying about a strange expression on Sir Richard's face. He was surprised to see me there, I expect – nothing more than that.

I pulled my hat further down over my eyes, wrapped my arms about me and set myself to doze.

It seemed only a blink of an eye later that my shoulder was punched. A typical way for Sir Richard to waken a friend, I thought idly as I yawned, stretched and then took off my hat to remonstrate with him.

Except it wasn't Sir Richard. Instead, I squeaked with alarm as I found myself staring into the face of Arch.

For a moment or two, I think I just goggled. There was a suspicious part of my brain that was suggesting that if this was a dream, it was a dream in exceedingly poor taste. A brain the quality of mine should have been able to summon up a vision of Cat, or perhaps Dorothy – but without her black eye. Anyone, in short, rather than this repellent vision.

'Oh!' I said.

''E's awake,' Arch said.

'Yes,' said Hamon.

'Do you think 'e'd like to explain 'ow 'e seems to have fallen out of London?'

'I hope so.'

'Because the last I remember, we spoke to him and told him we needed the money quickly, didn't we?'

'Yes.'

'But 'e didn't appear, did 'e?'

'No.'

''Ave you got your snippers, 'Amon?'

'I do, Arch. Yes.'

'Oh, good.'

'Wait!' I said.

'It speaks!' said Arch.

'It was a mistake! I had to come here because of the Coroner!'

'Oh, the Coroner.'

'Yes. He wanted me here to look into matters for him.'

'Oh, well,' Arch said, looking up at Hamon with an understanding smile. 'That makes sense, that does, doesn't it? No need for your snippers, if that's all that 'appened. We might as well go 'ome, eh?'

'Except,' Hamon rumbled.

'Hmm? Oh!' Arch slapped his brow. 'Oh, where would I be without you, 'Amon? I'd clean forgotten that the Coroner asking him 'ere still doesn't pay the interest or my loan, does it?'

'No, Arch, it doesn't, does it?'

And having reached that conclusion, both stared down at me again.

'I have the money,' I began.

'Oh, 'e 'as it,' Arch said. 'That's a relief, isn't it, 'Amon? So give us our six guineas, then, master.'

'Six?' I yelped. 'It was only—'

'Yes, but since then you 'ave led us a merry dance from London to this nice little village, 'aven't you? You still owe the base amount, and so far you 'aven't been interesting me in 'ow you're going to pay. So I think a little sum to reimburse us for extra effort, for wear and tear, for preventing us using our money to our own advantage – all that comes to a bit more. And if we add in the benefit to you of not losing a finger or two, perhaps we should make it a round eight guineas. So, where's the money?'

I confess, just at that moment it was very tempting to tell them about the box in the church. Hamon was staring at the little finger on my left hand, and I knew that he was thinking it would make a splendid addition to his collection of 'fingers I have snipped'. But I didn't know for certain yet that the box was the one Dick Atwood had spoken of. If I sent Arch and Hamon on a wild goose chase, they would start thinking more imaginatively than only one finger. They would be more likely to want to investigate behind my codpiece. I squirmed at the thought of his snippers down there. 'Come, now, Arch, you don't want to cause pain for no reason.'

'*I* do,' Hamon said.

I looked at him, careful not to glare. 'But you don't want to hurt your chances of getting your money, do you? It's not here. It's at my house.'

Hamon pulled a rusty pair of shears from his belt pouch and made a show of studying them. He clenched his fist about the handle, closing them. They made a metallic hiss as he moved the two surfaces together, and again when he released them. He held them close to my nose, where I could smell the dried blood on them. I wanted to turn away, but the man's eyes were hypnotic. And then the shears edged closer, until they touched my nostrils, the blades at either side of my nose. 'I don't think our chances would be hurt by your losing your nose or a finger, or something.'

'But if you injure me, I won't pay you,' I said. I tried to speak firmly, but it did come out as a bit of a squeak.

Arch leaned down into my field of view now. 'Trouble is, you see, my friend 'Amon doesn't trust you anymore. It's a terrible thing, suspicion, but 'e thinks that someone who doesn't pay 'is debts is a terrible person. 'E really does. And that means 'e is keen to express himself.'

'I—'

The door opened and Sir Richard entered. He had a face like thunder, and he glared at the two standing with me. 'What are ye doin', Jack, eh? Come on, stir yourself. We still have to find this miller. Are ye comin' or not?'

'I, I—'

'Get yourself ready, Jack,' Sir Richard said, adding to Hamon, 'My apologies, good fellow. This man must leave now. We have business to attend to.'

Hamon stood slowly from his crouch over me. 'He's with us now.'

Sir Richard glanced at him briefly. 'No, he's not. He's coming back to London with me.'

I winced and desperately tried to indicate with my eyebrows and eyes that Hamon was a very dangerous man. Sir Richard didn't appear to notice. 'Come on, Jack. On your feet. My brother won't wait.'

Hamon stepped between us and lifted his little shears, the blades together so it looked like a fat-bladed knife. 'You didn't listen to me, you old—'

Sir Richard's left hand whipped past Hamon's face, and I heard, rather than saw, the snippers whizz through the air, so close over Arch's head that I was sure I saw strands of his hair parted by the blades. His mouth formed a perfect 'O', as did his eyes as he ducked. The shears came to a shivering halt in the lintel of the door to the screens and garden. At the same time, Sir Richard had drawn his dagger and stepped forward. His blade's point was under Hamon's chin now and pressing upwards.

'And you didn't listen to me, you whoreson cut-purse! I'm not some fool visiting the big city for the day, who you can laugh at, get pissed, and cut the purse from. I'm the Queen's Crowner, and if you try to prevent me in my duties, ye'll learn what the inside of Newgate's like. They'd like a pretty boy like you in there. Unless you want to try to fight me now. Do ye?'

'No,' Hamon said. He would have shaken his head emphatically too, but that might have been dangerous.

'Good,' Sir Richard said. He threw a look towards Arch. 'You – yes, you, you gangling wastrel. If you don't want to swallow it, I'd take yer hands off yer dagger. If you try to pull a knife on me, master, you will not regret it for very long. Do I make meself clear?'

Hamon gave a pleading sort of a squeak, his eyes cast sidelong at Arch, who reluctantly took his hand from his knife's hilt. Meanwhile, Sir Richard's blade was pressing higher, and Hamon was forced to stand on his tiptoes to prevent a puncture. Sir Richard nodded, and then took his blade away and thrust it into its scabbard in a single, fluid movement.

He was about to walk from the room when he noticed I was still sitting on the bench. 'Did ye not pay attention? Get yourself on your feet, master.'

I trotted along beside Sir Richard with a sense of disbelief.

'Those friends of yours,' he said as we crossed a small stream. 'They didn't seem friendly.'

'I'm glad you noticed. They were going to hurt me.'

'Why?'

I saw no reason to deceive him. 'I owed them a small debt from gambling, but what was a few shillings has grown to guineas in a week.'

'Oh, he's one of them, eh? Lures his victims into his nets, and then won't let 'em go till he's skinned them and taken everything but the bare bones.'

'Yes. And Hamon takes that scenario seriously.'

'Hmm. You should get yourself rid of them somehow.'

'At the rate they're going, I'll never be able to afford to pay them. They want more and more.'

'Aye. It's how they work. So you need to find a way to make them seek some other victim, or else have them removed.'

That was an idea that had occurred to me. Because of my new position as unofficial assassin to Master John Blount, who worked for Lady Elizabeth's comptroller, I was aware of other men in a similar line of business, and had made use of a subcontractor on many occasions. However, I tended to use him when someone else was paying for his services. It was an unpleasant idea that I must use him for my own protection. I knew how expensive he was.

'I don't know how to. If I could, I would point them in another direction like a shot, but Arch is a hard man to evade. He even followed me all the way to St Botolph's.'

'I wonder how he learned where you had gone?' Sir Richard said.

I could guess. With only one servant, it wasn't hard to work out.

The church was quite full. A priest had been brought over from the next village, and he officiated with all the compassion and empathy of a chicken. Indeed, he rather reminded me of one, his head pecking down with every emphasis, his arms flailing together like wings to make a point. It would be coarse to call him a fool, but then I am coarse.

Dorothy stood at the front near her husband's body, her brood all about her. Roger was standing behind the priest, waving a thurible about and wafting incense that must have cost Sir Richard a pretty penny. He had not stinted on the costs of the funeral, I saw. Candles of wax were burning brightly, and the body was wrapped in a fresh, clean winding sheet. The congregation had turned out for the funeral, with many of the local peasants standing in the nave, hands clasped in prayer at the correct moments, while the priest rattled his way through the liturgy incomprehensibly.

The woman Sarah was at one wall, and there was a slight gap about her, as though she was ostracized, or perhaps because others feared her a little. She did look a rather daunting woman. Harknet was not far from her, and eyed her with unconcealed longing, I thought. It earned him a glare from Roger. Sir Richard himself was as upset as only a thorough-going hypocrite could be. I didn't get the feeling that his emotions were entirely genuine.

Of course, Dorothy survived only as far as the last mumbled words before collapsing in paroxysms of despair, wailing and weeping. Her two elder sons supported her on either side, while the youngsters looked on, two joining her in her demonstrations of misery. Ben stood stoically, wiping his eyes at regular intervals.

At the graveside we all stood about while Roger climbed down into the mud, and took the body as it was passed to him. The intention was to lower Peter gently, of course, but Roger fumbled it, and the body tumbled head first with a loud crack. If he wasn't dead already, he would have been killed by that.

It was a relief when the priest finally gave up at the graveside and we could make our way down the path and through the gate, away from that grim little church.

Sir Richard joined me on the ride back to London. There was little enough for either of us in the village, and I was glad of the company, bearing in mind that I could have met Arch and Hamon at any time.

As soon as we reached my house and Raphe let us in, his expression of pained resentment was enough to clear the question of how Hamon had known where I had gone.

'They came in here, and the big one, he held me with my back to the door, and threatened to cut off my tarse and ballocks if I didn't answer him,' he said in his familiar whine. 'He held a big pair of shears to my—'

'Yes, yes. What then?'

'They were going to kill Hector!'

'Who?' I said, surprised.

'My dog.'

I groaned, Sir Richard scowled, and Raphe continued quickly, 'I told them all I knew. I wasn't going to have my cods cut off. You don't pay me enough for that.'

'Fetch wine, you inveterate fool,' Sir Richard said, and dropped into my favourite chair. Sitting there, he looked up at me with a frown of bemusement. 'Master Jack, I worry about you. Ye get yourself into trouble with men like those two, and think you can ride away without needing to worry. They are exactly the sort of men who would never give up once they had found a gull. Although I *am* surprised that they made their way to St Botolph's. I would have thought that would be far enough away from London to worry them.'

'I know – there are not many of their kind who would travel so far!' I said. I was close to telling him that, as a retired cut-purse, I was perfectly well aware of what sort of men they were, and that I didn't need any warnings about them, but I reflected that informing a Queen's officer that I had been a cut-purse and was now an assassin might not endear me to him. Having seen how he despatched the threat posed by Hamon, I was under no illusions about his ability to capture me, if he desired. I took out the pistol and set it on the bench beside me. He looked at it, and then at me.

'Is that a threat to me?'

I looked down at it with surprise. 'No! It's just heavy on my belt!'

'Good,' he said.

Raphe appeared at that moment and poured us wine. In the silence of the room, the liquid seemed to make an appalling noise.

When he had left again, Sir Richard cleared his throat.

'I know ye saw me with the woman Sarah this morning.'

'Yes. I was going to talk to her, but you beat me to her door.'

'Yes. Not that she was very helpful. According to her, Harknet felt he owned her. He has made several advances to her, although she has told him to leave her alone. Not that it helped.'

'What of the vicar, your brother?'

'Ah, as to that, she said she spoke to him on occasion, but he was always thoroughly respectable and decent towards her.'

'Really?'

He gave me his most patronizing smile. 'I did tell you me brother was an honourable fellow.'

'Yes, you did. And I suppose you mentioned to Sarah that you were his brother?'

'She guessed. She said that he told her he had a brother who was a coroner.'

'She told you that?'

'Yes. Why?'

I shook my head, astonished at the foolishness of the knight. 'Because that means she saw more of him than you would expect a single woman to see of her priest. How many priests speak of their family and friends with members of their congregation? She was having longer conversations with Peter if she was learning about you.'

Sir Richard's face fell. 'That means nothing. She told me that there was nothing between them.'

'So she learned that you were his brother, that you were angry over his death, and then denied anything to do with horizontal exercise? Of course she did. She didn't want to upset you.'

'You see the bad in everyone,' he snorted.

'I've found it more realistic in my dealings with people.'

'Some people are not that bad. They can surprise a fellow.'

'And sometimes men will wilfully refuse to see what is in front of them,' I said, 'just as you refuse to see it in a wench with a pleasing smile and warm body.'

He glowered at his pot, drank off his wine and refilled the jug. 'Do you really think so?'

'Yes, not that it matters. You have two concerns,' I said. 'First, the widow and her children. You should help them. Second, you must learn where the miller has gone. We should try to find him and learn where he buried his daughter.'

*   *   *

He left me soon after, telling me that he was going to scour the drinking halls and alehouses all about the river. A man who had been a miller was most likely to want to stay near the river, he thought. Personally, I doubted that. Having seen his home and the lovely mill pond nestling quietly in the valley, I doubted that living near to the sludgy mess that was the Thames would hold much attraction for the man.

However, I didn't say so. Sir Richard was one of those men who must always be up and about. He had a need for action, whereas I was content to occupy myself. Just now I had two key problems to deal with: Arch and Hamon. '*Raphe*?' I bellowed.

'What?'

He appeared so suddenly that I thought he must have been listening especially to make me jump. On his face there was a nasty grin, as though he knew he had shocked me. About his feet, not barking for once, was the flea-trap. I glared at the mutt. 'Get out!'

Raphe grunted something, and, to my surprise, the dog fixed me with a mournful expression, in which hurt and regret were dominant, and slunk away.

I fixed Raphe with a serious glare. 'That thing stays out in the kitchen with you, not in here. Now. I would like you to find Humfrie.'

'Where is he?'

'That is the point of saying I would like you to "find" him. It implies that you will need to hunt him down. Because, Raphe, I don't know where he is.' I suggested a few places where he could be – mostly the taverns and alehouses about Ludgate – and Raphe resentfully agreed to go. I almost had to boot him from the door. It was a surprise: I had thought he would appreciate an opportunity of visiting various taverns. And then I realized: at taverns and alehouses he would have to spend his own money. Sitting in my kitchen, he drank my wine for free.

When he was gone, I sat back in my favourite chair and closed my eyes. Instantly, a vision of Cat came to my mind. She was so appealing, and all the more so when I was feeling lustful, as I was just now. Somehow the nearness of danger would often have that effect on me. I was feeling threatened after the morning's meeting with Arch and Hamon, and that left me wanting feminine companionship.

I had no idea where to find her, though. Cat was not the sort of woman who would stick to the same haunts, I felt. Her demeanour when I saw her at the Cheese indicated to me that she was anxious about something – or someone.

Of course, I knew a lot about women like her. I had met plenty of streetwalkers and inmates of brothels in my time, and if there was one thing that was obvious, it was that women in her line of work often lived in fear of their associates. She was plainly terrified of Henry.

He had not been a particularly scary man, in my estimation, it is true. The fact that I had seen his gun was not real had helped me when I snubbed him, but even then there was little violence in him. There are some men for whom violence is a way of life. Men like Arch and Hamon, for example. But there are others, such as Henry, who like to project it, but who simply fail. When Henry tried to threaten me, it came across as mere bluster. There was no conviction in it.

However, a young maid, fresh to her new career, trying to snare men like me while not getting hurt, I could easily imagine being terrified of Henry. He was strong enough to punch. I only had to think of Dorothy's face to realize how a woman could be forced to live in constant fear of being attacked and hurt.

Of course, Henry had not been present at the Cheese. Cat had been on her own there, which perhaps meant that she had run away from him, or, at the very least, she had left him.

If so, the poor thing was all alone, scared and lonely in the city. She would be desperate for a friendly face. And she would be grateful to be rescued, no doubt.

I smiled at that thought. But how to find her?

In my time in London, I had been lucky enough to make the acquaintance of several women who catered for the better quality of client, and Alice Pendle was one of the best.

I looked for her along Ludgate, where she was wont to idle her time between clients, and when I found her, she was peering at the bolts of cloth at a stall and discussing the merits of a green material that matched her eyes, compared with a reddish-gold one that set off her hair perfectly: it had delicious strawberry tints, and always made me think of summer, although her face and figure brought altogether more lustful thoughts. It was clear that the merchant was suffering the same conflicting emotions as she daintily tormented him, standing close to him, speaking breathily and making the poor devil redden like an apprentice on his first visit to a brothel. He was desperately trying to keep his mind on profits, but all he could see was the picture in his mind of Alice naked. It was the effect she had on men.

'Hello, Jack. How are you this wonderful day?' she said, when I sauntered up. She had an entrancing face, and it was easy to return her smile.

'I am well, dearest lady,' I said. 'I hope you are as well as you look. I have never seen a maid looking so bonny.'

'You still have the art of flattery, then,' she said.

Alice looked especially delicious that fine morning, and although she chuckled when I complimented her, she soon made it clear that there were no free rewards for my words. The merchant visibly sagged, wiping his brow as we left, and I expect he closed up shop soon afterwards, either to go and soak himself in a cold bath or to run to the nearest house of ill-repute. Alice was that sort of woman. I experimented and received a painful slap when my hand strayed, but she took my arm as we wandered along the road, and as we walked, I explained about Cat.

'She came here when?'

'Only a matter of days ago,' I said. In truth, I was surprised to hear myself say it. So much had happened in the last days that it seemed almost as though I had known her for months.

'And you first met her there,' she said, considering. 'It's not a territory I know well, but I have some friends who work about the Cheese and other places around. Leave it with me, and I will see what I can learn for you.'

'That would be wonderful,' I said.

'But that is all I can do for now,' she added with a yawn. 'Ugh! I was up all night with an alderman and his wife. He drank so much he soon fell asleep, but *she* was like a mad thing. Kept on all night. I need some sleep; I don't think I'll be working this evening.'

'Can I tempt you with a pot of hob or spiced wine?'

She gave me a cynical shake of her head. 'Save it for your woman, Jack. You don't want me draining you beforehand, do you? That wouldn't show you to best advantage with her, would it?'

We parted then, she to seek Cat, and I to find a jug of wine at my fire.

I made my way homewards, and as I closed the door, I knew that Humfrie was there. It was a simple enough piece of reasoning: nothing to do with his cloak on a hook or his staff at the door – he didn't wear a cloak and didn't need a staff – no, it was the sudden appearance of Raphe, his look of alarm and the lack of sound. Only one man I knew could instil that sort of wary caution in Raphe: Humfrie. Perhaps Arch and Hamon as well, after their recent visit, but I couldn't be certain of that. However, I was perfectly sensible to the extreme anxiety that the appearance of Humfrie inspired in young Raphe. There was something about the man, the way he moved so silently, his serious expression, his fingers' grip. When he shook hands, it was like being clutched by an iron statue. And I think Raphe had guessed that this man was dangerous, even if he didn't know about my subcontracting work to him.

'Humfrie,' I said as I entered.

He was sitting on a stool, back straight as a poker, and he turned to face me, his eyebrow raised. 'Master Jack. Your boy said you wanted to see me. Is it work?'

'It could well be.' I sat and bellowed at Raphe to bring more wine. Humfrie had already polished off one jugful, from the look of it. 'I've been dropped in an unfortunate situation with two men.'

'Ah. You want them removed?'

'I may do. But for now, what I really need is someone to stay with me in case they try anything.' The memory of a pair of bloody, rusted snippers came to mind, and I shivered involuntarily.

'Who are they?'

'A pair called Arch and Hamon.'

He allowed his face to crack into a smile. 'You wouldn't be the first to be gulled by them,' he said. 'They're known all about town.'

'I know. What can we do to keep them away?'

'What are they asking now?'

'Six guineas.'

He gave a low whistle. 'Well, if you will go about town dressed in silks and finery, I suppose they think they can take you for a lot. What was the original? Three? Four? Less?'

I admitted the depth of their rapacity, and he looked astonished. 'That's greedy of them. Naughty little bleeders! Anyway, all right. I could have someone see to them, if you want. It wouldn't cost six.'

'How much?'

'Two of them, maybe two each to have them done properly. That's about the going rate.'

'Four guineas?' I burst. 'That's too much!'

'If you say so,' Humfrie agreed accommodatingly. 'You know your own mind best, of course.' He sat back, and every so often his eye wandered to my cods. It was an unsettling glance.

'You think they really would try to hurt me?'

'I've no doubt of it.'

'Then, instead of killing them, why don't you stay with me for a while? Become my bodyguard.'

'Me? For you?' He considered. 'A guinea a week, then.'

'*How* much?'

He smiled happily. 'Just think: two weeks and it's one guinea each, isn't it?'

'You said it would be two guineas each.'

'I meant one per ballock of yours, if I save them,' he said imperturbably.

'Oh, very well,' I snapped. I wasn't of a mind to hear humorous comments about parts of my anatomy that could soon be removed.

'After that we'll have to think about whether you'll want

to carry on paying me, or whether it'll be better to have Hamon and Arch removed more permanently,' he said. 'You wouldn't want to pay too much, after all. Not even for them,' he added, grimly chuckling as he gazed at my codpiece.

When Raphe had replenished our jugs, I moved to the second piece of business. 'I have another slight problem,' I said. 'A strongbox that needs opening.'

'You lost your key?' he asked, his eyes going to the ceiling. How he did that, I don't know, but he could always sniff out the room where money was being stored.

'No, not mine,' I said with some asperity. 'It's another one. I've heard that it's full of treasure.'

'Oh? Whose treasure?'

'If you can get us inside that box, yours, mine and one other man's.'

'I see. Well, I have little else on just now. I've opened a number of locks in my time. I doubt this will provide me with a great difficulty. Where is it?'

I explained all about the chest and the priest, and Humfrie's face blackened. 'I don't know as I approve of stealing from the Church. That's not right.'

'It's not stealing from the Church. It was given to this priest by the abbot far away,' I said. 'And his abbey has gone, I understand. So whose is it now? The abbot and his monks have all been sent into retirement. I expect they are all dead by now, and meanwhile this treasure is sitting in a chest in the church of St Botolph. What good can it do there?'

'I don't know . . .'

'Well, at least come and look inside it, and then decide,' I said, and thus the pact was made.

'I'll do that and return to your house tomorrow.'

'There is one last thing,' I muttered as I sipped wine. 'There is another man. He's apparently killed his own daughter.'

'He's what?'

Humfrie's daughter was a chip off the old block. She was young, enormously attractive, vicious when an enemy, as I had learned to my cost, and the absolute apple of Humfrie's eye. He doted on her as a father should. I might have used a little dramatic excess while speaking of the miller, but it was in a good cause.

'Yes, I'm afraid so. This fellow, he was a miller in the village by the church, lost his wife some years ago and never sought another legitimate wife. His daughter was there, so . . . It is not a rare event, I'm sure, but the poor child was obviously distressed by his rapes. She looked to the priest for support and help, and when he appeared, the miller took umbrage. He murdered them both and then bolted for London. He's here somewhere, but I have no idea where.'

'I'll be able to find him,' Humfrie growled. 'And when I do, I'll feed him to the fishes.'

'It might be better to allow the law to take its course,' I said hastily. 'After all, this man has committed multiple offences against God and his daughter. His crimes need to be brought into the light, don't they?'

'I don't like it. I'll find him, but you'd best keep him from me,' Humfrie said. 'If I get too close, I might not be able to stop myself from doing something he'd regret briefly for the rest of his life.'

Humfrie knew the power of words. He didn't mean that the miller would only regret something momentarily before enjoying old age; he meant the man would have little time for regret since his life was about to end.

He stood to go, and I reminded him he was now my official bodyguard.

'Just lock your door. You'll be safe enough in here,' he said. 'Don't open the door to anyone. Besides, you said they were at St Botolph's earlier. They probably got stuck into the inn's ale and won't be here till morning.'

However, I was not to stay in the house. Later, I received a message from Alice, inviting me to meet her at the sign of the Blue Bear.

This was a better-quality tavern outside the city, not far from the Cheese, and Alice met me at the entrance.

'I've heard she'll be here soon,' she said. She covered her mouth as she yawned again. 'Should be any time soon.'

'How did you hear that?'

'She's new to the city and the life, but it's a place she comes to regularly. She has her routine already.'

That was a shame. I was sad to hear that little Cat was already so involved in the game. Women like her had their haunts, as I knew, but I had hoped it would take her a while longer to become so deeply inured to this way of life. Although it did, of course, mean that I would be able to see her whenever I wanted, since sleeping with her would become a simple financial transaction. So maybe it wasn't such a terrible thing after all.

It was a pint and a half of ale later that Cat appeared in the doorway. Again, I was struck by her apparent trepidation. This time she didn't hurry to the opposite side of the place, as she had when I saw her at the Cheese, but she did peruse the room carefully before entering. Satisfied that the place was safe, she came in and walked to a table. It was at the far side of the room, and had two advantages that I could see: it was close to a door to further chambers in case she wished to make a quick exit, and it gave her a good view of the rest of the room and the front door.

My own seat was at a small table beyond a pillar, so although I was hardly concealed, I was obscured from her view. She took a jug of spiced wine and sat demurely enough, while men entered, glanced at her, fetched drinks, stared at her, and obviously thought of the coins in their purses, and how much it would cost to whisk her away to a chamber where they would be charged by the hour.

When she was distracted by a scruffy serving boy, I rose and walked to her. 'Hello, Cat.'

She had been watching a new man enter and gave a little jump of surprise when I startled her. 'Peter!'

'I was sorry to miss you when you left. But more sorry to leave you alone in my bed that night,' I added with a grin of pure lechery.

'It was not very romantic with your friend there.'

'A man who could get between you and me is no friend of mine,' I said with perfect conviction.

Her eyes smiled at that, but then went to the door again.

'Cat, why don't you come back with me now? We can enjoy a lazy evening at my house.'

'I can't,' she said.

'I know. It's Henry, isn't it? You're scared of him. Well, you don't need to be. I could introduce you to people. There's a woman here, Alice, who has many friends. Some of them would be happy to help you and remove Henry, or just persuade him to leave you.'

'You think so?'

She didn't seem terribly enthralled by the idea, to my surprise.

'Yes. Come with me, and we can talk it through over a bumper of wine.'

She looked at me very direct then. 'Can you pay me?'

I was a little taken aback. Obviously, being in the profession she had adopted, money was a serious matter. 'Yes,' I said. 'I have money in my strongbox at home.'

She would be worth it.

It took a little while to get her back to my house. At first, she was reluctant and slow to walk, but as we went along the roads, and saw the people in the way singing, dancing, some behaving with lewd carelessness, not worrying about those watching, her attitude began to change. She glanced at me more often, her face losing the nervousness and anxiety, and beginning to calm. We crossed the road to avoid a group of drunken apprentices – a fellow soon learns to avoid them – and she clung to my arm as we stepped around a puddle, and as she did, I heard her chuckle. A short way after that, there was a small tavern, and I persuaded her to enter with me. We drank a pint each of strong red wine, and afterwards, when we walked, her arm was more closely attached to mine than before, and I could feel her warm bosom against my upper arm, and my heart felt full to bursting. I bent and kissed her. She was so sweet, so lovely and fine, I felt, for just a few moments, that I would like to marry her. Then I wondered how much she would charge for that.

As soon as we reached my house, I opened the door to her, and she was quick to step inside. I followed after. I ignored Raphe, kicking the mutt from my path and hurrying to the buttery to fetch wine and two pots, and with them we repaired to my parlour, where we sat on the rugs before the fire and drank, and gradually I persuaded her to lie down, and we kissed and cuddled and . . . well, whatever happened then is none of your business.

FIVE

Early the next morning I woke to the sound of pigeons and sparrows making merry, and glanced down at Cat's firm, pale body beside me. I can say, I think without exaggeration, that I had satisfied her in the hours of darkness. She had no reason to complain of my stamina. I rose, pulled on my hose and a shirt, and made my way down the stairs, calling to Raphe for some attention. When I reached my parlour, there was a knock at the door. The dog was curled into a small ball beside the fire at the foot of the ladder that led to Raphe's small chamber behind the chimney. The brute opened one eye, clearly decided I could do my own guarding and closed it again.

Thinking that Sir Richard had returned, wishing for a discussion about the miller and where he could have hidden, I went to the door and opened it.

A fist struck my belly, and the sudden pain made me curl into a ball. A hand grabbed my shirt, and I heard threads snap as I was hauled from the house bodily, whirled around in the air and slammed against the outer wall.

All the air was driven from my lungs. The brick and wood of the wall was painful enough, but the violence of the attack had knocked my skull against a prominent stone, and I was stunned. Stars flew about me, and I had to blink to try to clear my vision. All I knew was that I was pinned as effectively as a man with an arrow through his chest. Desperately trying to get a breath, I wheezed and coughed, and at last, when my eyes could focus once more, I goggled. It was Cat's man Henry.

But this was not the Henry I was used to. This was a fierce young man with molten iron in his veins. He was, in short, terrifying. I could quite understand how Cat would be afraid of him.

'Where is she?' he roared.

'In my house,' I said. 'Upstairs, I—'

'You have been ravishing her, haven't you? You put your foul hands on her pure skin! You've been swiving her in your bed, haven't you? I could gut you now for that!'

'I . . . What do you want of me?' I said, trying to keep my voice low. One does not want the neighbours to enjoy such discussions so early.

'She is mine, you understand me? *Mine!* And I won't have her trifled with by a half-arsed merchant, or whatever you are!'

I did consider mentioning that I was an assassin, but felt the time was not perfect.

'What did you do to her?'

'Me? I – um—'

'Never again, you understand? You will never do this with her again. Is that clear?'

'I – well, I suppose—'

'You're pathetic!' he said, which I thought was a bit rich from a man who had stood outside my door all night because he wanted to see what had happened to his associate.

'Well, look,' I said, and then I whimpered. There are times when lengthy debates are to be welcomed, and there are times when a man must recognize that his words could be, at best, superfluous. This was one of those times, because I became aware that, while his left hand was holding me by the shirt against the wall, he had a second hand. While I was discussing matters with him, he had drawn a knife, and now the chilly steel was resting just under my cods.

There is something about the criminal classes that associates a man's prickle and cods with revenge, clearly. First Hamon and Arch, and now this lobcock. I just wished the fools could find someone else's tackle to threaten.

Now, you may not have experienced something like this. All I can say to you is that when you first get the sensation that a razor-edged knife is resting against that most vulnerable of appendages, it drives all other thoughts from the mind. I was no longer aware of Cat or even Henry, truth be told. All I knew was the feeling of exceedingly sharp steel at the back of both ballocks, and the urgent need to get away from it. I was already on tiptoes, and now I tried stretching my head upwards, as though it could take my nether regions away from that horrible knife. It didn't.

'You won't touch her again, will you?' he snarled.

At this stage, my eyebrows were trying to climb to the top of my skull, in the faint hope that they could pull my body up with them. So far they didn't seem to be succeeding. I whimpered again, and then the knife was taken away. I dared not look down. It didn't feel like anything had been cut off, but when you are cut with a razor, there is no sensation at first. All I knew was that I didn't yet feel that hideous tingling that said an extraordinarily sharp blade had castrated me, and there was no sensation of running water to say that I was bleeding everywhere. As Henry rammed his knife into the sheath at his hip, I cast a glance down, past the fist gripping my shirt, to the ground at my feet. Yes. All seemed well. Just a codpiece that was askew, with a pair of laces sheered through.

The relief washed through me like a physician's purgative. I sagged, exhausted, and lifted my eyes to Henry, a weak smile stretching my mouth, just as I saw his fist clench.

It caught me under the chin, and I felt a big, thick blanket suddenly fall from the sky and smother me. I knew no more.

Some people I have known have been connoisseurs of fine wines, while others can claim to be professional in the way that they assess a good ham, a slice of beef or a capon. Those all seem eminently suitable areas of expertise compared with my own.

My speciality, you see, if I can call it that, lies in the miserable experience of waking from being beaten about the head.

I have woken in pleasant surroundings. I have woken in chambers richly decorated, but with the threat of danger all about me. I have woken in horrible rooms, in alleyways, in the cold and damp, and all have added their own particular flavour to my experiences. Usually, I come to in time to see someone trying to hurt me even more, or someone preparing to threaten me. However, this once, I was glad to stir myself without any apparent threat remaining.

Of course, the fact that he had already knocked me down

and threatened to remove my sausage and vegetables meant that his continued presence was less relevant. But it was still a positive aspect of this wakening, and I was not going to look a gift horse in the mouth.

The second issue, of course, is always the degree of pain that I felt. Today, I had the pleasure of what felt like a badly bruised jaw, two loose teeth, and a lump the size of a reasonable goose egg on the back of my skull where my head had been knocked back on to the projecting stone. I felt it gingerly and winced as I felt a stabbing pain. Yes, it was painful.

Of Henry, there was no sign. I clambered to my feet, clinging to the wall to support me. The stars I had noticed when Henry bashed my head against the wall had returned, and one or two attempted to strike me, but I evaded them, closing my eyes until they had disappeared and I could make my way indoors once more. The only thought on my mind at that moment was why on earth I hadn't insisted that Humfrie stayed with me overnight. There was, naturally, the desire to have some peace in order to be able to seduce Cat, but just now that seemed like a poor reward for the pain I had endured.

I tried calling to Raphe, but the result of opening my mouth and trying to call was so astonishingly painful that I decided not to try that again for some little while. There was a pattering of paws, and the useless mutt stood in the doorway to the kitchen, head to one side, as if questioning why I had to wake the household at such an early hour. I would have shouted at him, but my mouth and head hurt too much.

With great caution, I climbed the stairs to my bedchamber, wondering whether Cat would still be there, or whether I had been unconscious for so long that Henry had come up and taken her away with him.

She was still there, curled up in my bed like a kitten. When I sat carefully on the edge, and then rolled over to lie on my back, she stirred and stretched luxuriously, eyes still closed. When she finally gave a groan and relaxed, she turned to me, opening her eyes and smiling with a slow lasciviousness.

And then her eyes widened, the smile fled like a snowflake in a fire, and she jerked away from me.

'Peter! What's happened to you?'

'Your man Henry happened to me,' I said. I opened my mouth and tested it. It seemed to work, and I ran my fingers over my chin to see how my jaw felt. I winced: it didn't feel good. She gently removed my hand and moaned at the sight. 'You poor darling,' she said.

I couldn't disagree. My hand went to my cods to see if there was any blood.

She chuckled. 'You want another go? Even after Henry did this?'

'No, you . . .' I stopped my tongue before I could be too rude. After all, a second bout might be possible. I was not foolish enough to refuse a sympathetic bedding. 'He tried to cut my ballocks off.'

'He . . .' She glanced down at my cods and delicately moved my tarse out of the way to view matters more clearly. 'Oh, you poor thing!'

I felt my heart stop. 'Is it bad?'

'It is terrible,' she said, shaking her head. I tried to sit up on my elbows to take a horrified look, but she pushed me back down. 'I can only think of one way to cure it,' she said, and climbed into the saddle with a smile.

At first, I had a horrible thought of what damage Henry could inflict on me, were he to learn that I had been enjoying little Cat once more, and then I began to fear for the damage *she* might do to me. As matters stood (if you will excuse the pun), I thought my poor pikestaff could be ripped from me, if there was a deep enough cut, but even as I became aware of such concerns, I was rescued by the hammering on the front door.

There is something about the sound of my door being belaboured in that manner that always has the effect of making lust and desire flee. While my brain was willing enough, other organs were not.

'I suppose you might as well go and see who it is,' Cat said regretfully, casting a glance of disappointment towards my malfunctioning vitals.

I hurriedly grabbed my hose and pulled them up. The laces of the codpiece were still dangling, but I was able to fix them with some simple knots, and I pulled a shirt over my head as

I made my way downstairs, avoiding the bruises on my head and jaw.

'Who is it?' I demanded at the door itself. I had taken the precaution of picking up my gun, and its weight was comforting in my hand. There was something about the firearm that inspired confidence, even if, as I feared, this was her damned man again. No one else would knock with such violence, other than a man who thought his wife was inside. Or so I thought.

'Open the door, man! I have matters to discuss. 'S'blood, you're fretful, fellow!'

'Sir Richard,' I said, drawing the bolts. 'I give you joy of the morning, sir! I am very happy to see you.'

He was frowning at my face. 'What happened to you? Did you insult a horse, that it would kick you like that?'

'This was no horse's kick, but a man's fist.'

'By heaven, the man must have a punch like a maul! Your face has been sorely bruised, my friend.'

'Yes, well, he was offended by my seeing his maiden.'

'Seeing, eh? I hate to think what he would do if he thought you were swiving the maid!'

I glared at him. It had little impact, other than to make him laugh.

'Where is your misbegotten servant?' he asked. 'Why are you opening your own door, when you have a man to do it? You would own a cat and catch your own mice?'

'I don't know where he is,' I admitted. I didn't want to have to say that the fool was yet abed. Sir Richard would have thought it reprehensible to allow a servant to sleep so late, forcing his master to open the door to guests.

Sir Richard shook his head, walked to the buttery and bellowed at the top of his voice, 'Raphe! You useless piece of dog turd, get yourself out of bed and down here before I come and fetch you!'

He turned to me with a grin. 'That should fetch him out! Where's his dog?'

I nodded and winced. His voice had entered my skull and now seemed to be rattling around inside like a loose cannon-ball. It felt as though my head was going to come adrift. 'I don't know. It was here last night, useless brute. I've seen more useful slugs than that thing.'

'Stop yer moanin'. Anyone would think you'd been seriously injured.'

I forbore to mention the near damage done to my manhood as he led the way to my parlour. 'Why did you come here so loudly?'

'Why'm I here? Why, because I've had no success,' he declared, and strode to my best chair. The fire was not yet lit, and he stared at the charred embers with disgust. 'I had thought that the miller would be easy enough to find, but although I've spoken to men up and down the riverside, no one has been able to help. The damn fools take my ale and wine, but none of them has anything to say about strangers appearin' in the last few days.'

'What can happen, I believe, is that some men will take money from strangers to hide them,' I said sarcastically.

'Aye, of course. But I have spoken to thief-takers from the Tower to the Black Friar's, and they know all the men in their areas. There is not one man of thirty or more from east of London who's appeared in the last week or so. The only people here are those who have been around for an age, or so they say. I'll need men all along the river to find a new fellow.'

'And both sides,' I pointed out. 'There are many who would be happy to hide a fellow in the Bishop of Winchester's lands south of the river.'

Sir Richard balled a fist and smacked it into his cupped left hand. 'Peter's murderer can't be allowed to escape!'

'Peter and the girl's murderer,' I pointed out.

'Yes, the poor miller's daughter. She must have suffered in her life, poor child. It's hard to imagine what she must have endured from such a violent man.'

'Yes,' I said, thinking of Dorothy and her black eye.

'Where is that boy of yours?' Sir Richard muttered, going to the door and bellowing again for Raphe.

'Perhaps he has gone out to the shop?' I wondered.

'Perhaps he's still lying abed,' Sir Richard said. 'You should go and check to see if he's all right.'

I had my hand to my head at that moment and incautiously

nodded. It felt at first as though my head must fall from my shoulders, which made a spasm of pain shoot through my shoulders and spine. My chin accidentally hit my hand, and I felt a pain so intense that I wished my head had been removed.

'I'll go,' I said.

Raphe was nowhere to be seen in the house, and I concluded that he had indeed taken himself and his 'Hector' to the market to purchase viands or other edibles. I was somewhat surprised, since he had not displayed much in the way of enthusiasm for shopping in the past, nor any great ability for rising early in the morning.

When I returned to my parlour, I was surprised to find that Cat was already dressed and was sitting demurely with Sir Richard, engaging him in conversation about his brother and the search for his murderer.

'What sort of man would kill a priest, Sir Richard?' she asked with a sort of enquiry that displayed the prettiest delicacy of spirit.

'Alas, my child, there are many who would harm a man of God, no matter what the colour of his cloth. Just as there are many who would dare break into a church to steal the valuables. Thievery is nothing new, sadly. But to kill a man like my brother . . .'

'I am so sorry.'

'Thank you. But to kill him for an imagined fault, that is surely the worst of all crimes. He was no womanizer, no matter what others might say. I will not have his name impugned in that way. He should be remembered as a kind, good man.'

'He did appear to be popular with the feminine members of his congregation,' I said.

'There were many who sought his advice and sympathy, I have no doubt. But Peter would not do more.'

'And he deserted Dorothy and their sons.'

'He had no choice in that matter. The law forced him to do so.'

'What will you do?' Cat asked.

Sir Richard gazed at her, and as he shrugged, I was struck by the evidence of his misery. The man had never before, I suppose, had to accept defeat. He was a man to whom submission was a fresh experience. For knights like him, being beaten was something that happened to other people. He had been born to a good family, had been granted an education, had risen to his post of Coroner, and in all that time he had known only success. He inflicted punishments on others, he recorded their crimes, he arrested them – and he had never felt this struggle to achieve. It had always been there for him to grasp. And now, in the most important matter of his life – his own brother's murder – he was lost.

I saw his confusion and I was sympathetic. This man had, after all, rescued me from Arch and Hamon. 'Perhaps it would be best to return to St Botolph's and organize for a proper search for the miller's daughter?'

Cat nodded. 'Yes, that would surely be sensible, Sir Richard. You must find her, to make sure that she has a Christian burial.'

'But her murderer, and me brother's, is here, somewhere. I can't just up and leave town.'

Cat nodded thoughtfully. 'But there may be more you can learn. Someone may be able to give you a scar or a birthmark that will allow you to identify this murderer. Or perhaps he didn't leave the village at all. Perhaps he is there even now, and hiding in the woods as an outlaw would.'

Sir Richard slowly considered. 'It is possible. It would explain his not being here.'

'Perhaps that would be best, then,' I said. 'You should ride back and see what may be learned there.'

'I will need help,' Sir Richard said.

'Peter will help you,' Cat said. 'He wouldn't want you to go alone, would you, Peter?'

'Peter?' Sir Richard said, turning to me.

Just at that moment, I was in no mood for a ride, no matter how brief. At least, not on horseback. Besides, I wanted to see Humfrie. 'No, Sir Richard. I am sorry, but I cannot join you today. I have been belaboured, pummelled and sorely beaten. It's a miracle that I am still able to—'

'Peter?' Sir Richard said again.

'Sir Richard, I cannot join you today.'

'Peter?'

I gave him a cold stare. He returned mine with an expression of pure cynicism and a raised eyebrow that told me in so many words that he knew he had me for lying to the wench and using a pseudonym.

I know when I am beaten.

I did insist on breaking my fast before departing. And with Cat there to aid me, I was able to enjoy a little exercise as well. She had, bless her, a tear in her eye as she waved me off from my bed, her hair tousled, the sheets and blankets all disarrayed, and my fervent desire to remain with her playing havoc with my ability to leave. She was such an enticing, entrancing maiden.

Sir Richard had suggested that we should meet at the stables just down from Aldgate. I made my way thither, shoving my pistol into my belt with as much enthusiasm as I could muster. I put the balls and powder into a bag and pulled the strap over my head so that it hung over the gun, making the weapon less obtrusive. With my head thundering painfully, it was not so easy. I walked with my back hunched, my head down. The bruise at the back of my skull was more painful than the bruise at my chin – not that it wasn't a close match. With every step I took, the rearmost injury seemed to pound, while that forward gave a stabbing pain. Different, you see, but equally painful in their own ways.

The way to the stables took me down an alley to a narrow street which could only take a standard car, and it was as I was about to cross the street that he caught my arm.

I squeaked. Instantly into my mind flashed a picture of blasted Henry once more. The hand on my arm jerked, and I was pulled around to meet the glowering features of Hamon.

You can tell how confused and injured I was at the time by the simple fact that I considered this a good thing. My only thoughts were of that weighty fist approaching my chin and all the pain that had ensued. 'Oh, it's you,' I said, with evident relief.

Hamon had a fleeting look of embarrassment cross his face before he fitted a fresh malevolent scowl to it and leered at

me. 'You think me turning up is going to be good for you?
I'll have you know that I have my snippers here,' he said,
patting his pocket.

'That is fine. However, I am in a hurry,' I said, gabbling
rather. 'Have to be away, you see. Got to meet a man.'

'Yes: Arch.'

'I would like to,' I said, trying to pull my arm from his
grip. 'But I have an important meeting. People are depending
on me. They're expecting me.'

'And Arch is expecting you. I don't want to keep him
waiting. Nor do you.'

'Let me go!'

'For one thing, it's difficult to find a decent servant nowa-
days, isn't it?' he said, smiling to display a row of unpleasant
teeth.

I almost fell over as his breath caught me. It rocked me
back on my heels, and I coughed and almost retched. 'Why
does he want to see me now? I have told him I'll get the
money shortly.'

'He doesn't trust you.'

'*He* doesn't trust *me*?' I exclaimed, and I was offended by
the implication. After all, it was he who had forced me to
gamble and increased my debt daily.

'I'll put it like this: you'll come with me now if you want
to see your servant again,' Hamon said. 'At least, all in one
piece, anyway.'

That put a different complexion on things, of course. It was
one thing to mislay a general boy of all work and quite another
to mislay a boy who was related to my master, John Blount.
I had always had the impression that Raphe was more a local
spy, whose main task was to furnish my master with any
improprieties I might commit, rather than to support my well-
being. Since Master Blount thought me an excellent assassin,
he perhaps did not consider that I required assistance in
self-defence.

'You have my boy?'

'You're quick. Yes, we have Raphe. He's at Arch's house
now. And you're coming, too.'

'Let me just—'

'And every time you delay matters means a joint of his fingers with my snippers.'

Arch's 'house' was a small building that leaned alarmingly against a stone wall enclosing a merchant's home. On one side of the wall was a delightful garden, I imagine, with roses and a vegetable patch, a small pasture, some cattle and pigs mingling with the merchant's horses; on the other side was a hovel little larger than the pigs' sties. A dog was barking furiously. In London there were always dogs barking furiously.

Hamon pushed me inside, and I stood still while the world stopped reeling and my head stopped whirling.

'So, Master Peter, yet again you 'ave been disappearing. And that after you were so rude to me and 'Amon. We didn't appreciate that, did we, 'Am?'

'No, Arch, we didn't. He made us feel foolish, didn't he?'

''E did, 'Am, 'e did. And that's not polite, is it?' Arch said. He was sitting in a rather uncomfortable chair that looked as though it had been made by a blind apprentice who had never passed to become a craftsman. 'Which is why we decided to take a more direct approach to you, Peter. Since you wouldn't come to us willingly, we thought we'd persuade you to come with a more firm proposal.'

'Where is Raphe?'

'Oh, you want 'im right away, do you? I'm sorry, master, but you'll 'ave 'im back when I 'ave my money. 'Ow much was it, again?'

'Six guineas,' Hamon said.

'Oh, but there's interest to add to that now,' Arch said. 'Interest over another day makes it, let's see . . .' He made a show of counting on his fingers, but then again it might have been proof of his mental acuity. 'Ah, yes, a guinea and ten shillings more to last night, so now it's another two guineas to add to the six you already owe. There's another tuppence ha'penny, too. Only we'll let you off the ha'penny.'

'How could it have grown to eight guineas?' I demanded. 'It was only a ten-bob debt!'

Hamon stood. I could almost hear the joints squeaking as

his limbs moved, but it could have been the mechanics of his brain. 'Are you saying Arch is dishonest?'

I didn't want to get into a fight. 'Where's my servant?'

'Somewhere safe. Where's my eight guineas?'

'At my house. I can fetch them for you.'

'Oh, yes. Last time we trusted you to bring us the money you owed, you disappeared for days. Remember? And the time before that. In fact, I forgot our journey all the way to St Botolph's. That was expensive, wasn't it, 'Am?'

'Yes, Arch. Very expensive.'

'So I'll need two more shillings for that. Which means eight guineas, two shillings and tuppence.'

I could have accused him of extortion, of bullying, of theft, but any and all would have led to Hamon pulling his snippers out, and I had no desire to become disconnected. I was attached to my various appendages, as I think I mentioned while Henry was threatening to beat me to a pulpy mess and cut off my tarse and ballocks. 'What do you want me to do?'

'Let's go back to your 'ouse now. You can fetch us our money, and then you can 'ave your servant.'

'Not right now. I have a job to do at St Botolph's.'

'That's fine. You can go right away, if you want. Of course, your servant will look a bit useless after a while. One joint every 'alf 'our means if you ride all that way and back, 'e won't have any fingers or toes left. It'll make 'im a bit less useful as a servant.'

I glared at him. Arch sat back with a self-satisfied look on his face. Hamon was twirling his snippers with a certain amount of glee.

I had no choice.

'Very well,' I said.

The house seemed oddly silent when I arrived. Without Raphe or Sir Richard, it was as quiet as a church before Matins. I had never appreciated just how still and empty a place could sound when there was nobody inside. And it felt colder, too. I suppose that was because no one had lit the fires.

My first thought was that I hoped Cat would make herself scarce. My second was that she had already done so. For the place to be so calm, she must have collected her belongings and gone. I clenched my jaw at the thought. I could have done with her now.

'Where's the money?' Arch demanded.

'I'll fetch it,' I said.

'Very good. And we'll come too, just in case you 'ad any ideas about running away again.'

'I don't know what you mean.'

Hamon chuckled nastily.

'Come on, where is it?' Arch said. 'Lead the way, Peter.'

This was growing intolerable. I dared not let the pair of them see my special hideaway. Were they to discover my money chest, I had no doubts that they would in short time knock me on the head, take all my money and fly off into the distance with a merry laugh at my expense.

On the other hand, I had no means of escape. All I had on my person was my pistol, but that was only sufficient for one of them, and I might not hit a vital organ, which would mean that the men would both set upon me, and I had little doubt that the result would be painful and short-lived – as would I be, too.

'Come on!' Hamon urged.

I had no choice. There was no second route by which I could escape. My options were strictly limited. With a grunt of resignation, I made my way through to my upper chamber. There I unlocked the padlock from the door and entered. Arch and Hamon were close behind me. Arch fixed his eyes on my chest and beckoned to me. 'Key.'

'I'll do it.'

'And I'll say it again: *key.*'

I heard the slither of steel being drawn, and there was a sharp prick of a knife point over my liver. Hamon was behind me, and his dagger was a strong incentive to do as I was bid.

With very bad grace, I unbuttoned the flap of the pocket at my belt, reached inside and withdrew my keys. I weighed them in my hand, seriously contemplating, just for a moment, hurling them through the open window. This being my money room, I had caused iron bars to be fixed over the windows, and I could surely throw them out into the road. But if I did, someone else would find them. Besides, if I were to throw, what were the odds of missing my target and the keys striking the bars themselves, falling conveniently back into the room as I expired with Hamon's knife in my back? I considered the chances of my death to be very high. And I am not, generally, a gambling man.

I flung them to Arch, and he smiled as he caught them in his left hand. 'Thank you,' he said, and inserted the key into the lock, turning it.

The well-greased mechanism barely made a sound as the key turned, and Arch lifted the lid with a smile on his face.

I knew the sight that would meet his eyes. There were a number of little leather purses inside. Each contained several coins – gold and silver. One bag had only gold coins. It was a small fortune in money, all the proceeds of other men's deaths that I kept. It was my share. The rest had gone to my accomplice, the man to whom I had subcontracted the actual killings.

I saw Arch's fixed smile as he took in the contents of my box. He reached out with a hand while a look of wonder filled his face. And then he looked at Hamon and me.

This was the moment I had been dreading. Once he knew how much money was in my box, he was certain to give Hamon the order to kill me. I was now only an impediment to Arch and Hamon's enjoyment of my money. I meant nothing else to them.

This was the moment, I knew: it was the moment at which I should leap forward, dart past Hamon and flee through my house, leap the steps and bolt out into the street. If I stood here, Hamon would remove me with one thrust of his knife.

The only problem was that my legs had turned to aspic. It was a miracle that they could hold me upright, let alone assist me in an attempt at flight.

'Ah—' I said.

'So, 'ow much is there in 'ere?' Arch said.

'About a hundred and thirty guineas,' I admitted.

'I think you 'ave real problems,' Arch said, and slammed the lid, shoving the box towards me.

I stared at him. It was a surprise that he could kick the box across the floor, since it was made of solid oak and was heavy enough when empty. I lifted the lid and stared at the box.

It was empty.

I goggled. My mouth fell wide.

'That,' Arch said, 'was priceless. Your face! You couldn't 'ave acted that! You were so shocked there was nothing in there! Someone's robbed you, boy!'

'Raphe!' I breathed. 'The little . . .'

'You think so?' Arch said. 'I doubt that shit-for-brains has the capacity to think of stealing all your money and concealing it safely. Besides, 'ow would 'e do that while working for you? Any case, the real question that matters here is 'ow you plan to pay me now.'

That was an aspect that had escaped my attention while I was staring down into my empty chest. My entire concentration was fixed on that empty space before me. Now, of course, Arch had reminded me of the other rather pressing issue, which was how I could keep my head on my shoulders, or my liver unpunctured, now that all my worldly wealth was gone.

'I will have to borrow money to pay you.'

'Very good. Who from?'

'My master, I suppose.'

''E'll have the full nine guineas, will 'e?'

'I'm sure he . . . wait – *nine*?'

'It's not 'ere, so I'll 'ave to wait a little longer, won't I? I've worn out enough shoe leather to 'elp you already. Now I need some added interest to make all my efforts worthwhile.'

'I will get you your money,' I said through gritted teeth.

'Oh, I know you will. You don't 'ave any choice.'

I felt Hamon's hand on my arm again, and the point of his dagger pressing at my back once more.

Hamon led me out of the room, back to the stairs, and then Arch walked to the bottom, while Hamon held me at the top. He pushed, and I hurriedly descended, with Hamon a scant step behind me. We walked to the front door, where Hamon held me, and Arch stepped outside, beckoning Hamon to bring me.

'Where is your master?'

'I'll take you to him,' I said.

It was one of those moments that occur sometimes when a man has to choose whether to throw all on a die or to pocket his losses and accept defeat. Of course, the problem with accepting defeat in this case was my probable ruination. Master Blount would be unimpressed to learn that I had fallen foul of a pair like Arch and Hamon. He would be more concerned still to consider that I had not done my best to kill them both.

I threw the die. It rolled and came up with a six. That, at least, is what it seemed like. I stepped sideways as we passed a nag being mercilessly whipped as she slowly pulled a cart in the street, and pulled out my pistol. Hamon had not bothered to take my dagger or see if I had another weapon on me. Now he would live to regret his arrogance. He was watching the nag, but something warned him of my attack, and he turned to face me just in time to see my fist gripping the handgun. His mouth formed a perfect 'O' as I brought the butt down on his head. He said nothing as the solid steel butt hit his pate, but seeing his eyes roll upwards was a joy I have seldom experienced. I smiled as his body tumbled to the ground at my feet. Then I pointed the barrel at Arch.

'Arch, I fear I cannot go to my master today. Just now I am more concerned with who has robbed me.'

'You knocked 'Am down! You could have killed 'im!'

'That thought had occurred to me. Sadly, I think not,' I said suavely.

Arch appeared to notice the pistol. 'You drawed a gun? On me? Are you mad? Do you know 'ow dangerous those things are? Point it somewhere else!'

'Yes, Arch, these things are very dangerous. They go off at a moment's notice, for the least reason. And, Arch, if you try to step even a half foot closer, I will kill you. I know how to use this thing,' I added with a certain pride.

It was true. In the last weeks I had spent time learning the mechanism and how to load it. At Moorfields there were a number of trees that testified to my ability to reload and fire the thing. Admittedly, not necessarily the same trees at which

I had aimed, but at this distance even I could not miss. The look in Arch's eyes told me he knew it, too.

'Well, that's wonderful. What are you going to do now? You do realize, you've made an enemy of 'Amon and me, don't you, Peter?' Arch said. 'Run away now, boy, and you'll need to watch your back for the rest of your life. And it may not be very long.' He smiled nastily.

'I am going to go back to my home to work out how someone could have robbed me, and where the whore's child could have hidden my money. And then I might pay you the ten bob I owe you,' I said with deliberate firmness, trying to stop my voice quivering.

Arch smiled then. 'Ten bob, you say? Ten bob? I don't think that covers the debt.'

'I'll pay that much,' I said loftily, 'because I am a man of my word. But if you try to force me to give you more, beware! It will not end well for you.'

'I see. Well, there's not much more to talk about, is there? You pay us ten bob for the debt, and then I'll want nine guineas more for the servant's release.'

'You don't hold any cards,' I said. 'You have my servant. I have no interest in him. However, he is related to my master, John Blount. You may not know of him, but he knows of you both, and he is a powerful man in the government. Cross him, and you will make an enemy who will destroy you.'

Arch nodded, but he still smiled. 'Oh, really? You think your boasts of powerful friends will impress me?'

'No. But Master Blount employs his own assassin. No one knows who he is, but he kills silently and his bodies disappear forever. Cross Master Blount by hurting his boy, and you will live briefly but very painfully.'

'You'll regret this, Master Peter. No one crosses me neither. You 'ave made an enemy of me this day.'

I walked to him, the wheel-lock in his face, the barrel touching the tip of his nose. 'No, Arch. You've made yourself an enemy of me. And I will not be kind if you try to pursue me again. Where is Raphe?'

He sneered a bit, but evidently the barrel of the pistol was persuasive. 'You go find 'im yourself!' He added a suggestion that was frankly impossible as well as rude.

'Right.' I had a good idea already where Raphe was.

I suppose I should have rescued Raphe before anything else, but I was not of a mood to liberate him until I had searched for my money. Running through the streets, it took me little time to get home. I pushed at the door and it opened easily.

'You didn't leave the door locked.'

Humfrie was standing in the hallway, looking at me disapprovingly.

'I didn't think it was that important while Arch and Hamon had a knife in my back,' I said bitterly. 'Luckily, I had my own life-preserver, in the absence of my bodyguard!'

'What, they came back?' He looked shocked.

'Apparently so.'

'You look like you've been playing at baiting bears,' he said with a professional glance at my eye and chin.

'That was Henry.'

'Who?'

I ignored him and continued inside. There, I went through to my money room and stood staring at the empty money box.

'What is missing?' Humfrie said.

'My money!' I pointed at my empty chest, and although it will sound foolish, I was close to weeping. 'They must have broken into my house while I slept. Or this morning, when I was on my way to meet Sir Richard,' I said brokenly.

'You think?'

'They picked the door's lock, made their way up here, unlocked this door, took my money and walked out through the door like innocents.'

Humfrie looked dubious.

'What?' I said.

'How did they know the place was empty? How did they know they could walk straight in? How did they know you'd have your money box up here? How did they know to come just at the time when Raphe was not here?'

'I don't know!'

'Perhaps they were watching you?'

I felt that like a cold drench.

The padlock on the door was a strong one, and that on the chest was robust and supposedly enough to prevent even professional thieves. They had yet managed to carry my money away. It was all gone.

I had a strong suspicion that I would never see my money again. I wanted to weep.

And then I remembered Raphe. He might have seen someone watching the house; he might have noticed someone suspicious, if there were men watching the place. And then I had another thought: he was still held by Arch. Arch may take his vindictive nature out on Raphe himself. And that would mean I would never hear about anyone watching the house. I might never get my money back!

Humfrie was watching me with a look in his eye that suggested he was beginning to wonder about my sanity.

'Come with me!' I shouted.

'Where?'

'We have to go to Arch's house.'

'I thought you wanted me to defend you against him? You should stay here.'

'No, you fool! Arch has Raphe, and Raphe might know something about my money!' I snapped.

Everything depended on my finding Raphe and finding my money again. In a hurry, I grabbed my bag holding the powder and the pouch of lead balls, and ran from the house, counting on Humfrie to follow.

If I wanted to talk to Raphe about those who had stolen all my money, I needed to get to him before Arch and Hamon took out their snippers. I could not leave him to their tender cares. Not when it involved my money!

I ran all the way to the house where Hamon had brought me to see Arch. Raphe had to be close. Arch had said as much, after all.

'Oh, please don't let them hurt Raphe,' I prayed. I wanted to get to him first, and if I could, by all the Saints, I would make the wretch regret his theft. 'Come on, Humfrie!'

There were people in the alley, but all denied any knowledge of Raphe. No one had seen any sign of him, nor of Arch and Hamon carrying a rug or sack that squirmed. Walking back to Arch's house, I tested the door. It was unlocked. He must have thought no one would dare to rob him. A dog began barking again, and I cursed it.

Standing in the main chamber near his chair, I gazed about me. Humfrie had followed me inside and now stood watching me like a man eyeing a dog suspected of rabies. I walked up and down the place, and while standing at the wall, I stared about me with growing dismay. Raphe had to be nearby, I was sure of it, and yet there was no sign of him. There was nothing to be seen. Only this room and another above. There was no one upstairs. In a fit of temper, I stamped my foot. The floor-board moved, and the noise rang dull and hollow. I stared down. Perhaps there was an undercroft, some kind of basement room beneath this. I should have realized. There was no entrance that I could see, no trapdoor or loose planks, so I hurried outside. At the side of the building, heavens bless us, the barking dog was Hector. He stood bellowing his fury at a trapdoor. Humfrie pulled it wide, and I peered down. 'Hello? Raphe?' The dog slipped past me and sprang down inside.

I heard a moaning then, and a thrashing sound, a drumming noise as if someone was kicking with his boots at an empty barrel. I stared into the gloom and tried to discern anything, but it was impossible to see in the darkness. The dog was up in the far corner, barking again. Reluctantly, I set a foot cautiously on the uppermost rung of the ladder, and gradually lowered myself into the chamber. 'Raphe?'

The drumming on the barrel grew louder. Humfrie waited at the entrance while I hesitantly made my way towards the sound and found three large barrels standing in a corner. The dog was scrabbling at them, trying to dig around them, appar-ently. The noise of drumming came from behind them, and when I rolled the nearest out of the way, I found a huddled figure behind it.

As my eyes grew accustomed to the dim light, I could make him out. Raphe was bound hand and foot, with a rope that was attached to a ring in the wall. A gag had been forced in his mouth, tied in place by a thong that went about his head twice.

It was tempting to laugh at his predicament, but I was concerned that Arch and Hamon could return at any time. Hamon would not be happy after being clubbed. I drew my knife and began to saw at the ropes binding him. In short order, I had him freed, and he pulled the gag from his mouth and spat repeatedly to clear his mouth of the flavour while Hector leapt at his face, slobbering in a repellent fashion.

'I've been here hours,' Raphe said with disgust. 'They didn't even give me a drink of water.'

'Yes, they are horrible people,' I agreed affably, and then I cuffed him about the head. 'Do you want to wait here for them to come back and cut your ballocks off? Then stop moaning and let's get home!'

For once he was abashed. 'Yes, sir.'

And it sounded as if, just this once, he intended to give me respect.

Back at my house, I threw open the door. Raphe and Humfrie slipped inside with Hector, and Humfrie locked the door behind us. Then I politely asked Raphe to follow me upstairs. 'Look at this,' I said, pushing him into my money room where the chest lay wide still. 'What do you have to say about that?'

'You've been robbed!'

'You think so?' I said sarcastically. Humfrie had joined us and stood at the door now. His silence and fixed posture seemed to make Raphe still more anxious. 'And who could have done that, eh?'

Raphe was gazing into the chest with an expression of bemusement. Now, his face hardened and the lad I had grown to know returned. Gone was all gratitude for his rescue, and in its place a sullen resentment.

'You saying I did it?'

'You? No! Why would I think that? Who could possibly think you would be guilty, eh? No, I want to know where my money is, that's all. Do you have any idea who could have taken my money?'

'I thought you only came to rescue me because I meant

something to you, but, no, it was just because you thought I might know where your money was.'

That was when I lost my calm exterior and displayed some of my inner emotions. 'Of course I care about the money, you blockhead! How do you think we can stay here without money?' I bellowed.

He gaped at that. 'You can always get more, can't you?'

'I could sell your skin, I suppose!' I rasped. I grabbed his shirt, thinking to beat him, but he surprised me by knocking my hand away.

'No! You won't hit me, master! You should think about whom you trust.'

'What, like you?'

'Yes. I've taken nothing of yours.'

'So, who could have taken all my money?'

He pulled a face. 'Whom have you trusted?'

I drew myself to my full height. 'I trust no one.'

'No? What about your woman?'

'What?' I laughed. 'You expect me to believe that a lovely young creature like little Cat could have done this? You reckon she could have picked these locks? She left my bed without waking me, came in here to rob me, then went back to my bed?'

'Not without help. There was a man with her. He picked the locks, ran downstairs, and he had a cart back out there in the street. When she could, she threw the money from the window. I saw him there, catching the bags and putting them on the cart under some hay. I was in the kitchen and saw him, so I went out and followed him to where he put the money, and watched him unload his cart and lock it up before trundling off. That's why I was up so early this morning with Hector.'

'Seriously?' Humfrie said.

'Yes. Master Jack had slept with her, and this morning her man came here and knocked Jack into the middle of next week, and while he was out, the man came in and picked the locks. I saw him.'

I restrained the impulse to grab him and kiss his spotty face or lank, greasy hair. 'Show me where he took my money,' I said.

He was reluctant, but finally assented on promise of a reward, and led me through the streets up near to North Gate. Here there was a row of lock-up chambers set into the wall itself, each arched. They were mere shallow scrapings in the wall with a door to close them, like deep, brick-built cupboards. Above them was the wall's walkway, and someone had thought to set these cupboard-shaped chambers for storage. No doubt someone was making good money from renting them. A man should never underestimate the ability of a Londoner to make money.

Raphe took me to one that had three bolts and a massive padlock on each to stop the bolt moving. 'There,' he said, pointing.

Now, I have never been a great one for the mastery of locks, but I knew several men who were very capable with such work. I turned and looked at Humfrie. He shrugged and stepped to the locks. Picking one up, he studied it with a quizzical look on his face, and then took a metal spike from his belt. He inserted the fine end into the lock and felt about with a frown on his face. There was a click, and his face eased. He moved to the next.

In the space of only a few minutes, the door was open, and each of us was clasping a money-bag to our chests. I had bound two together, resting over my shoulder, and we began to make our way home again. 'Humfrie,' I said. 'There has to be a safer place to store this money than in my house.'

He frowned. 'I might know somewhere,' he said.

It was the middle of the afternoon when I finally managed to make my way to the stables with Humfrie, feeling wary and anxious, keeping a suspicious eye open for Arch or Hamon. I knew that Sir Richard would have left hours before, probably growling about the unreliability of modern youths and complaining bitterly all the way to St Botolph's.

When I thought of beating Hamon over the head with my pistol's butt, a cold sweat broke out over me. I didn't like to think of meeting Hamon again in a dark alleyway. His snippers would soon go to work, I feared, and the thought, were I not riding on a pony at that moment, would have made me cross my legs protectively. What with Henry's knife at my nadgers the night before and the thought of Hamon's snippers, all of my limbs and appendages felt threatened. I knew Hamon could be very dangerous on a good day, and I had a distinct feeling that any day I saw him again would be a very bad day indeed for me.

Later, when we were on our mounts and jogging along, I had the opportunity to think of my day's work so far. At least I had a feeling that at last things were going my way. My head ached, but the worst of the pain was receding from my chin. Now it was focused on the lump at the back of my head.

It seemed clear enough that Cat had robbed me. That was hurtful. I had been besotted with her, and to learn that she was lifting her skirts merely so that she could distract me was most upsetting. It was probably why Henry had arrived at my door, knocking me down, so that he could enter the house while I was unconscious, and then picking the locks. And when he was done, he slipped out while Cat was professionally nursing me. And she had been very gentle and professional, I admitted, with a smile on my face. With a memory like that, it was hard not to smile.

But Henry's face would keep intruding. He was a bully, of course, and I had already seen that Cat was scared of him. Mayhap, just as with Dorothy, Cat had been forced to do his bidding with the threat of a thrashing if she refused? Dorothy had won that horrible black eye, and Cat was no doubt similarly harmed, or threatened with the same dire injuries, were she to refuse his demands. In Dorothy's case, it was a matter of the favours she offered in bed, perhaps, while in Cat's it was a case of betraying me, her lover, so that her husband could rob me blind. As he had.

'What are you grinning about?' Humfrie asked.

'Nothing.'

'Must have been a good "nothing" for you to wear that smirk.'

'I was just thinking.'

'About the woman, I suppose?'

'I'm just astonished that she could have organized to have me beaten and robbed. She was so . . . so . . .'

'Aye, well. There's nothing to say she was involved willingly. What if the accomplice was watching where she went? He followed her without her knowing. Then, late at night, he knocks on your door, and you open it. She knew nothing about him being there. He knocked you down and hurried upstairs, picked the locks and made her help him get the money out.'

'She could be innocent, you mean?'

'Well, bearing in mind the sort of wench she is, I couldn't put it stronger than that, but yes, she might be.'

That was a thought to bring a grin back to my face. After all, I had my money back, and it was secured in a place Humfrie considered safe, and if he was right, it would be possible to renew relations with Cat later. All felt good.

Were it not for Raphe, I would now be in a dire circumstance that did not bear thinking of. He had proved himself, as, in a way, had Hector, by telling us where Raphe was being held.

And then the smile was wiped from my face. Because London also held an angry Hamon who would snip me apart, piece by piece, if he were to get the chance. That was an alarming thought.

So, instead of sitting in my house and waiting for them, here I was, riding for St Botolph's, where at least I knew Sir Richard was able to help protect me. As long as he would.

The inn was almost empty when I arrived. Humfrie took our mounts round to the back, and as I walked to the inn's door, I saw young Ben, who was playing with a hoop and trying to get it to move along the road, but every time he set it down, it stuck to the mud and wouldn't roll, but instead toppled over. He was staring at it disconsolately when I dismounted.

'Hello, Ben,' I said.

'Oh, hello.'

'Where is everyone?'

'They're all out at the millpond. They say that they're going to find the miller's daughter.'

'Oh?' I was about to lead my pony to the rear of the inn and the stables, but there was something in his serious expression that made me hesitate. 'You don't think they will?'

'No, she's not there.'

'Where is she, then?'

He looked up at me. 'Wherever she wants to be. I've seen her. She looked scary, all white like a ghost, with blood all down her front. She was so scared and upset.'

'When was this?'

'On the evening of the day they say she was killed. The night before we found my father. I saw her walking down the street there,' he said, pointing. 'It was terrible. I haven't barely slept since then.'

I have never seen a ghost myself, but the lad's expression told me all I needed to know about the horror. Blood all down her front, and her winding sheet smothered in her gore. 'I think that would have scared me, too,' I said. 'So you think they're looking in the wrong place?'

'If she could come here, she might be anywhere,' he said, logically enough.

'Well, seeing a ghost doesn't mean that her body is moving, too. It's a picture of her, I believe, just as though someone had picked up a painting of her and moved that along the road. But her body is almost certainly up near the mill. It would be too much like hard work to bring her all the way down here, wouldn't it? Just think of the weight of a woman's body like that. No one would carry it too far.'

Except they might, I thought to myself. If she was a slim little thing, and he was a hulking great miller, well used to lifting sacks of grain and flour, it might be nothing to him to throw her over his shoulder and trudge away for mile after mile. If he could have lifted Sir Richard's brother all the way to the road, why not a much lighter figure?

I bade Ben farewell and deposited the pony with a particularly scruffy version of a groom. I decided to go at once to the mill and see how the search was progressing.

The grim atmosphere of lowering malevolence which I had noticed the previous time I had gone to the mill with Sir Richard was considerably lessened by the sound of shouting and hallooing in the woods as the local peasants rattled about the place. In all honesty, it is sometimes hard to understand these lower folk. What, I ask, was the point of their bellows?

They were not calling to an injured person, but to a dead one. There was clearly little possibility of her responding to their cries, unless she was, as poor young Ben suggested, actually walking abroad as a wraith.

The last time I had walked down this track, I recalled, I had thought I had seen a figure behind me, moving through the trees. I glanced over my shoulder. No, there was no one there. It would be ridiculous to think that the woman's shade might try to hunt me down. What had I done to her?

But the thought of a woman clad in a winding sheet that was all besmottered with her own gore suddenly made me keen to move a little faster through the woods. I picked up my pace and started to trot towards the mill.

Sir Richard was standing in a patch of grass some tens of yards from the mill itself. He held a length of stick in his hand, from which he had cut all the twigs, and was using it to point at specific areas that he wanted searched. All about him were peasants from the area. I could see Dorothy's two older boys, and even the innkeeper was out near the mill's leat, prodding half-heartedly with a stake into the water and mud. I made my way to the knight. I had left Humfrie at the inn to make his own enquiries. I did not think I was in danger from Arch and Hamon at the mill with so many other men searching for the miller's daughter's body.

'You finally deign to grace us with yer presence, eh?' the Coroner called when he saw me.

'My apologies. I have had some troubles today.'

'Oh, some *troubles*, eh? I don't suppose they include wanderin' back to yer house to take a tumble with the maid?'

'No,' I said coolly. 'They included rescuing my servant, who was threatened with death, discovering my house had been burgled and apprehending the men responsible.'

He gazed at me blankly. 'Eh?'

'Oh, and recovering my money, as well. Still, I am sorry to have been delayed,' I said smoothly. 'Have you found her yet?'

'No.'

'It occurred to me that the woman was probably not terribly

heavy,' I said, and explained my thinking: that the miller was strong enough to carry the maiden to the road or the village.

Sir Richard nodded. 'I don't know. I just feel it in me water that she's here somewhere. There's something that feels unpleasant down here, if ye see what I mean.'

'It's cold and grim, right enough,' I said. I shivered. The place did feel as if it was saturated in ghosts. 'I wouldn't be surprised to find that there were hundreds of bodies buried here.'

'Aye, well, so far there's been nothing,' Sir Richard said with a slash of his stick at a wayward stalk of grass that displeased him. 'I don't understand it. The girl's got to be here somewhere. He must have killed her, from the look of the blood in that chamber. Besides, no one has seen her since Father Peter was murdered.'

'No one but Ben,' I said without thinking.

'Eh?'

'Oh, he thought he saw her. Probably dreaming, though,' I explained.

He didn't look convinced. 'He said he saw her in the roadway, you reckon?'

'In a winding sheet and blood all over her,' I agreed. 'Like I said, it was a little boy's nightmare, I dare say. The fellow ate too much cheese or drank more of the inn's ale than he should have.'

'Might be worth havin' a word with him,' Sir Richard said. He looked at me with that suspicious expression I had first noticed at the inquest. 'Is that all he said? What was she doing?'

'I don't know – he said she was walking along the road, I think.'

'Alone? He didn't mention her father, or anyone else? Perhaps her father was chasing her, before he caught her and killed her?' Sir Richard said. 'He could have been there, somewhere. I'll need to speak to the lad and make sure there's nothing more he can tell us.'

'Why, do you think he might be able to dream where she is now?' I laughed. It was easy to be humorous down here, with the knight looking so serious. It made me feel rather superior. I had come a long way from being a pickpocket only a few short months ago. I was proud of my new position. The status that I was granted and the sense of importance that I had earned from my job with Master Blount conspired to give me a feeling of superiority. Which was earned, after all.

'Sir Richard!'

It was Roger of Ilford. The man was ill-clad for a search of this nature. He was at the farther edge of the woods, and Sir Richard and I made our way to him. 'Well?' the Coroner asked.

'There is a track here, as though a body could have been dragged through the undergrowth?'

Sir Richard nodded, bending and peering along the line of broken twigs and scuffed earth. 'You could be right.'

Before he could encourage others to join in searching at this spot, there was a scream, and then laughter.

Sir Richard stood, glowering. 'This is no laughing matter!'

'Sir, over here, sir.'

A man stood waving. He was dressed in clothes that were filthy from mud and lichen, but as we approached him, he pointed. 'I found this,' he said.

There, in the damp soil, was the tip of a piece of leather. I pushed at it with my boot, but it bent and returned to the vertical. The earth all about here was scraped clear, so it appeared to me. I bent and pulled at the leather; to my surprise, it was difficult to bring it out.

'That's odd,' I said. 'It almost looks like a poor-quality shoe. Look. There's a thicker piece of leather, like a sole, and the two are sewn together.' I pulled again, and this time a length of soil moved.

'I'd leave it there for now,' Sir Richard said, and bellowed to the peasants to come and help dig.

I shook my head. 'It's just an old boot,' I said, and pulled hard. The boot gave a sad sucking sound, and suddenly I fell back. Standing, I stared. The soil had given up the boot, while exposing a dirty, brown quintet of toes. I had pulled off a dead man's boot.

'Those ain't a woman's toes,' Sir Richard said professionally.

'No?' I said, wiping my hands quickly on my tunic. They felt horribly dirty for some reason. I could almost feel contagion creeping like lice up my fingers. The toes seemed to be waving at me; my vision was hazy.

'Aye. Looks like a man's,' Sir Richard declared. 'Let's have him out, fellows. Dig away! Hoy, Jack, are you feeling unwell?'

While Sir Richard organized three men to dig and bring up the body, I found a small bush and threw up behind it.

Once the body of the man had been retrieved from the boggy soil in which he had been buried, we walked back to the inn. Sir Richard had ordered that the men should fashion a stretcher from timbers. They took two boughs and strung a rope between the two, back and forth, and laid the body on top.

'I didn't expect that,' Sir Richard said as we walked alongside the figure.

'No. Nor did I,' I admitted.

The figure was that of a man in his early middle years, a great hulking fellow with a black beard and hair. He was, so we were informed, the miller. And that, in short, was the cause of our confusion.

Sir Richard had the man taken back to the inn and set out on the same trestles in the lean-to building at the rear that his brother's body had occupied. Meanwhile, he and I, along with a sizeable proportion of the peasantry, adjourned to the inn itself, Sir Richard and others demanding drinks by the fire. While Sir Richard sat, I went to speak with Dorothy. Humfrie was nowhere to be seen.

'Mistress, we would like to speak to your son Ben.'

'Why? What has he done?' she asked with concern.

'Nothing at all. It's something he told me earlier, about a dream he had. However, first, may I ask you how you fare? Your eye is at least open again. The swelling has reduced. I was worried for you, mistress, when I saw how badly swollen it was.'

'Yes, well, I am well again.'

'Why did he do that to you?'

'He didn't mean it,' she said quickly. 'Sometimes he doesn't know his own strength.'

'That, mistress, is no excuse.'

'In any case, perhaps he was right.' She sighed. 'Since Peter's death, I haven't known what to do for the best.'

'If he does it again, he will answer to me,' I said firmly.

She smiled at that, I am sure because she was impressed with my words and attitude. After all, I cut a dashing figure standing there, offering myself as a protector and support.

'He won't,' she said.

'I hate to ask this, but there are many stories, as you know, of your husband's infidelity. Do you think they are true?'

Her face hardened. 'He was a good, loving husband until the new law. They forced him from me, and then these people here accused him of over-friendliness with other women! Do I believe it? No! My husband was always a loyal, decent man. But he was a priest. When he went to Sarah, it was because she had lost her husband, and he went to offer her support, I think. When he went to the miller's daughter, that was because she was scared of her father. When he went to any member of his congregation, it was in order to help those people. All these stories about him being a womanizer, they are false, *horrible* stories spread by those who want to think all priests are untrustworthy, especially the ones who were prepared to change their gowns. There are many here who hate the old religion, and they disliked my Peter because he came back to it from the new Church.'

She swept out to the back room, and soon I heard her calling for Ben. After a few moments she returned to serve, and a little later Ben appeared at my side.

Sir Richard glanced at him and then pointed to the floor in front of him. 'Come here, lad. Sit and talk to me for a while. Would ye care for a pot of ale? Warm from the hob, eh?'

He poured and passed the ale to the boy, and Ben sipped carefully, his serious eyes fixed on the Coroner.

'Now, boy, this man here says you spoke to him and told him about a horrible dream.'

'A dream? No, it was the miller's daughter, out here in the roadway.'

The Coroner exchanged a glance with me. The boy clearly didn't realize he had dreamed it. If not a dream, it must have been a ghost. 'And she looked as though she had been stabbed?'

'All her front, sir; she was smothered in blood. It was horrible. It was like when we kill a hog. We pull it up on a tripod, hanging by the back legs, and when the throat is cut, the blood gushes. I thought the lady had her throat cut, too. The blood was all down her front, sir.'

'I see. And when you saw her, did you think that she looked angry, scared? How did she look?'

'I think she looked sad, sir. She always did. I think she . . .' His voice trailed off and he turned to glance at his mother. She stared back at him, then at me. Some men moved between us and broke that gaze, and I was relieved. It felt as if I'd been the target of a lance-tip. Ben turned back to Sir Richard. 'Everyone used to say that her father was cruel to her, sir, ever since her mother died. He used to hit her, sir,' he added, his voice dropping. 'And they said he did other things to her, too.'

Sir Richard nodded to him encouragingly. 'Yes?'

'Well, they said he couldn't marry, so he treated her like his wife. They said that the priest went to them to try to persuade the miller to leave her alone.'

'Who said that?'

'Most of the men here. Only one said other things.'

'What sort of other things?' Sir Richard rumbled.

'That the priest was only keen on visiting the *women* of the village, sir,' Ben said, his voice dropping as he recognized the anger in Sir Richard's face.

'Boy, I am very grateful to ye,' Sir Richard said. 'Can you tell me who said that?'

'It was Master Harknet,' Ben said, looking terrified by the Coroner's expression.

'Do not fear, master,' Sir Richard said. 'The truth won't hurt you, and I won't be angry with you for speakin' it.' He leaned back in his seat and eyed the men in the room. 'Is he here, Master Blackjack? Do ye see him?'

'No, I'm afraid I don't.'

'Hah! The whoreson whelp wouldn't dare come here in case I was already inside, I suppose.'

'I doubt that would trouble him. He knows nothing of your relation to Peter,' I said.

'Hmm. I suppose that is true,' the knight conceded. He

scratched at his beard. 'What now, then? I suppose I should speak to him and see if he can bring anything in the way of evidence about Peter, or whether he is spreading rumours out of simple malice, but I don't know that I can stop meself from hitting him if I hear him speaking about Peter in that sort of way.'

'You have to restrain yourself,' I said. I sipped more of my ale contentedly. It had been a hard day, but I had retrieved my money, Arch hadn't caught up with me yet, Raphe was alive and may be grateful to me before long for my rescuing him, and that meant my master, John Blount, would be grateful that I had liberated his fellow. All in all, I felt I had achieved much in a day that began so badly with a punch to my chin. I casually glanced about the room, refilling my pot from the mulled ale, and sipping cautiously. It was quite warm there. When I turned back to Sir Richard, who was being most uncharacteristically quiet, I found he was watching me with a little smile. His shrewd little eyes looked like gimlets, the way he was staring at me.

'What?' I said. And then, 'Oh. No, I really can't.'

'Of course you can, Master Blackjack. It won't take you long. Just find out what he really knows, and what he guessed at.'

I was grateful for Ben's assistance in finding the place.

Harknet lived south of the road through the village, with a smallholding of perhaps five acres. It was teeming with live-stock, too. Pigs and sheep, a cow, two donkeys and, from the row as we approached, a couple of dogs as well. Ben stood at the gate and gave me an anxious look before haring back up the track towards the inn.

'Harknet?' I called. The dogs were redoubling their efforts. I think they were indicating that they had an appointment with my liver and were looking forward to getting acquainted. Not that it bothered me terribly. I reckoned that if I was attacked, firing my pistol would probably scare them into the middle of next year. It certainly terrified me every time I pulled the trigger and saw the flames spout from the barrel, the effusion of smoke, sparks and foul smells that were given off every time. It was a truly terrifying weapon.

The door was flung open, and the dogs suddenly pelted down the path towards me. I had to leap backwards nimbly and pull the gate behind me, but even then it was touch and go. I feared that one of the beasts, an ill-favoured monster with slavering jaws and particularly large teeth, I noticed, might attempt to leap the gate. He could clear it in a single bound, I felt sure.

'Harknet, hoi! Come and take these monsters away before I kill them,' I said loudly. I already had the gun in my hand, and was pointing it at the nearer of the dogs while I stared at the house. There was a light, and I saw a lantern, just as there was a sudden grip at my gun. When I looked down, to my horror, I saw that the vicious brute had caught the gun's barrel in his mouth, and he was chewing at it like a stick. 'Get off it, you fool,' I muttered, trying to wrest it from him, and when I looked down into his eyes, I saw a sudden gleam.

I have heard it said that a dog always knows when a man is scared of him. The dog will always take advantage when he senses fear. Not that he had to work hard to sense my nervousness. He clamped his jaws on the gun more firmly, the barrel passing through his mouth from left to right, and he shook the gun like a hound breaking a rabbit's back.

Now, I could have told him that doing that was not going to be enjoyable for him. Shaking the gun meant twisting it from side to side in my grip. My finger, naturally, was on the trigger, and at first I didn't realize what the whirring noise was. Nor did the monster, whose face took on a quizzical interest, one eye turned down to peer at the mechanism – because my finger had pressed the trigger. The clockwork was performing its function to perfection, spinning the great wheel, and the pyrites was resting on the wheel. Suddenly, a shower of sparks flared.

The dog yelped and dropped the fiery stick just in time. As he did so, there was the flash in the pan, and then a loud report as the gun fired. I swear, the flames were six feet long, and they lashed at the hound's arse. It gave a loud yowl and disappeared into the thick grey coils of greasy smoke. The billowing clouds concealed everything for some moments. And when the smoke cleared, there were no dogs. They had high-tailed it back to the house.

I took the precaution of reloading the gun, swabbing it clean of sparks and cinders, tipping more powder in, and then wrapping a slug in cloth and ramming it home. As I walked to the house, I dropped a pinch or two of powder into the pan and rewound the mechanism, setting the dog back against the wheel. By the time I had reached the door, it was primed and ready.

'Harknet!' I called. 'I want to talk to you.'

'You tried to kill my dogs!'

'No, I didn't. Your dog tried to attack me.'

'You didn't have to kill him. What'll you do to me?'

'I want to talk to you. If I don't, your next visitor will be the Coroner, and he won't be as accommodating as me.'

Slowly, the door opened. Harknet stood a little back and stared at my pistol as I walked inside. His dogs were cowering together under the small table. Neither showed any enthusiasm for playing with my exploding stick, and the big devil who had grabbed it kept his eyes on it all the time, ignoring my face. He looked like a toddler watching the belt, waiting for the blow to strike.

'Have you heard that they found—'

'Miller's daughter, yes.'

'No. The miller himself.'

'Caught him, eh? That's good. He'll suffer for all eternity for—'

'Just listen and try to understand,' I said irritably. 'There is no sign of his daughter, only the miller. Someone killed him – stabbed him, I think – and buried him at the side of the millpond.'

He gaped and slumped into a seat. 'What?'

'Do you know anything about this?'

'Me? No! Why should I?'

'But you have said that the priest was the sort of man who would go to comfort the women of the parish?'

'Yes. He was an incontinent fellow, the same as all these priests who have enjoyed carnal knowledge of women. Once they taste the pleasures of the flesh, they cannot stop themselves. They—'

'Really? So they are turned into ravening beasts by a single kiss, you think?'

'No, it's more than that! Once they have lain with a woman, she opens their eyes to pleasures that they should not have discovered. It was the greatest failing of the heretical new Church the old King imposed on us all!'

'The one you supported, you mean? I've heard you were the most enthusiastic supporter of that Church, and reported all those who you felt were keeping to the old Roman religion.'

He paled. 'It's not true! I was persecuted for my faith, because I was always true to Roman Catholicism,' he asserted, but his eyes would not meet mine as he said it.

'Oh, well, if that's the case, we can put it to the others in the village, if you like,' I said. My sarcasm was intended to hurt. 'After all, if you were never keen on the new faith, they must have lied when they said you reported them for not attending the new services.'

He glowered sulkily.

'However,' I continued in a more conciliatory tone, 'I am not here to discuss your personal views, only your proof of the infidelity of the priest before he died.'

'Not after he died, then?' Harknet sneered.

I snapped. 'Fine. You do not wish to talk to me. I'll go and fetch Sir Richard. He won't be as understanding, but I've had enough of your arrogance.'

'No! No, I beg. I will help you all I can. Anything but him!' He glanced away. 'He terrifies me.'

'In that case, kick those dogs outside so I can sit, and fetch some ale or wine so we can speak comfortably.'

He did as I asked, and soon we were sitting with a jug of cider between us and a cup each. It tasted like something the dogs had thrown up, and I was sure it was eating into my teeth as I drank. It landed in my stomach like acid, but after I forced down the first cup, I ceased caring. It was almost soothing then – which was itself worrying.

'I don't know how many women he seduced,' Harknet said, distracting me from my concerned staring into the cup. He shook his head slowly. I could understand that. I wanted to myself – but then I realized he was not shaking his head at the cider, but at the folly of men.

'I know he tried it on with Sarah, and I know he slept with the miller's daughter. As to how many others, I couldn't say.'

'You say you "know" he tried it on with these. How do you know? Did you see him in their beds?'

'A man doesn't have to be seen in bed for a fellow to know what he's been getting up to. I saw him with the miller's daughter, and he was . . . *affectionate* with her. As to Sarah, she told me he tried it on with her. She went to him after her husband died, and Father Peter went to her and suggested that they should pray together. He bade her kneel, and he knelt behind her, and then she felt – well, it wasn't his crucifix. She was up and denouncing him in a moment, and he was ashamed and fearful that she might speak to someone, so he made profuse apologies and left her.'

'She said this to you?'

'Yes.'

'Sir Richard spoke to her, and she denied anything of the sort.'

'Perhaps she was awed by him or just fearful of him. He is an alarming man. And then there is his position. And his relationship to Father Peter.'

That was true enough. Especially since she knew that he was the dead man's brother.

'He might have told her he was Peter's brother,' I agreed.

'He wouldn't have to. Most of us knew.'

'Knew he was Peter's brother?'

'Yes. Peter often told of his clever brother who had become a knight and was now a Crowner. When Peter died, we all guessed his brother would come to investigate. And the similarity was hard to miss. I doubt Sarah would wish to upset him with tales of how his brother tried to swive her while she prayed, do you?'

'What of the miller's daughter?'

'Her? He wouldn't have had to work hard with her. She couldn't help but seduce men, no matter who they were. Even her own . . .' He stopped and looked away.

'Her father?' I said.

Harknet was quiet for a few heartbeats. Then he sighed. 'Yes. Everyone knew it. He lost his wife, and with his temper and drinking, no other woman would have been stupid enough to take him on. So instead he took his own daughter.'

It was not unknown. Incest was deplorable, but in the quieter areas of the countryside like this, when a man was desperate and couldn't find a legitimate wife, he would sometimes make use of the women available. A daughter was as legitimate as anyone else to a drunk with fire in his ballocks. 'Talk is easy. Was there ever any proof?'

'I saw him with her. I was taking a load of grain to be milled, and when I got to the place, I saw him. He had her pressed up against the wall, her skirts up around her waist, and he was kissing her all over her neck and face. Quite disgusting!'

'How long did you watch them to discover it was disgusting?' I asked.

'Don't be impertinent! As soon as I saw them, I turned the donkey round and came home again. It was horrible. An offence against God's laws!'

'You saw her face?'

'Yes.'

'And his?'

'I didn't need to see his face. She was turned towards me, and I saw his back. A big man. Who else could it have been?'

'So you only saw his back? Did he turn? Did you see his face?'

'No. What of it? There was only her and her father living there.'

'What clothes was he wearing?'

'A shirt, hose.'

'The miller's clothes?'

'I suppose so. It was the miller, after all.'

'Did she respond? Did she return his kisses, or try to spurn him?'

'Oh, no! She made no effort to spurn him!'

'So that is that, then,' Sir Richard said. He sighed. 'Harknet thinks Peter was a womanizing lecher.'

'What did Sarah say when you spoke to her?' I asked.

'She said what I wanted to hear, I suppose. That Peter was a good man, a shoulder to lean on, that he was always there for his congregation, that he was there when Sarah needed him, after her man died. Peter was a decent, honourable priest.'

'But she knew beforehand that he was your brother. She didn't want to upset a Queen's officer, did she?' I stated. It was hardly surprising. Telling a man to his face that his brother had tried to rape her was not going to be conducive to happy relations.

'And he said that the miller was . . . was doing that with his own daughter?'

'Yes.'

Sir Richard shook his head, appalled by the depths of human depravity. 'How could a man do such a thing?'

'Yes,' I said, but at the back of my mind, there was something about the story that sounded a little odd: off key – or just wrong. I had known cases of incest. Back at home at Whitstable, I knew several girls who were little more than the playthings of their fathers. But they didn't respond willingly. They hated the unwanted attentions. One I knew threw herself from a cliff and was buried at the crossroads just outside town as a suicide. The hypocritical son of a whore, her father, wept like a baby, as though he had no idea what had led her to self-murder, but I knew, as did many of the people standing there at the grave. I heard that later the local priest went to the grave and begged God to accept her soul. No one thought it was her fault. I had never heard that she or any of the other girls had accepted their father's unwanted attentions. The younger ones didn't fight, but they all knew it was not right. Most wept and endured. None kissed their rapists back.

'And it doesn't help us, either,' he said. 'If the miller killed Peter, who killed the miller? And where is his daughter's body?'

'She must still be around here, I suppose. We shall have to continue to search for her tomorrow.'

'Once this new fellow's inquest is out of the way, aye.'

'Have you looked at him to see how he died?'

'Plain enough: a stab in the chest.'

'But not frenzied, like your brother's killing?'

'Not that I could see, no. Just one blow, but struck with violence.'

A thought struck me. 'Your brother was a cool, collected fellow. Could he have struck that blow? One thrust with a good knife and the miller was dead.'

'Perhaps. Who killed Peter, then?'

'Perhaps the daughter? She stabbed him in a mad passion, after seeing her father killed.'

'And she buried her father? Think how heavy he must have been. She'd have been a strong wench to drag him all the way to that grave.'

'No, Peter did. Perhaps he felt remorse at the murder?'

'Which means Peter had a row with the miller, he killed the man and then dragged his body to the soft ground, where he could dig a shallow hole and leave the body there.'

'Yes!' I said.

'And when he returned, the daughter had built up so much rage at the slaying of her father that she stabbed him like a berserker.'

'Yes!'

'And then she picked him up, threw him over her shoulder and carried him all the way to the road. Does that make sense to you?'

'She could have done.'

He raised an eyebrow. 'She's been described as a slim little thing, a light maiden, small and dainty. Remember?'

'Perhaps, but she was in the street and covered with blood. Ben said so.'

'If she was a small, dainty maiden, perhaps she had an accomplice? A young woman could have inspired a man to help her.'

'Yes,' I said. 'Perhaps she had another man here. Another lover?'

'Another man? Really? How many lovers do you think she had?' Sir Richard said, peering at me. 'Any other ideas?'

I racked my brains. 'Could it be that Peter stabbed the miller, another man helped the maid to bury him, and then they both followed Peter and killed him by the road?'

'Why would they?'

'Well, if he was taking advantage of the girl, maybe she saw him kill her father, and then had a friend help her to punish Peter?'

'And perhaps pigs might sprout wings and fly? No, I don't think so. The idea that Peter could kill a man is ridiculous.'

'You said that about him carrying on affairs with women, but he did.'

'Peter simply could not have killed a man. Now, if you say that he was a womanizer, I will accept that. I must. But the idea that he was a killer? No.'

'Perhaps he saw the daughter kill her father, and she knew that he had seen her, and ran after him and killed him?'

'You are forgetting that the first stab wound was while he was not wearing his clothes. No, he was purposefully slain without a shirt on, and then the stab wounds were added when he had been dressed.'

'So he was stabbed in a bed?'

Sir Richard pulled a grimace. 'He was stabbed in a compromisin' position, I would guess. So who killed him? Not the girl, unless she had left him in bed, and went to fetch a drink and decided she didn't like him anymore. And then someone helped her carry him to the road. Her father? And then she killed him, too. Or she killed her father because he had killed her lover? Ach! There is a logic to this, if I can only find it.'

'Perhaps,' I said. I pictured in my mind's eye the scene: a young woman lying in bed, being bulled by Peter; the miller arriving, drawing his knife in a trice, stabbing once, the priest dying almost instantly; the girl beneath screaming and sobbing; her father smacking her, pulling the body from her, clothing him, throwing the body over his shoulders, walking up to the road through the village, letting Peter fall to the ground and leaving him there before walking home, where his daughter met him with a blade and stabbed him once. And then she picked him up and . . . no. The miller had been a big man in life. Perhaps the girl could have picked him up, but she could not have carried him all the way to his grave. Not on her own. She would have to be a strong, heavy-set peasant to pick up a man like the miller.

'She couldn't have dragged his body to where she buried

him,' I said. 'Surely a dainty little woman couldn't have pulled a man his size all the way to his grave.'

'Daughter of a miller, don't forget. A woman who's grown lifting sacks of grain . . . It's possible she could have.'

'I can't help thinking it would be more likely that a man like Harknet would kill him than his own daughter.'

'Him? Why? Harknet already has little reputation, other than being a turncoat when it comes to his religion. What advantage would he get from killing the priest?'

To that, I had no answer.

While we were talking, my eyes had strayed to Dorothy. The bruised eye was taking on all the colours of the rainbow now. I went to her, asking for another quart of ale. She nodded, turned and twisted the tap on the nearest barrel. Soon my blackjack was filled with a foaming brew.

'Delicious!' I said.

'I am glad,' she said.

'When you found your husband's body, it must have been a terrible shock.'

'Yes. It was there in the road. I didn't know what to do,' she added, her eyes filling once more.

'I am sorry, Dorothy,' I said. 'I didn't mean to upset you.'

She rubbed her face with the heel of her hand, avoiding the great bruise, and avoiding my gaze. Since seeing her in the church, at best she had treated me with suspicion. 'I'm fine. It's just so sad. He was always such a strong man, you know? It seems impossible that he could be gone. I can still hardly believe it.'

'It must have been horrible.'

'Yes.' Her voice was quiet and reflective. 'I had hoped to win his sympathy, some support. I had dreamed that he would take me back, that he would relinquish his post in the Church and come to help us.' She shook her head. 'In my dreams, I had thought I would be reunited with him. And then to learn that he had been murdered . . .'

'It must have been dreadful. Although, since you were here with the innkeeper, surely that would have coloured your husband's feelings?'

'What do you mean?'

'Well, you know, sharing Nyck's bed. That must have been a bitter pill for a husband to swallow.'

'What would he expect me to do? I have no man to support me!'

'No, of course not, but surely—'

'We were fortunate that the landlord wanted help with the inn. It was only when I was rejected by my own husband that I sought comfort. I was lonely, and I needed a man's support.'

'Yes, of course,' I said.

'And, yes, now I feel great affection for Nyck. He has been very kind to us.'

'I see.' No, I didn't. But she had been desperate, and perhaps she had hoped that sleeping with the innkeeper would make her husband jealous and bring him back to her. The devious ways of women was a closed book to me. There was one thing that was still confusing me. 'Mistress, at the inquest you said that there was only a short time between you seeing your husband in the roadway and catching up with him, when you found him dead.'

'That's right.'

Yes, it was confusing me. You see, arrant coward that I was, I could not understand how this woman could say that she had been the last person to see her dead husband without knowing that it must make her suspected as the murderer. I said as much to her.

'I was taught to tell the truth. I had sworn to tell the truth at the inquest, and I did.'

'Although you were clearly mistaken.'

'What do you mean?'

'Well, we know you couldn't have seen him there. He died in the bed of the miller's daughter. That is where all the blood was. And it must have been some time before, if he was cold. A man just killed would be warm to the touch still.'

'But I did see him. I swear it!'

'You saw his face?'

'No, but it was him. I recognized his clothes.'

'He was wearing his religious garb?'

'Well, yes.'

'You don't think another man could put on similar clothing to confuse people?'

She gaped at me. 'Put on a priest's clothing?'

'It has been known,' I said.

'No one would do such a wicked thing!' she protested. 'It would be a terrible sin!'

'Worse than being burned at the stake for murder and petit treason?' I asked.

She glared.

'So, I ask you again, as the woman who knew him best: are you quite sure it was him? Did you see his face? Did you hear him speak? Did you recognize his manner of walking? Did you see how he held his head? Did you see how he held his arms, how he paced, how he went faster or slower than he usually did?'

She looked at me with a sneer and was about to respond when another customer demanded a drink, banging his cup on the bar. Dorothy glared at me and went to serve him, leaving me leaning on the bar, waiting.

Soon she was back.

'I am sorry, mistress, I didn't mean to question your words,' I began, but she suddenly held up her hand. There was a faraway look in her eye now, and no anger.

'I think you might be right. Peter had a slight limp. When he was a young man, he fell in a rabbit hole, and it broke his leg. He was never recovered from that. When he moved quickly, that injury always showed – but the man I saw on that day had no limp. He moved along swiftly. He had his head down, too, but I thought that was just Peter trying to ignore us as we followed him.' She frowned, staring into the middle distance. 'It wasn't him, though, was it? I was bitter and angry because I thought he was turning his back on me and the children, and all the while he was already dead. Stabbed to death and left at the roadside.'

And then the tears really started in earnest.

I almost touched her shoulder in sympathy, but pulled my hand back; I didn't want another misunderstanding. A movement made me look up. There was a figure in the doorway, and as soon as I saw him, he slipped out. It was Dick Atwood again!

Grateful for a reason to leave Dorothy, who was standing with her apron over her face, shoulders jerking, I downed some of my ale and then turned and went after him. I had never had the feeling that I could trust Dick. I was certain he must know something about what had happened to the priest. And then it occurred to me that his build was not dissimilar to that of Father Peter. He had a similar breadth – was of a similar height, too. Someone seeing him run away from them could easily confuse him for Father Peter, I thought – even a wife who loved him and knew him, if her vision was blurred by her feelings of betrayal, her emotions confused by his apparent disregard. The hurt her husband had caused her had made her mistake someone else for him. And that other person had been clad in clerical garb. Which might mean he had known that the priest was already dead. And if that, what better time to go to the priest's home and church to see whether a legendary box of gold might not be available? I darted into the back room and gazed about me, but Atwood was not there. Turning, I went out through the front door and stared up the road. I couldn't see him, so I turned to look the other way, and as I did, I felt his knife at my throat.

'Evening, Jack,' he said with a chuckle in his voice. 'How are you?'

When I say that I grabbed his hand and pushed his knife away, you will be able to tell how angry I was feeling. It is usually my habit, born of long experience of the dangers of courage, to squeak and bolt when confronted by a weapon, especially one in the hands of Dick Atwood. Indeed, one part of my brain was looking on in horror as I said, 'What have you been doing? You imitated the priest, didn't you? You dressed up like him, because you knew he was already dead, and you went on up the road to the church to search through all his things, didn't you? It must have been a shock when you heard his widow calling to you, but you thought you had the perfect way to walk to the church in full view of everyone, didn't you? Dressed like a priest, no one would stop you.'

'Interesting,' Atwood said. He wore a vaguely perplexed expression, staring at me rather like a man who had stroked his family pet only for it to bite him. Well, I didn't care. He had insulted me and my intelligence for the last time.

'Well?'

'You do realize that I have not the faintest idea what you are talking about?'

'Of course. As usual, you are the innocent abroad, aren't you? Except this time you're quickly getting out of your depth.'

'Yes, well, this is all very interesting,' he said, 'but I do have to be getting on with things. Have you managed to discover where the gold might be hidden?'

'What?'

'The gold,' he said patiently. 'Where it might be? The abbey's gold from Ilford, remember? You were going to help hunt for it?'

'Me?' Of course, I hadn't forgotten. The box of gold in the church had weighed as heavily on my mind as . . . well, as a box of gold would. 'No, I have no idea. You must have searched the church on the day that the priest's body was discovered, I suppose?'

'I did go up there and look about quickly,' he admitted.

'And?'

'There was nothing there that I could find. But it did occur to me that it could have been hidden in a grave or somewhere similar. The only problem is, it's hard to get up there to search, and, in any case, the only fresh digging that there has been was the priest's own grave. All the others appear to have been there for an age.'

He looked sad at the thought.

'Then maybe he spent it. Or there never was any money,' I said. 'You have been hunting a chimera all this time.'

'Perhaps. But he who never dares will never succeed in any undertaking. Now,' he added, smiling disarmingly, 'what will you do next?'

I was immediately suspicious. When Dick Atwood tried to be charming, it was always time to run or put on armour. I took a step back. 'Finish my ale,' I said.

'But, Jack, if the story I was told is true, there is more than enough for both of us. We only need to find it, and we can do that. Just you and me, Jack.'

'You may not have noticed, Dick, but there has been a series of murders here, and I am here to help the Coroner.'

'A series?'

'Yes! Father Peter, the miller and possibly his daughter, too. No one has seen her for days.' I gazed at him with suspicion. 'Have you something to do with them?'

'Me, Jack?'

'Have you?'

'I'm hurt you could even think something like that, Jack.'

'That's not a denial.'

'Jack, just think: I saved you at Woodstock.'

'You tried to kill me during the Wyatt Rebellion.'

'That was ages ago,' he said airily, waving a hand as if to dismiss the past.

'Did you have a part in any of those deaths?'

'No, Jack. I didn't. On my honour.'

That was a commodity of little value, he had sold it so often. 'Not a one?'

'No! So, are you going to help me find that gold?'

'What will you do?'

'I am keeping watch over you, Jack. I am guarding you.'

I made a rude noise. 'From whom, exactly?'

'There are people here who are not all they appear to be,' he said with a smile. 'I have been following you to protect you from those who might decide to hurt you.'

'Such as?'

He sighed. 'Dick, if there is gold here, many people would wish to get their hands on it. Even a Queen's Coroner might be tempted.'

'The Coroner knows nothing of any gold!'

'He is the dead priest's brother, isn't he?'

'So?'

'One brother may have a good idea of the other. He might easily learn that his brother had, say, a box of gold. And even a knight would not turn down a box of gold.'

'You say that Sir Richard could have killed his brother for

a box of gold? You are a fool! The only reason he's here is to learn who killed his brother!'

'You think so? Well, in that case it cannot hurt for you to seek the gold yourself.'

What could I say?

'Oh, very well.'

I walked back inside. Sir Richard was at the fire, telling bawdy stories from his youth, it appeared, from the way that the men about him were laughing and hanging on his every word. The rest of the men had started to dribble away, and the room was growing quieter.

Watching Sir Richard, I could not believe that Dick Atwood was right. The knight was not exhibiting perpetual misery over his brother's death, but that was not his nature. He was a man who lived every day to the full. His brother was dead, and Sir Richard would mourn him, but he was a knight. A man who was trained to fight and kill. He was used to death, still more so since his job required him to study many corpses every year. A man like him would quickly grow accustomed to death, even of a close relative.

Dorothy was not at her place. I guessed that she had fled when her tears took her over completely. In her stead, the innkeeper glowered about the room. His expression did not ease when he caught sight of me.

Sighing, I went over and placed my blackjack on the bar. 'Another, please.'

'So long as you won't start getting loud and fighty,' the man said.

'I never get aggressive. I only ask questions when I need to.'

He was bending to the barrel's tap. 'Well, you can keep your thoughts to yourself here.'

'What do you mean?'

'Leave Dorothy alone. You have upset her.'

'I could say the same to you,' I said with some heat.

He slammed my blackjack on the bar and stared hard at me. 'Meaning what?'

'Meaning there was no need to punch her and give her a black eye.'

He stared at me some more, and then, to my anger, started to laugh.

'You think it's funny to punch a woman, do you?' I said, and would have thrown my ale over him, but if I had, I would have had no room for the night. Besides, he was used to lifting barrels of ale. He was quite strong. I decided not to provoke him further.

He lowered his head, the amusement slowly departing, until he was eyeing me with a curious firm and steady gaze. 'You should be careful whom you accuse of things like that. I took her in, her and her boys, and I look after them and feed them.'

'And thrash them.'

'When they deserve it, yes. This is my inn: my home. If that little scrote clambers up my trees, I'll whip him because he's been told not to often enough. A man has to be master in his own house.'

Well, I couldn't argue with that. Ben had been deliberately flouting the innkeeper's laws. 'But punching Dorothy, that—'

'What?'

'You punched her. Blacked her eye for her.'

'That wasn't me!'

'Eh?'

He shook his head. 'You have no understanding, do you? The poor woman's lost her husband, and yes, I let her share my bed. But I don't beat my women. She is there of her own choice, seeing as how her husband had deserted her. It was very troubling for her and the boys.'

'So you added to their troubles, you mean?' I tried to sound accusatory, but it came out as thoroughly confused and nothing more.

He saw my blackjack was not yet empty and filled a pot for himself. 'Look, her boys were very upset when they heard that their father had left them, you understand? They were deeply unhappy. Hardly surprising. The older fellows, Ed and Walt, wanted to talk to him, and that was why the lot came here. But he refused to see them. The poor woman was at her

wit's end, so she asked whether I might have any work, and
I took pity on her and them, but I have never raised my
hand to her.'

'Oh, I suppose she accidentally fell into a door?' I said.
'I've seen that sort of injury often enough, Nyck, and it doesn't
come from tripping!'

'I didn't say it did.'

'Oh!' I suddenly realized what he meant. 'You mean her
husband did it? She pestered him so much that . . . no, he was
already dead, and at his inquest there was nothing, not a mark
on her.'

'Not him!' the innkeeper sighed, and rolled his eyes. 'Ed!
Her oldest. He may not look much, but he does have a temper.
When he's taken a half gallon of my ale on board, he can grow
wild. And just now he's feeling extra sensitive, what with his
father deserting them, and him feeling that he's the head of the
household now, and has all responsibility for the family. That
was why he punched Dorothy. Poor woman. I found her sobbing
her heart out on the floor in a pool of ale she'd been carrying
to a customer.'

'Why did *he* punch her?'

'He doesn't like the fact she's sleeping in my bed. He's
mostly a man, but he's still a boy in a lot of ways, and he
argued with her, saying they should leave here and go back
to Ilford, especially now Peter's dead. I can't blame him. If I
was his age, in their position, I'd feel the same, I'm sure.'

'Will they go?'

'Ed and Walt might. The others, well, they'll stay with
Dorothy, and for now she's content to stay with me. She has
work here, a roof and a bed, and I'm not demanding. Her
children are safe enough. If the older fellows want to make
their way in the world, that's their choice. I won't stop them,
and I don't think she will either. They're welcome to go. But
that little bastard Ben had best clean up his behaviour and
learn to do as he's bid, before I take the skin off his arse with
my belt,' he added.

'The boys have been that badly affected?'

'How would you respond if someone murdered your
father?'

I couldn't answer that. My own memories of my mother were somewhat hazy, because she had died when I was very young, and it was my father who had raised me – after a fashion. How would I have reacted if my sire had suddenly left me with her? Probably with great joy, knowing the vicious old brute as I did. Anyone less affectionate and thoughtful was hard to imagine. My mother was surely a kinder, more loving person. She must have been. I would have been happy with her.

'So he decided to take his mother to task because she was sleeping with you?'

'Of course. And obviously I gave him a slap, and knocked him into the middle of next week, but I felt a bit bad. I couldn't blame the lad.'

I was unsure how to comment on that. Leaving the bar, I walked to a bench and sat. The Coroner was still bellowing a joke, and the guffaw he gave when he reached the final line almost made the actual point rather incomprehensible. I certainly couldn't hear it myself. With his eyes turned to tiny slits, his great fist pounding his thigh in delight, Sir Richard looked like a Cardinal after a feast. He waved his pot of wine (he had changed from ale) as he began a fresh tale.

It was deafening in there, with Sir Richard telling his comic tales, and the audience tending to laugh along with him – although whether at the sight of his delight in the telling or because even a single one of them actually managed to discern the story as he spoke, I don't know. I know I could make no sense of them.

Still, it meant I had some time to think. I took my ale out to the room where I had spoken to Harknet the day before. I sat there with two other men who had the look of men who wished to find peace, and who believed it existed at the very bottom of their pots. One, from the sour odour, was drinking, or rather belching, cider, while the other was content with good ale like me. He was nodding, his head slowly leaning forward and then suddenly jerking upright. It was no surprise: the warmth from the fire in this smaller chamber was noticeable, and I could feel my own eyes growing heavy as we sat

in there. It was hard to remain alert when the room was so
well heated, and when the ale was so good and strong.

There was something at the back of my mind that was
fighting to reach the front, but I couldn't tell what it might
be. At last, after trying to keep awake, but realizing that I was
emulating the dozing man, I stood, yawned and walked outside.
A little cool, fresh evening air would work wonders, I thought.

Besides, there was something I had to do.

I walked from the village, out of the patches of light that
glimmered and sparkled on the puddles in the roadway. The
churned mud was treacherous, and I thought to myself how
much harder it would be to bring a body up here, carrying
it over the shoulders like a great sack, one arm clinging to
the corpse's arm, the dead man's leg hooked by the other
arm, trying to stagger out of the village. And then – what?
To just reach the outer limit of the village's territory and
drop the body as though evicting the man, his corpse, his
evil behaviour and every other aspect of him beyond the
village's responsibility.

A man who could do that was a serious fellow, I thought.
If it had been the miller, he was a thoroughly dedicated fellow
– and determined. The body I had seen was definitely that of
a strong fellow who could pick up a body without much
trouble, but Peter was still a fair weight. Bringing him all the
way up the hill from the mill, through the village, and throwing
him down there at the outer limit would have taken a fair
effort. Even Dick would have found that hard work. Roger
the sexton wouldn't have been able to manage such a weight.

And then the man, the miller, went back to his mill and was
killed there – possibly stabbed by his own daughter. It was a
horrible thought. What had led him to such a death? Was it
his own jealousy for the priest who was playing hide the
thurible with his daughter, leading to his being so incensed
that he had killed Peter? And that act had so enraged his own
daughter that she had killed him.

But that was where my imagination failed. How could a
young girl have picked up a man who was powerful enough
to lift Peter? How could she have carried him to the grave

she had scraped? It was surely too far for a young woman to bear a man. So she must have had an accomplice. Or someone else had murdered her and hidden her elsewhere. She appeared to have disappeared from the village and, indeed, the world. Were there two deaths here – or three? It was alarming in the extreme to think that there could be another body to be found.

I gazed along the road ahead. It was dark, the trees were rattling in the wind, although there seemed very little breeze down here where I was. Overhead, the clouds scudded across the sky at speed, concealing and then revealing the moon. It was beautiful, the grey clouds looking as though each was rimed with frost as the moon's light made them glow, and then dimming. I turned and glanced up towards the church, and saw a pale light from within. I smiled: I knew what that meant!

And then I screamed aloud and threw myself sideways as a white, silent figure hissed past me. I instantly remembered young Ben's words – the thin, pale form of the miller's daughter, blood-beslubbered, the portent of death – and would have covered my eyes with my hands, had I not seen the wraith-like form move on along the line of the road before disappearing in among the trees that lined the way.

I stood, brushing the leaves and dirt from my legs. One shin had caught a stone and it hurt damnably now. Turning, I hobbled back to the inn.

Back home at Whitstable, the sight of an owl would not have been enough to unman me, but since I had been living in London, I had not seen a great white owl like that, and the creature gliding past me, silent as a ghost, had been enough to scare me to my core.

I needed another ale.

SIX

That night it was brought to my mind that other men can sleep through even a thunderstorm. At least, that was what it sounded like. There was a constant rumble, a crackle and then a whisper of the wind through the branches high overhead.

To put it another way, Sir Richard snored. And unlike those with more sensitive souls, he didn't have the decency to wake himself.

I rose and walked out, away from that intolerable noise.

Out in front of the inn, I looked up the road.

The sun was a glow in the sky to the east, and I eyed it sourly. I have never been a fellow who enjoys rising early. It has been necessary from time to time, but so is an occasional blood-letting. It may be needful, but that doesn't make it a joyful experience. It was out there that the girl's ghost, supposedly, was seen by young Ben. I shivered at the thought. It is fortunate that I am a sober, unimaginative man. Others would have been struck by superstitious fear. I had a fleeting memory of an owl, but quashed it.

Looking along the road, I had to wonder: if it was the miller's daughter whom the boy saw, what was she doing up here? Was she simply following her father as he came up here to drop off the body of her lover? Did she not trust him and sought to see where he was going? Perhaps her father had told her he was taking the priest to the church or somewhere similar? And she was smothered in blood, so Ben had said. Peter had died in her arms, and then she killed her own father. Well, at least it wouldn't make her shift any more bloody than it already was.

'Hello.'

'Sweet Mother of . . .' I nearly jumped out of my skin. 'Humfrie, don't do that!'

'What?'

'Walk up on me when I'm not expecting you!'

'You asked me to come here and meet you.'

'Since you are here now, did you have any luck?'

You see, having experienced some danger since I arrived here in St Botolph's, it had occurred to me that I might be well advised to have a friend on hand and available, who could assist me in case of trouble. I had asked him to follow me about the place. Oh, and there was one other thing I had asked of him: the box.

He pulled a face. 'I went up to the church, like you said, and opened the chest, but it only held vestments for a priest. The long robes, a scarf and some other items. Nothing of any value.'

'So you left them all there.'

'I don't approve of robbing a church.'

His long face told me as much.

'So that is that,' I said.

'Yes. Although . . .'

'What?'

'It is probably nothing, but while I was there, I thought I might as well take a look about the place.'

'And?'

'When I went up the tower, there was a place where some dust had lain in an alcove. It was a sort of square shape in the dust. I did wonder whether there could have been a box.'

'But it was not still there?'

'No. There was no sign of it apart from the mark in the alcove. I didn't find it in the church itself. If it is there, it has been hidden very well. I looked most of the night. Up in the loft, over the screen, in the vicar's private chambers . . . I have to say, almost anyone could have broken into those rooms. The locks are ancient, and could be opened by a child.'

'Only a child with your sort of experience,' I said.

'Perhaps.'

He gave me the rough dimensions of the box, if box it was, and I took a careful note. Apparently, it was some ten inches by a foot, but there was no indication how tall it would be, of course. Only the outline of the base. 'I need to get my head down,' Humfrie said.

'Yes, of course,' I said. He had been up all night, after working the previous day as well. 'The inn here has some chairs that are comfortable.'

He nodded. Then, as he was about to turn away, he shot me a look. 'You were going to ask about the man who was raping his own daughter?'

'Yes. That is confusing, I know. We found nothing about him in London because he's here. Someone killed him.'

'Oh,' he said, and he grew thoughtful.

'What?' I said.

'Only this: you asked about the cart, and there *was* a cart that week. A man and a woman from around these parts. They stabled the beast and sold the cart.'

'A man and woman? They had nothing to do with this matter, then.'

'I suppose not,' he said, and yawned. 'And now I must get my head down. Hmm. Once I could go three days and two nights without sleep. I was younger then. Now I suffer if I don't doze after lunch.'

He stifled a yawn as he made his way to the inn's door. Soon, I guessed, he would be adding his own snores to those of Sir Richard. His could hardly be more loud or disruptive, I thought.

In the east the sky was glowing golden, and clouds on the sky's edge were lit as if from within by a flame. It was a glorious sight, and I stood there, entranced for some minutes, my mind completely empty, but for the joy of God's creation as shadows appeared, like pools of dark water left behind as the light took over the ground. And I knew a strange peaceful-ness. I was at one with the world, calm, content, satisfied and at ease.

The inn was waking, with the noise of grooms preparing for their fresh day, a lad in the inn's hall preparing a fire for the guests, dogs barking along the road, cockerels crowing, birds twittering and chattering in the branches overhead, a rat scurrying across the road in front of me, shoulders hunched as if ducking to avoid detection.

It was strange, I felt. The rat was moving like a man, hunched and alarmed, evading any glances. It was almost as if he knew I was there.

That brought a fresh thought: if the miller's daughter was there, why had she been so happy to be in plain sight? If she was following her father, appalled at his murder of her lover, why was she not bent, following her father with caution, trying to avoid being seen? In fact, why was she there at all? Could she have been there to help her father, rather than remaining concealed from him? Why bring him up there, anyway?

What was the point?

The sun rose, and with it I began to walk about the town. I was reluctant to go inside and listen to Sir Richard's snores. I felt that my ears needed a rest from them as much as from his booming voice. In preference, I walked away from the inn, aimlessly. I had no particular route in mind, nor a destination, but when I passed along, my feet finding their own path, I suddenly realized I was already halfway to Sarah's house.

She was a peasant, I reasoned, and would surely be up with the sun. And at least this time I could be sure that Sir Richard was not with her. I remembered that shamefaced look about him as I saw him in the entrance that last time I saw her; I was still unsure what that look was for.

It was a good-sized house, and I approached it warily, remembering Harknet's dogs, but this was free of brutes, I was glad to note. I knocked, but there was no answer, and after a few moments, I made my way round the house to the rear, where I found a well-tended vegetable garden and a privy. The door opened as I stood at the back door, and Sarah appeared.

'I knocked, but there was no answer,' I said.

'Yes, I was in there,' she said. 'Since I'm alone now, I can't always be at the door when someone knocks. I used to have the dog, but . . . anyway, what can I do for you?'

I gave her my best grin. Women can never refuse me, because I have a transparently open face. I have been told that I have the most trustworthy features of any man alive, and certainly women tend to find it so.

'I heard that you were widowed. I was sorry to hear that. When did your husband die?'

'Die? Oh, no, he's still alive. It was the same for me as for Dorothy. My husband was told he had the choice of remaining with me or he could remain in the Church. He took the obvious choice. Which was less of a troubling affair for me, because my family had the money in my marriage. Of course, he tried to claim that, as my husband, he had full claim on all my wealth, but since he was leaving me on the understanding that our marriage was never valid, I countered his demands with the fact that since he was never my husband, he never had any claims to my money. He tried to wriggle on that, but it was a hook of his own making, and I was happy to see him suffer on it.'

'Where did he go?'

'I don't know; nor do I care. The Church doesn't want distressed women appearing in churches up and down the land, so they don't tell us where our husbands have been sent. I suppose they think it's easier that way. Personally, I don't care. He was happy to leave me, so I am happy to see him go.'

'But it must be very hard to be alone now.'

'You think so? Now I work to please myself, without having to please a man. It is a great deal more relaxing.'

It was very brave of her, and I told her so. She laughed, for some reason I couldn't quite fathom.

'Would you like an ale?'

'Yes, please.'

When she had fetched a jug and two cups, she set them on a bench near her back door, and we sat down and gazed over her garden.

'Losing my husband was shocking at first. It showed me that I was worthless. The Church didn't care about me, and thought I was not even married; my husband valued his work more than me. No one cared. So I hid myself away in here. But then I thought, "Well, what have I done that makes me so foul?" And the simple answer was, nothing! I had worked hard to make a man happy, and he had chosen to leave me. That was his weakness. But I refused to allow it to shape my life. Why would I?'

'So you felt jealous of Dorothy when she appeared with Peter?'

'Jealous? What did I have to be jealous of? She had been as badly treated as me. I thought Peter a fool, just like my own husband. It seems so cowardly for a man to desert his wife – still more his children – on the whim of a . . . Well, you know what I mean. No, I am not jealous. Dorothy and I often chat about things.'

'I see. What of the miller and his daughter?'

'Him?' Her face changed.

'Saul, the miller, was a horrible man,' she told me.

She had brought me into her house and installed me before her hearth. We both held cups of steaming ale served from a pot beside her fire. The light gave her features a golden glow, and I could see how her husband would have found her an appealing woman. She had a kind, soft expression, but just now it was hardening as she thought of the miller.

'He was a brute. Polite enough to most people, but when he had been drinking, he was foul. When I was married, he was as respectful as a man should be, although he was one of those men who would always stare at a woman as though she were naked. But a woman grows accustomed to such behaviour. No, what distressed me and many other women was the way he treated his poor girl, Jen. Just like a wife.'

'He raped her.'

'Yes. She was a slight, sweet little thing. Dainty, gentle, kind. But so tired and worn always. She had to slave away for her father, and when he was in his cups, well, he treated her like a whore to satisfy himself. And from that it was a short step to selling her body to those who would pay for her. All the men here knew it. Some argued with him, saying it was a disgrace that a father should treat his child in such a manner, but if they pushed the matter too far, he would resort to blows. People were all scared of him. Then, there were others, who were prepared to benefit.'

'How so?'

She stared at the cup in her hand. 'He wanted money for his ales. When he had none, he sold what he could. He sold his daughter to any who would pay.'

'He was very violent?'

She gave a short laugh. 'Violent? He would fight with anyone. His fists were the most used in the whole of Middlesex.'

'So many would have wished to hurt him?'

'What do you think?'

I considered. 'Would his daughter, Jen, have sought to defend herself?'

'Never. She was always timid and obedient to him. Away from him, she was clever and witty, but when he was about, she grew quiet and submissive. And then she met a boy who changed things.'

'Who?'

'He was a fellow called Hal, from a farm down near the river. A big, strapping fellow, who was not the brightest, perhaps, but he adored her from the first moment he saw her when he came through the village to London. Saul found them together, and swore he'd kill Hal if he found him on his land again. I think he feared that his little girl would be taken away from him. And she would have been, too, if Hal had been given a chance. But, of course, Jen wouldn't go against her father's instruction, so Hal went away again.' She shrugged. 'And then all this happened.'

'What of Peter? You told Sir Richard that his brother was an honourable man, but some say he was a womanizer and lecher.'

She gave me a very direct look. 'He was honourable, in his own way. I did not lie to the Coroner. But he told me that he was the priest's brother, so I sought to save his feelings and perhaps did not tell all the truth.'

'Which was?'

'He tried to be familiar with all the women of the parish.'

'Do you think he could have been enjoying an affair with Jen, the miller's daughter?'

'If he had paid Saul the miller, yes, of course. He only ever wanted the price of his next drinks. I doubt any man could have rejected her,' she added, sadly staring into the fire's flames. 'But this is not the sourness of an older woman. I can look at a woman like her and understand why men would find her appealing. I am only sad to think that such a fresh, young thing could be so sorely mistreated. Selling her to any man . . . I am sorry that her father died so quickly. He should have suffered more.'

'I was told Peter tried to get into your bed, too.'

'Were you? My, tongues do wag in this village. Yes, he once tried it on with me. He wanted to assault me in the church, but I made it clear to him that I was no foolish peasant woman who had no understanding, and if he tried such a thing again, he would discover that a woman's fist could be as painful as any man's, when directed at his . . . well, you take my point.'

'Yes, indeed. But you don't think he tried it on with Jen?'

'Oh, I'm sure he did. But she would not have accepted him, and unless he paid, her father would not have allowed him. So he would have gone to seek fresher pastures that were more readily available to him.'

'Where? Would he have attempted any other women?'

She smiled. 'I very much doubt he got anywhere. Yes, he would have tried, but we are a small village, and all the women know each other well. I wouldn't let him near me, and I doubt many others would have either. No, I think he died a frustrated man.'

'But you didn't talk about that with the Coroner?'

'No, of course not! He would be upset, no doubt.'

'But you didn't tell him anything before he mentioned he was brother to Peter?'

She laughed. 'We all knew they were brothers! You could see it by looking at them, but we had all been told before. Peter let everyone know his brother was a Coroner; he threatened us with Sir Richard if we didn't do as he wanted.'

I saw Humfrie as soon as I returned to the inn. He could only have had two hours of sleep, and yet he looked the same as he did after eight. Which was not, perhaps, to his credit. He had that leathery sort of flesh that looks slightly grey no matter what the light illuminating it.

Sir Richard was in the chamber, chasing egg yolk about a platter with a thick haunch of bread. He looked up as I entered. 'Have ye met this fellow? Calls himself Humfrie, but has a good brain in his head.'

'Really?'

Humfrie cast a look at me. He appeared to have been chatting with the Coroner. Personally, if I had been a professional assassin, as I was supposed to be and as he was, I would have avoided talking to a man who was so deeply involved in the law as the Coroner.

'I think you have some work to be getting on with?' I said to Humfrie coolly.

'There's no hurry.'

I bit back the comment about the valuable box that sprang to my lips, but glared at him.

'Where have you been this morning?' Sir Richard asked when he had finished his eggs. He set his platter aside and gazed at me.

'I went to talk to Sarah.'

'Oh, and what did she have to say?'

'Only that your brother did indeed have an unsavoury reputation and had attempted to have his way with her.'

'Even though she told me . . .'

'She was trying to protect your feelings. She thought you would be hurt if she told you that your brother, whom you had just lost, was less Godly in his behaviour than he might have been. And apparently he used to tell people that you were a Coroner. She knew you were his brother before you came here.'

'The woman could be lying now.'

'She could, but why would she? What she did say was that the miller's daughter had a friend. A strong man called Hal, who farmed down near the Thames. He came through here, saw Jen, and the two became lovers, so Sarah believed. The miller wanted nothing of that because he wanted his daughter all to himself, so he threatened the youth to leave. Perhaps this Hal came back, killed the miller, and eloped with the girl?'

'Would she have agreed to elope with a fellow who had killed her father?' Sir Richard said.

'If her father was anything like . . .' I had been going to say 'my father', but it didn't strike me as the moment to share that. 'Like the rumours suggest, I would think that it would be highly likely that she would be grateful to run away with someone who had killed him.'

'It would fit the circumstances,' Sir Richard mused.

'Except for the fact of your brother's death,' Humfrie said.

'Oh, aye. It doesn't explain his murder.'

'Nor the interesting fact that she was seen in the roadway about here with blood all over her,' I said.

'She may well have been covered in gore when her father died,' Sir Richard mused.

Humfrie shook his head. 'The body found on the road was Father Peter, not her father. Her appearance here seems surprising. Master Jack told me that he felt your brother was lying in bed with the miller's daughter when her father found them and killed Peter. He carried the body to the road to drop it off – why did his daughter join him? Then, when they returned to the mill, she stabbed him. Or her friend did.'

'Hal,' I said helpfully.

'Yes. So he killed the miller and buried the body, and then he and this Jen fled the village.'

'They probably made their way to London. They could make money there, selling her body. A new wench will always be able to make some money in London,' I said.

And it was then, as my thoughts turned back to darling Cat, that I felt my smile leave my face. Cat, the slim little temptress, the whore who looked so anxious, and who was so keen to hear more about the murder of Peter, who spoke to me and the Coroner about the matter, who had a large, hulking man with her, who was apparently so jealous of his waggle-tailed woman that he would knock on the door and break a man's head just for sleeping with her. A slim little woman, who had a slight accent, who was experimenting with a new life in London, although she seemed experienced in so

many ways. And Alice Pendle had said she was new to the
city.

I knew them as Cat and Henry – but since they knew me
as Peter, that was a fair exchange. They needed money and
had tried to rob me to get it. Cat and Henry – were they Jen
and Hal?

'What is it, man? You look like a constipated goat!' Sir
Richard said unhelpfully.

I stared at him. I did not want to tell him that he had enjoyed
a meal with the woman we were hunting for. Besides, there
was a more urgent task now. Humfrie had to find the box from
the church.

'Nothing, Sir Richard, but I want to go to Mass, and I know
my friend Humfrie will also want to come.'

'Aye, I'll join you both. May be interesting to see how the
folks all behave.'

In the church there was an overwhelming odour of incense
that all but had me choking as we entered.

There can be few more difficult situations than standing in
a church, trying to behave respectfully as a man should on
entering, only to inhale a thick fume and be overwhelmed by
a fit of coughing that almost had me on the floor. I was standing
at the front with Humfrie, when the wafts from the censer
caught in my throat. Several horrified stares pinned me to the
spot, with the people obviously assuming that I was suffering
from some sort of possession. I saw a child pointing at me
with a kind of fascinated horror, as though expecting me to
roll about on the floor and begin spewing frogs or snakes, or
some other superstitious nonsense.

Luckily, the spasms left me, and I could continue with the
service without disrupting matters further.

The sexton, Roger, was officiating in the absence of either
the priest or the local sexton. He gave me a condemnatory
glare until I had fully recovered, and then proceeded to sing
the strange words that seemed alien to me now after so many
years of hearing English spoken. There was a strange mixture
of reactions in the congregation. I saw Harknet had set
himself up as the arbiter of good behaviour, and was standing

up at the front, while Sarah was also there, but in her case nearer the back. Gazing about me, I saw no sign of Dick Atwood, but I did see Nyck, although Dorothy was plainly keeping the inn open. No doubt she would come to the next service, bringing her brood with her.

Her story was still confusing. She had been so convinced and convincing when she had spoken of seeing a man dressed as a priest and then falling over her dead husband. But her story was not convincing, of course, since her husband had been long dead by then. Which is why I had immediately thought of Dick Atwood and accused him of dressing in the priest's clothes, not that the devil had admitted to doing so. He had rather slavishly refused to comment, in fact.

But that itself was strange, I realized. Atwood rarely worried about confessing to acts that might be illegal or immoral, but this time he had not. I would usually have expected him to shrug his shoulders and admit what he had done, when found out, with a little smile of self-effacing humour. But when I accused him of dressing like a priest to disconcert Dorothy and her boys, he had not made any comment, other than to say it was interesting and that he had no idea what I was talking about. That itself was unlike him.

Of course, he must have been the man dressed as Peter. Who else could it have been? Dorothy had seen a man looking like her husband, and . . .

But wait! She said she had seen a man, someone looking like a priest. But what if she had been lying? She knew her oldest son was bitter about the family's situation. The boy had a violent temper when he was drunk, as he had proved when he punched her. Perhaps . . . Suddenly my mind raced: what if she believed her boy could have murdered Peter in order to avenge his family for his father's desertion? Could the lad have murdered Peter at the mill and then brought him all the way up here? More to the point, could Dorothy have believed that he might have done?

One boy would have found it difficult to move the man so far, but two boys, perhaps, could have dragged him or carried him . . . But no. Peter was too big even for Dorothy's two oldest boys.

I turned to stare at the door to the church. She was back there at the inn. I would have to ask her.

The censer swung and more fumes billowed like clouds on a windy day. I could feel a tickle at the back of my throat, tried to clear it, but instead got a lungful of thick, scented fog. I felt my eyes start almost from my head, and then, spluttering and wheezing, I had to escape the place, Humfrie at my side.

'Are you quite well?' he demanded.

'I just breathed in too much of the incense.'

He nodded, but there was a touch of suspicion in his eye, I thought.

'You stay here and see if you can work out where the box might lie,' I said. 'I need to speak to Dorothy again.'

'Why?'

'I reckon she believes the murderer might have been one of her boys. If she realizes it couldn't be them, she may be more helpful.'

Dorothy was sweeping the inn when I arrived.

'Mistress, please, could you speak with me for a little?'

Her eyes went cold, as if shutters had been dropped over her soul. 'If you think I am available, you had best leave the inn this minute!'

'No, Dorothy! It's the murder. You never saw another man there, did you? You believed it was your son who killed Peter, so you invented the figure you saw. You wanted to blame someone else – anyone – didn't you?'

'No, not at all!'

'Dorothy, it couldn't have been one of your children! Believe me! It was someone else.'

'Well, of course,' she said, looking somewhat flustered.

'Whoever killed Peter was a big man, strong enough to haul his body up there to the road. Your boys aren't big enough to have carried him all the way from the mill. Not even Walt and Ed together, likely enough. What would they have been doing at the mill, in any case?'

'Do you swear to me that you don't think they had a part in this?'

'Yes, I swear it on the Gospels. I truly do not think them capable of it. But I think you feared for them because you are a mother. And I think you saw something that made you believe others could suspect your son.'

'It was less that than the fact that all know Ed has a dreadful temper when he has been drinking, and he had been that evening.'

'Where is he?'

In answer, Dorothy called to the lad. He had been in the parlour and was sleepy when he appeared, rubbing his eyes. When he caught sight of me, his expression darkened. 'What, has he insulted you, mother?'

'No. Just come here and tell him what you told me.'

'You said you wouldn't tell anyone.'

'And now I have. This man is trying to help, I think.'

He looked up at me. His mother recognized the decency in my clear features, but her whelp was of a less forgiving nature, it was clear.

'Tell me what you saw,' I said. 'Because it is just possible that your life could be in danger, otherwise. After all, if you saw something, and the real murderer realizes, it is likely that he'll try to kill you to silence you forever. Once a man has murdered once, a second and third killing are no difficulty.'

Ed glanced at his mother. 'Which is why I said not to talk of it,' he said accusingly.

'Now she has, what will you do? Punch her again or start speaking the truth?' I demanded.

He sulked a bit at that, but then started to tell what he had seen.

I won't give his words verbatim. He rambled, and there were many expostulations of his innocence and the cruelty and unfairness of life towards him and his family, but, in essence, his evidence was this: he had been angry with his father and had a loud rancorous argument with him in the street, as Harknet had mentioned, I now recalled. His mother had heard them shouting at each other, and heard Ed saying that he would have his revenge on his father for deserting them. That evening, he had seen his father and followed him

down to the mill. He had been going to attack his father, but
then he saw someone else in the woods who was obviously
stalking his father.

'Did you recognize him?' I asked.

'No. He was in among the trees. But he was a big man.
Beefy.'

That could be almost anyone. 'Then?'

'My father went into the mill, and I heard voices. I
stalked the mill, creeping quietly, and it took me some while.
And then, when I was almost at the door, I heard a scream
and a shout.'

'What about the man following him?'

'I didn't see where he went, but I don't think he was there
in the woods. He must have left.'

'Or gone inside the mill as well,' I said. It could have been
the miller, or perhaps Jen's boyfriend Hal. Or someone else
entirely.

'I suppose.'

'There was no means for you to recognize him, though?'

'No.'

'What were you doing there, Ed? Did you hope to see your
father with Jen? Was that it?'

'I don't know,' he muttered, and suddenly all pretence of
adulthood left him. He had his arms wrapped about his
breast, and he looked over at Dorothy imploringly, twisting
his torso this way and that. 'I just thought if I saw him with
her, I'd be able to forget him, you know? If I saw he was
betraying Mother, and us, then I could leave him and we
could all go and find a new life without him. It was just . . .
I don't know.'

'You didn't have a weapon? You didn't mean to steal up on
him and stab him?'

He shook his head. 'My own father? What do you think
I am?'

'So what happened?'

'The door burst open, and I saw her: Jen, all covered in
blood, wailing and moaning, and wild, like a mad woman!
She pelted up from the mill, straight past me, and stood panting.
Then she ran back and stopped yards from the door, before

running back towards me again. I slipped behind a tree, and she went on past. She looked so scared, so horrified . . . It made me feel the same.'

'What time was this?'

'The middle hours of the night.'

'What did she do?'

'She ran past me, up to the road. I know that Ben saw her up there; I tried to tell him it was just a dream, but he didn't believe me.'

'No one chased after her?'

'I didn't see anyone. I waited there a while, and whoever it was in the woods didn't come back, not that I saw, anyway. So I followed Jen back towards the village. I didn't see her. I came back here and shut myself inside. I didn't want to see her again. All that blood!'

'She didn't scream or cry out that you heard?'

'No, just moaned and groaned like someone with a real bad fever.'

When I saw Humfrie, I told him I was going to return to London. I was convinced that Jen and her Hal were Cat and Henry. It was the merest chance that I had happened upon them, of course, but chance was a wonderful thing on occasion.

Humfrie and I set off as soon as we could, and we were in London again by the middle of the afternoon. We left the ponies at a stable and made our way through the streets to Ludgate, searching for Cat and Henry. It took some little while, but I returned to those taverns where I had seen her before, and at the Blue Bear I felt lucky. I sat in the dark, while Humfrie sat at a table with a clear view of the people entering, kicking my shin whenever a likely looking woman walked in.

It was the fourth woman, just as I was beginning to develop a painful bruise, which proved to be her.

I rose and walked to her, while Humfrie moved to the door to prevent a sudden escape.

'Hello, Jen,' I said.

Her head shot to me, and instantly her eyes were shaded with fear. She was about to try to bolt, but I stood foursquare before her, blocking her path, and Humfrie stood behind her when she turned in that direction. In the end, she had to accept that she had no choice, and when I saw the urgent desire to fly turn to resignation, I sat beside her.

'It must have been horrible, seeing what Hal had done, Jen,' I said.

'How did you learn my real name?'

'It wasn't difficult to work out. After all, you and Hal have a certain skill at getting money, don't you?'

'Did you take it back?'

'Of course. You didn't think you could get away with robbing me, did you?'

'We didn't think you'd realize it was us.'

'My head is still sore after his punch.'

She grinned weakly. 'Didn't I make up for that?'

'You're good, but not *that* good,' I said. A serving wench passed, and I asked for a jug of wine and three cups, beckoning Humfrie to join us. 'I know it all, I think, maid. Your father forced you into his bed, sold you to other men for their pleasure—'

'It was horrible!' she said, shuddering, looking away from us and staring down at the floor. 'I knew it was wrong, but what could I do? I would have run away, but in the end I went to our new priest. I thought he would be able to help me. Except he had other ideas. A few days ago he appeared and paid my father to sleep with me. It was horrible. I knew then what men thought of me.'

I almost put a hand to her shoulder, to show her that I didn't think of her like that. I thought it might help me later, but memories of Dorothy's response when I had attempted to show her sympathy stayed my hand.

'And then Hal came,' she said with a quiet smile.

'You fell in love with him and he with you, and you both began to plan how to save you from your father.'

'We didn't even think of that, no. It was just good to be with him. We were not careful, though. We were outside once, and Harknet came down the lane and saw us, I think, but we didn't care. We love each other.'

'Which is why he hit me so hard when you were in my bed,' I said ruefully.

'I was really shocked to see you after he hit you,' she said, but there was a chuckle in her throat.

'But your father sold you one last time, and Hal couldn't bear to see you with another man, so he lashed out and killed Peter. And then your father saw what you had done, and Hal killed him too, and you . . .'

Her face had fallen. 'What? What do you mean? My father was killed? He's dead? No!'

'You pretend you didn't know he had died?'

'I . . . he can't be dead! That's not what happened!'

'Then what did happen?'

'Father told me I had to sleep with Father Peter when he asked. Father Peter didn't say anything, but his eyes told me if I didn't sleep with him . . . I told him in confidence, but then I saw. If I didn't do as he wanted, Father Peter would tell Father that I'd confessed and accused him of incest, that he took me every night in his bed. I knew what father would do to me if he heard that. Father Peter knew too. I had no choice,' she added, her voice so quiet that I could barely hear her. 'That last night, Father Peter appeared late in the evening while Father was away. He demanded me. I think he had been drinking. He scared me. I let him do what he wanted.' She lifted a hand to her eyes and wiped away the tears angrily. 'I had to go to the privy later, and when I got back, he had been stabbed. There was blood everywhere! I've never seen anything like it. I knew Hal was in the village. He had been to London and was staying overnight in the stables, so I went to him. He came back with me. To hide what had happened, we dressed Peter and took him up to the road, to make it look like he had been attacked by some outlaws. Hal stabbed him. Again, and again, and . . . It was horrible, but it made sense to make it look like a real attack.'

'What of your father?'

'He had been in London that day and must have come back early. I don't know when. I found the pony and cart when I was packing my things, but I didn't find Father. I

thought he was up at the inn, and hadn't bothered to say he
was back. He often did that. He would go up to London
and when he came back he'd spend all the money on ale or
cider. When I saw the pony, it made sense to take it and
make our way to the city. We just decided to get away, to
come to London. We knew I could make money on my back,
even if Hal didn't like the thought. And we thought, maybe
we could gull fools into my bed and threaten them with
exposure or worse, for money.'

'Fools?'

She had the grace to look apologetic. 'I am sorry. You looked
such an easy mark. I didn't want to hurt you.'

Well, it was hurtful, but I consoled myself with the thought
that she had at least wanted to come back and stay with me.
Even though that was to find out how to get hold of my money,
of course, so not terribly consoling.

'So you say that you were not in the mill when your father
was killed?'

'I don't know,' she said, holding her hands out in a
gesture of openness. 'I don't know when he was killed. Who
killed him?'

'We should take them to the Coroner,' Humfrie said.

'Is there any point?' I said. 'They know little enough.'

She was looking at me with the expression of an orphan in
the snow who spies a warm fire. 'I've told you all I know,'
she said.

'See?' I said.

'The Coroner will want to speak to her,' Humfrie said
flatly.

'Is there any point reopening the matter?' I said. 'The
Coroner wants to know who killed his brother, but does that
mean Jen needs to go and admit to all the sorry details?'

Humfrie looked at me and let out a long-suffering sigh.
'Her evidence could be useful to help find the murderer.'

'How? Her father returned while she was elsewhere. Peter
was there, but died while she was in the privy. She found the
body of the priest, but someone else took it up to the road,
and someone else killed her father.'

'So she says. He will still want to question her.'

'Well, if he does, he can find her and ask her,' I said. 'And now, maid, I suggest you come back with me. Although I am afraid that my strongbox has been moved to a safer place, so there is no need to try to knock me on the head to rob me. Besides, Humfrie here will be guarding me all night. Won't you, Humfrie?'

He gave me a bleak look.

That night was one of those dark ones in which the fumes of a thousand coal fires gave a yellowish tinge to the fog. The fog was thick, and swirled about us as we walked, and I felt my cough begin to return. At least before it had been the swirling patterns of incense. These thick London fogs are different. They're unpleasant at the best of times. The smoke catches at the back of the throat, and the eyes grow sore from the whirling mists. In fact, there was so little vision that at one point I realized we had taken the wrong turning. I was about to mention it to Humfrie, but when I turned, I couldn't see him either. The London air really can be awful.

I linked my arm more closely with Jen's – for now I had to grow accustomed to calling her Jen – and was about to stride onwards when a figure appeared before us, a figure with an expression of affronted surprise on his face. I was about to dart back, but realized that it was only some statuary. I recognized the statue, but was not certain of the location. I knew I had passed this place before now, but for the life of me I could not place it on the map I held in my head.

And then there was a second figure. Perhaps this one would be more familiar, I thought, and stepped forward to view it, only realizing when I was already too close that this one had a horrible familiarity.

''Allo, Peter,' said Arch.

I bleated something and turned to flee, but there behind me was Hamon. But this was not the usual surly, grimly cynical Hamon I had grown to dislike. This was a new, obstreperous Hamon, who clearly had a desire to treat me to an extensive testing with his snippers.

''Amon wants a word with you,' Arch said.

*   *   *

They took us back along the road, then up a side alley, and suddenly I knew where I was. This was the way to the back of my house. At the little gate that led through the wall to my yard, we were pushed through, stumbling over the lip of the doorway, and forced to stand in the cold while swirls of thick smoke coiled about us.

'You hit me,' Hamon said. He pulled the gate closed behind him and began to move menacingly in my direction. 'You're going to regret it.'

I was sure he was right. In fact, I already did. His face was twisted into the sort of grimace worn by a demon who had just stabbed his own foot with his trident.

'How about I . . .'

'And you don't 'ave the money to repay your debt, do you?' Arch said. 'That means you're goin' to be taught why it's not a good idea to take my money under false pretences. Know what that means?'

'Yes.'

'It means you're pretending to be someone you ain't. It means pretending you 'ave money, when you ain't!'

'Well, you won't get a penny if you hurt me,' I said. Jen was with me, and I was tempted to pull her in front of me, but she slipped behind me, and while I tried to grab at her, my hands flailed. I dared not take my eyes off Hamon. He was grinning evilly, and as I watched, his hands went to his belt. His left hand pulled his dagger, while his right reappeared with his snippers. He clenched his fist, and I heard that horrible slithering of steel as the blades slid over each other. It made my bowels turn to water, and I was about to fall to my knees to plead, desperately thinking about anything I could offer, making little moaning noises as I watched the weapons approaching, when something made me lift my chin. A new courage had stiffened my spine. I stood straighter and took a step towards him, and even Hamon hesitated at the sight.

Now, this will sound like lunatic bravado, I know. If you have read my past chronicles, you will know that I tend to avoid displays of courage. In my experience, courage is vastly overrated. Personally, I prefer a show of simple terror. It tends to create a more substantial atmosphere, I find, in which I can speedily effect an escape at the first opportunity.

However, there was one thing here that gave me to consider that bluster might be useful. It was the fact that I had observed the wicket gate opening behind the two. As I watched, Humfrie stepped in. He had a hand in his tunic. Now he withdrew it, and I saw that he clutched a light string. There are times when a man's confidence in his fellow being is forced to accept that it has been dealt a blow. I would have remonstrated with Humfrie, had Hamon not already approached painfully close to me. But now I saw Humfrie whirl the cord about his head twice and then snap it forward. As I watched, it wrapped itself about Hamon's throat, and Humfrie pulled hard. The cord tightened, and Hamon dropped both weapons, scrabbling with his fingers where it had sunk into his flesh.

It happened so quickly that Hamon can have known little about his danger. If he had thought, it would have been the work of a moment to slice the string with his snippers or dagger, but before he could register what, or who, had caught him by the throat, the devilish string was constricted and Hamon off balance. As it bit deeper into his throat, his face became suffused, swollen, and he fell backwards, his fingers tearing bloody trails in his flesh as he tried to obtain some purchase on it. He was slowly strangling as Humfrie kept a careful tension on the cord.

Meanwhile, Arch had realized his own danger. Of course, he could have run to Hamon and cut the cord, but the sight of Humfrie's face as he relentlessly tightened his cord was enough to dissuade me from going nearer. Plainly, Arch felt the same, especially as Hamon's movements grew slower and more strained as he succumbed. His face was growing purple, and his imminent demise lent a certain logic to Arch's next manoeuvre. Ignoring the fate of his companion, he darted to the wicket gate and threw it open. In an instant, he was through it. I began to move to give chase, but before I could, he returned – this time flying horizontally like a bullet from a gun. I winced to see how he landed on the packed earth. I could hear the thud over Hamon's choking.

A moment later, a grim-faced Henry – or, I should say, Hal
– appeared in the doorway. He looked as though he wanted
to perform a clog dance on Arch's face, but as he entered
and pulled the wicket closed behind him, Arch stood again,
dusting himself down, grimacing as he brushed his left side
in a way that made me feel positively cheerful. With luck,
I thought, he might have broken a rib or two. I have heard
that they are very painful. The thought was enough to make
my smile widen.

'Oh, Arch. Have you met my friends?' I enquired. As I
was passing Hamon, who lay struggling on the ground like
an upside-down beetle, I kicked him as hard as I could in
the cods. A sort of strangled, hissing gasp was all the sound
he could make just then, but already Humfrie was moving
to him, wrapping the string neatly about his hand as he went.
When he reached Hamon, whose face was now blackening,
he quickly whirled his hand about the injured man's head,
unwrapping the cord from his throat. Hamon gasped, his
body clenching like a fist as he drew in his first painful
breath, his hands at his throat, head moving so that his chin
was on his breast.

Humfrie replaced the cord in his pocket, withdrawing a
lead-filled leather cosh at the same time. He paused, eyeing
Hamon like a saint viewing an unrepentant sinner, and then
tapped it against his head, just above the ear. Hamon stared
up at Humfrie, and then his eyes crossed and rolled up to
become hidden, even as his head fell backwards to the ground.
He wore a rather fetching, foolish smile on his lips. He snored
too, although more quietly than Sir Richard.

I walked to his friend, Humfrie at my side.

'Arch,' I said, 'I don't seem to be able to get this through
to you, but I am not repaying silly amounts of money to
someone who is trying to extort it from me. You decided
to attempt to rob me. It won't happen. More to the point,
if you try anything like it again, you will die. I hope you
understand me.'

'You wouldn't dare,' Arch sneered.

Humfrie's hand seemed to blur, and Arch collapsed on
the cobbles, wheezing like an ancient peasant climbing a

hill. He was clutching his middle with both hands, head bowed.

'I won't say it again, Arch. I have friends who will make very short work of you. Go and find another lamb to fleece. Try pestering me again and I'll have no option but to make your life short and painful.'

I was rather proud of my imposing tone as I said this. It made me feel sophisticated and lordly. I took Jen's arm, walking to my back door. There, I turned.

'Hal, please join us for wine, but before you do, would you mind throwing those two into the road, please? No need to be gentle.'

My parlour felt a warmer, cosier place when we were all seated. Hal was toying with Hamon's dagger and snippers. I confess that I was glad to see that they were in his care, rather than Hamon's. In my mind, I could envisage walking along a quiet alleyway in the dark and hearing those devilish blades sweeping against each other. It was a mistake, I thought, to let Hamon and Arch live, but there were as many problems with killing them there, in my yard, as there would be with any other course, as Humfrie said.

Raphe was not there – he was still at Humfrie's home with the contents of my strongbox. I had sent him there as soon as we had recovered my purses, and once I had changed the locks to my secure room and procured a new strongbox, I would have them returned. Meanwhile, I busied myself in fetching cups and flagons of wine for my guests. Jen helped, and it was delightful to be with her in my little buttery, her hips butting into mine as we drew off wine, her delicious buttocks before me as she bent to gather linen from the box under the table – it was sorely tempting to carry her upstairs for a grappling gallop, but it would not have done. I had experienced Henry's – Hal's – irritation with my earlier enjoyment of her bounties, and just now he had possession of Hamon's weapons. I didn't like the thought of Hal with snippers any more than I liked the thought of Hamon with them.

We were through the third flagon of wine before my nerves

felt fully recovered. Humfrie sat in the corner away from the fire, staring at the flames, while Hal and Jen held hands and stared at each other, occasionally answering my own questions.

'You say you did not know your father was dead?' Humfrie said, after I had thrown a fresh log on the fire.

Hal glanced across at him with a scowl on his face. 'What, you think we're murderers? You think Jen would kill her own father?'

Humfrie said nothing, but stared at Hal with a sort of wonder, as if astonished to hear such foolishness.

It was Jen who answered, 'No. I didn't know he was dead.' She shook her head and lifted her chin boldly. 'But I'm not sorry, either. He was no guardian of mine. Selling me to Peter and others when he wanted money!'

'To whom did he sell you?' I asked. A sudden suspicion tweaked my attention. 'Not the new sexton, Atwood?'

'No. I never saw him. The other one, Roger, he came to me a few times. Father liked him. I suppose he thought it was good to have a priest and a sexton on his side.'

'Roger?' I said. I was surprised. The man had seemed to be devoted to Dorothy, I had thought. But a man who was lusty would make do with any available wench, as I knew.

'Yes. I liked him. He was gentle.'

'I see.'

Except I didn't. I had thought the man so besotted with his master's ex-wife that no one else would suffice for him. Not that it mattered. 'It was unfortunate that your father returned so soon.'

'Yes. I don't know why he came back early. Usually, he would go to the nearest tavern or alehouse when he had finished his business. More often than not, he would just go to the inn and drink till he fell asleep. Nyck always allowed him to stay there. It was easier than fighting with him. Father would get into a horrible temper when he was drunk.'

I felt a sudden interest. 'Was there one particular person with whom he would fight more than others?'

'He was likely to fight with anyone there,' she said. 'A

little while ago, he tried to fight one of the boys living with
Nyck.'

'One of Dorothy's sons, you mean?'

Yes. That was when I realised what had happened.

SEVEN

t took little time to work it all through in my mind, and the next morning, as I jogged along on the road that was growing unpleasantly familiar, I ran through the obvious facts of the case.

As I had thought in the church when I was choked by the censer, Ed had good reason to hate his father, for the hurt given to his mother and the rest of the family. He had a vicious temper, too, as his mother's black eye had proved. Ed was not a child; he was almost as big as a man – and as strong. His mother had made up the story of seeing her husband walking ahead of her on the day she found his body, because when she found her dead husband, she realized that her son must have killed him. Ed went down to the mill and saw Peter in there. He ran over and stabbed his father to death and left him there. Ed couldn't hope to carry his father all the way up the mill's lane and out to the main road, not all on his own.

So he hurried back to the inn, asking for help from Nyck and Dorothy, and they went with him to bring the body up. Only the miller arrived just at the wrong time, and Ed killed him, too.

Yes, it all made sense to me. A shocking matter, for a fellow so young to be so steeped in blood, but that was the way of things. He would soon be turned off in his turn with a hempen halter. A shame, but there you were. Felons could not be tolerated.

Sir Richard was riding casually, his right leg hooked over his horse's withers, chewing on a capon's leg with evident satisfaction. We had called on him to join us as soon as Humfrie and I had decided to make our way back to the inn. I hadn't told Sir Richard what I intended, but he appeared content to enjoy the morning's ride. Sir Richard enjoyed his capon's leg and thigh, and after tossing the bones away, he took a swig from his leather bottle, giving a sigh of contentment as he did so. I could smell the strong wine from where I was, and threw him a contemptuous glance. He smiled at me, casting a look to either side, and then turning to speak to Humfrie, who jogged along quietly behind us.

We clattered into the inn a little after noon, and the smell of pottage and fresh buns reached out on the cool air with welcoming wafts of pure enticement. I salivated at the odours, and I was filled with urgency as I threw the reins to a waiting stable-boy.

Entering the inn, I strode to the bar and rapped loudly. This early, there were only two ancients sitting in the nook near the fireplace, and they cast me the suspicious looks of elderly peasants the world over, their conversation, such as it was, instantly halting.

Nyck appeared in the doorway and rolled his eyes to see Sir Richard, Humfrie and me, as if we were little better than tax collectors. Still, he quickly recovered and nailed a welcoming smile to his face. 'Good morrow, masters. What may I serve you?'

'A pint of sack,' Sir Richard said. Humfrie and I were more moderate in our demands, asking for a quart of ale each. Then we walked to the fire and took our seats at the bench by the wall, ignoring the two ancients. Soon Ed came out with Nyck, carrying two jugs brimming with ale. His master carried a wooden tray with a jug of sack and three cups. Mine was a pottery mug glazed in a revolting brown colour that made it look like a turd, but the ale was welcome, and I sank three cups in quick succession. When Ed made as if to leave, I halted him with a raised hand.

'Master Ed,' Sir Richard said, 'when your father was killed, where were you?'

'I don't know.'

'Don't know? It was only a little more than a week ago. I'm not asking what you were doing when you were still in clouts.'

'I don't know.' He had reddened, and the boy's head stuck forward truculently.

'We shall have to make our own assumptions, then,' I said.

'What does that mean?' Nyck said.

'That we think Ed here might well have walked down the lane to the mill, and there slain his own father,' I said.

The result was, I confess, gratifying.

Ed's mouth fell wide and emitted a soft groan. Nyck gave a half-hearted curse and fell back as though struck on the head, and from the doorway there came a gasp of horror. Even as I glanced in that direction, I saw Dorothy clutch at her breast and fall against the door's frame. Nyck rushed to her, but she was already toppling, and before he could reach her, she had swooned quite away.

Sir Richard strode over and helped Nyck pick her up and carry her to the bench nearer the fire. With Nyck rubbing her face and the heat from the fire, as well as a goodly portion of Sir Richard's sack, she started to stir, and as soon as she could take in all our faces, she clutched at her son and Nyck, and her face was, well, tragic, really. I felt bad having to put her through this.

'No! You can't be serious! He had nothing to do with his father's killing!'

'*You* thought he did, didn't you, Dorothy?' I said. 'That was why you invented seeing your husband walking that morning. You knew that would help throw us off the right path, didn't you? Saying you had seen him would send us off searching for the strange man who looked so alike to your husband. Did you mean to make us think that the verger here was the guilty man?'

She had the grace to look ashamed at that.

'Yes, I realized Atwood was remarkably similar to your husband in build. And persuading us to look elsewhere stopped us looking at your son.'

'Atwood is a foul man. When I went to church, he put his hand . . . where he shouldn't. I wouldn't be surprised if he was the murderer! My son had nothing to do with it!'

'But you thought he did, didn't you?' I said.

'No!' she burst.

Sir Richard was watching this all the while, but then his eyes turned to Ed himself, and thence up to Nyck's face.

The innkeeper nodded slowly. 'There's no point, Dorothy. I'll tell him the truth.'

*   *   *

Nyck's face was pale. He let his head fall, and when he began to speak, it was as if he was talking to the floor.

'He came in here late at night, Miller did. I was out in the back, and he was in a fighty mood, insulting everyone, pushing them around, and then he knocked Ed down. Ed couldn't do anything about it. Look at him – he's only a boy, really. So I told Miller to stop it and leave the boy alone. But instead he came towards me and started shouting. I said to him, he should go. He wasn't welcome in that state of mind. And I said to him, if he came into the bar in that kind of mood again, I'd not serve him and he'd be told he couldn't come in anymore.'

'What did he do?' Sir Richard said.

'He shouted and blustered and complained, and when I thought he was about to hit me, and I was about to run for a club or a knife, he suddenly calmed. He was sulky, but he nodded. I think the idea that he wouldn't be allowed into the place again was enough to make him appreciate how much he liked it here. Eventually, he agreed to go home, and then I started to clear up in here and get the regulars to realize that I had a bed to go to even if they didn't, and I was about empty when he came back again. This time even more drunk, I thought. He was rolling like a wherry in a gale, and I was about to shout at him when he started trotting forward and fell there.' He pointed to the basket of kindling beside the fire. 'I shouted at him, and kicked him, and it was a while before I realized he was dead.'

'That was why the stones under the basket were wet,' I muttered. It made sense. There had been a damp patch on the day I first arrived, and it was because the innkeeper and Dorothy had tried to clean up the blood.

'I didn't know what to do. In the end, all I could think of was removing his body, so I took it down to the mill—'

'How?' Sir Richard demanded.

'Eh?'

'On yer back? In a cart? How?'

'I have a barrow, and I put him in that.'

'Then what?'

'I wheeled him down to the mill, and put him inside.'

Sir Richard shook his head. 'It won't do. In the first place, you're lying about the barrow. You couldn't carry a man his size down that path with all the potholes in the dark. In the second, why did you bury him? In the third, where was Peter all this while? And Jen?'

'She must have left for—'

'So you walked in and stabbed Peter in the back?'

'No!'

'What do you say you did, then?'

'I took him into the mill and put him just inside the doorway.'

'And then?'

'I came back here, washed the stones where he had bled, and tried to put it all from my mind.'

Sir Richard shook his head. 'Who helped you?'

'I did,' Dorothy said before Nyck could argue. 'I heard the clatter as Miller fell down. He knocked over the cooking pot when he fell, and I thought someone was attacking Nyck, so I went down to him, and found him with the miller's body. I thought he had killed the man at first.'

'So you both went to the mill and delivered the miller like a sack of old grains?' Sir Richard's voice was calm, but he still shook his head. 'You expect me to believe that?'

Dorothy shook her head. 'It's the truth. We went down to the mill and left the miller in the room near the door.'

'And someone else accommodatingly went there after you, dragged his body out and buried it.'

'Yes.'

'Jen, his daughter, was there. Yet you say you didn't see her?'

'No.'

'And the body of Peter was there, I suppose. Your husband.'

Dorothy glanced about her at the faces and gradually sat upright. 'Sir, I will swear on the Gospels if you like. I had no idea he was there, but there was a foul smell about the place, like metal. I didn't think at the time, but perhaps it was his blood?'

'That would mean that his daughter was still there.'

I interrupted. 'Or that she had already fled up here to fetch her man, as she told us.'

'But she also denied knowing that her father was dead,' Humfrie said.

'So she had already been to find Hal, had him return to the mill with her, and removed the body of Peter,' I mused. 'But if that was the case, who concealed the miller, and who stabbed him?'

'The same man, I would imagine,' Sir Richard said. 'He was at the mill, he killed Peter, and then made his way to the inn, where he met the miller and stabbed the fellow. When the miller made his way inside, the murderer waited outside to see what happened. Perhaps he thought the miller would survive and name his murderer? And perhaps he would have,' he added thoughtfully. 'No matter. When he saw that the miller was dead, and that his body was being transported to the mill, he went along, too. But for some reason he decided to conceal this second murder. Why?'

'Because he didn't want people to blame someone else?' Humfrie said. 'He could see that the second murder would implicate someone. Perhaps someone dear to him.'

'Who could that be?' I said. I thought they were clutching at straws, personally. This all sounded like mere guesswork. To my surprise all those present gave me a long stare. 'What?'

Humfrie asked if he could have another ale. 'Because, Master Jack, if anyone heard that the miller had been murdered, shortly after he had sold his daughter again, the same daughter he had been molesting and abusing for so many years, the natural guilty party, in everyone's estimation, would be either the daughter or her new swain. Or both. So, if someone adored her – was infatuated with her, perhaps – he would try to protect her, wouldn't he? He would bury the evidence, the body.'

'And afterwards,' Sir Richard said, 'he would be delighted to learn that the Coroner and villagers all believed that the girl had been murdered by her father, and that he had escaped to London. A search would ensue, and the object of his deepest affections would be safe. Quite touchin', really.'

'So who is this murderer, then?' I said.

'The fellow who adored the miller's daughter as much as

Hal,' Humfrie said, and as he did so, the door opened and in walked Atwood.

Atwood glanced about with a half-smile, but I confess that my own mouth gaped. I had not considered that it might be him, but his sudden appearance made it all fit! I knew Atwood of old, of course, and I knew him to be a murderous devil at the best of times, but this surprised even me.

'You loved her?' I burst out, and Atwood raised a languid eyebrow to me.

'I beg your pardon?'

'No,' Humfrie said, and cast a look at me that seemed to mingle confusion and alarm. 'This man is not the murderer.'

'How can you tell?' I said, and then Atwood fixed his full attention on me, and I recalled that my business was not of a nature that would win universal approbation. I glanced at the Coroner and was silent. Atwood nodded approvingly.

'I came in here to warn you that there are two disreputable gentlemen approaching the village,' Atwood said. 'I think you know them as Hamon and Arch, Master Jack.'

''S'wounds,' Sir Richard said. 'What the devil are they doing back here now?'

I said nothing, but I had the feeling I was about to learn very soon. 'Are . . . are they alone?' I asked hopefully.

'No, they have a pretty little cavalcade behind them, with the worst degenerates I have seen in many a long year.'

Sir Richard nodded. 'We are grateful to you for keeping an eye on them, Master Atwood. How many are there?'

'Five, so seven in total.'

I had an idea. 'I could go outside and attack them in flank when they arrive,' I said, thinking quickly. If I were to leave through the back, I could soon be mounted, and I was sure that I could outride Hamon and Arch back to the city. They were no horsemen, if I was any judge.

'No, best that you stay here,' Humfrie said.

'We are more than enough to keep a force of seven at bay. Master Atwood, I think, has some experience of fighting, as do I. And you, of course, Master Jack. Humfrie, you have the look of a man who can hold his own in a fight. Innkeeper, you must have a stout cudgel or two that we could use, I dare say?'

'Of course.'

'There, so we are five against seven. Not bad odds. How far are they, Master Atwood?'

'They will be with us very soon, I fear.'

'Then let us prepare. Ah, a good, strong oaken stave. I thank you, innkeeper. Atwood, you keep an eye on the front of the inn. They will no doubt separate their force with a view to taking us by surprise, but if we pummel those trying to force the front, the others will be easy to subdue in their turn. So, Nyck, if you and Humfrie could guard the rear of the inn, we can take the front. Jack can wait in here. I shall go to the small chamber over there, and when they enter, we can take them front and rear.'

I listened to his plans with the enthusiasm of a boy waiting for the first lash of the cane. The idea of being trapped here, while the ravening hordes of outlaws attempted to break in, just to punish me for refusing to pay their exorbitant demands, was intolerable. For a moment I actually considered trying to force myself between Humfrie and Nyck, but the two fools had effectively blocked my path, and the only other escape that was open to me was the door at which Sir Richard stood, his sword in his hand.

Today all knights and gentlemen of quality were aping the fashions of the continent for fine, sharp rapiers, but I was glad to see that Sir Richard put his faith more in heavy steel. He had drawn his weapon, and now he stood gazing out at the roadway. 'Here they come,' he said, and for once his voice did not make the foundations of the building tremble. He slipped backwards into the chamber where I had spoken to Harknet all those days ago. There, he was all but invisible to anyone entering the inn.

And enter they did, all too soon. Arch came first, pulling off gloves and staring about him. He still wore his smile, but his face held a lunatic blankness. He gave a cry of joy to see me, and slapped his gloves against his hand. 'Didn't I tell you,'Amon, that 'e'd be 'ere? How very pleasant it is to see you again! And now we 'ave a little matter of thirty guineas you owe us.'

Hamon came in behind him and stood staring with detesta-
tion on his face. He pulled out his snippers from his belt. His
voice was strained, and he was forced to swallow as he spoke.
'I've been looking forward to this all the long ride here,' he
said, and I heard that foul swish of blade against blade once
more.

The two entered the bar, and three followed after them.
Hamon looked towards Atwood. 'Get out! You don't want to
be in here.'

Atwood, whom I had expected to begin fighting as soon as
the men entered the room, nodded equably and drained a pot
he had found nearby, before beginning to edge his way around
the group. I was about to call him back, when another sound
was heard. It was that of an oaken cudgel striking a pate with
full force.

Suddenly, from the rear entrance to the inn there came a
wailing and screaming. 'He's broke my 'ead! He's broke my
'ead!' from a man who appeared in the doorway now, a hand
to his brow. Even as I watched dumbfounded, I saw Humfrie.
He lifted both hands and brought them down, gripping a thick
staff. There was a cracking noise, and the man in the doorway
fell to his knees. He looked about the room pleadingly, before
suddenly toppling over sideways.

'Get 'im!' Arch said, pointing at me.

I squeaked with alarm as Hamon reached for me, but before
he could, there was a bellow behind the group, and Sir Richard
launched himself into the fray like a berserker. His pommel
struck one man on the head, whose eyes widened like an owl's,
and then he slid to the floor. Atwood had drawn a knife from
somewhere, thrown a pot of ale into another man's face and
now had the fellow in a firm grasp, one arm about his throat,
his knife at the fellow's throat even as Sir Richard launched
an attack against the third man.

But I had no eyes for them. I was staring at Hamon.

Have you ever seen a man stalk a hare? The creatures will
often sit stock-still, as though they could be missed, but perhaps
it is only that they fear turning away from their hunter. Because
that was how I felt, staring at Hamon. I dared not take my
eyes from him, as though the only thing that prevented him

capturing me and using those damned snippers was the power of my gaze.

And then he was almost on me. I made a squeak that was as ineffectual as a mouse's complaint on feeling the hawk's talons, and I would have run, but there was nowhere to go. In the end, in a futile attempt to warn him off, I grabbed for my dagger.

Now, I don't know how it happened, but I missed the dagger's hilt. I suppose I have never been a terribly enthusiastic knife-fighter. I have seen men, bloody and battered, leaving the ring in London after demonstration bouts, and it never enticed me to attempt the same. Once you have seen one knife fight, with all the gore involved, and heard the cries of the injured, you have seen enough to persuade you not to indulge in such a dangerous activity. That was the case for me, at any rate. So I had never attempted to reach for my knife in any great hurry.

But my hand did find something. A metal grip. I pulled and the thing came free, and as I pointed it at Hamon, I saw his snippers approaching my face. I squealed in anticipation, closed my eyes and thrust forward to defend myself. There was a flash, a roar that deafened my ears, and when I opened my eyes, there was a thick mist, like a sea fog early in the morning at Whitstable. I could hear a shrill call, and when I had blinked a few times and could hear again, I saw that it was Arch, who was hurling imprecations at me. He raised a knife over his head and was about to throw himself on me when Humfrie intervened, and I saw his club strike Arch in the throat. Arch gave a horrible choking gurgle, dropped his knife, and both his hands went to his throat. Humfrie swung again, and the club struck Arch's skull with a dull thud. He went down like a badly filled bag of beans.

At the end of the battle, there was one man unscathed, whom Sir Richard had pinned against the wall, and a second, who begged for mercy, and whom Atwood released with a show of disappointment. Sir Richard set the two to binding their companions, all but for Arch and Hamon. Hamon was in no need of binding. The slug from my pistol had caught him in the breast and found its way out through his back. Ben found it later, and I believe he took it as a souvenir, bits of material from Hamon's coat and shirt, bones and all. Personally, I took one look at it and wanted to throw up. But the youngsters of today are made of sterner stuff. In any case, Hamon was dead. The hole in his breast, the singed material of his shirt and the thick blood that clotted all spoke of the horror of the gun's effect. It was enough to make me want to throw the thing away, but then I hooked it back on my belt and tried to halt the quaking of my hands.

Arch was dead, too. Humfrie's blow had been a little over-enthusiastic, and the cudgel had broken his windpipe. Striking him on the head was a merciful end, for else Arch would have had a slow, strangling death, unable to breathe. I did wonder how much of an accident his blow was, for Humfrie had always been an enormously accurate antagonist, but a quick look at his expression told me this was not a question I needed to ask.

The others were all alive, and the two survivors carried them to the yard behind the inn, where they were seated on a low wall, their hands and ankles bound. They were allies of Arch and Hamon only in so far as they had accepted two shillings each to join the little band. Each had expected a short ride, a swift punishment and then a ride back with coins in their purses. The sudden change in their fortunes had left them bemused, if the blows had not.

When the gang was all bound, Sir Richard demanded that the two helpers should carry the dead bodies to the church. They were reluctant, but with Sir Richard and Atwood walking with them, they acquiesced quickly enough. Having seen the short work made of their companions, they had no wish to incur Sir Richard's wrath. They also appeared to eye me with alarm as I made a show of cleaning my pistol and reloading it. I wound up the mechanism and put the key back in my purse before setting the gun on my belt once more. It was useful work, because the concentration involved stopped my hands from shaking. My expression was probably a little threatening, because the two took one look at me and hurried with their task.

We reached the church in little time. Atwood opened the door, and the two men carried their burdens inside.

Roger was at the font and, on seeing us with the two, he hastily crossed himself and turned to stare back the way we had come. 'I must—'

'No, Roger,' Sir Richard said. 'You have work here.'

'But she is well? Mistress Dorothy?'

'Never better. Now, these two.'

He nodded, but even as he knelt beside the two bodies, muttering his way through the *Viaticum* and the prayers for the dead, it was obvious that his mind was not on the task at hand. When he stood and made the sign of the cross over the two figures, Sir Richard eyed him and said, 'We are in the church, Sexton. I would like you to confess now. It is past time.'

'I don't know what you mean!'

'You know. You went to the mill that evening and, to your disgust, you saw the priest bulling the little maid, Jen. She was a sweet little wench, wasn't she? Sweeter even than Mistress Dorothy, whom you adored. And the same man had abused them both. Peter had deserted Dorothy, and now he was enjoying Jen, the miller's daughter. As soon as she rose from her bed, you went in and stabbed him, didn't you? A hard, cruel blow that pierced him through and through. And then you left him there, thinking it was no better than he deserved.'

'I didn't think that! God help me, I knew it was entirely wrong, but what else could I do? The man was insatiable! He even tried to rape Sarah here in the church! He told her it was an especial prayer, and then he tried . . . but she had been married, and she knew the difference between a prayer and a . . . How many others would he assault, if he wasn't stopped?'

'And then you came back here to try to – what, pray for forgiveness?'

'Yes. But when I had passed the inn, I heard a wailing from the mill, and as I listened, I could hear steps. I had to hide, and I concealed myself in bushes, and poor Jen came flying up the road, her shirt all besmottered with gore, hurrying to the stables. After a little, I saw her appear again, with that boy, Hal, and the two took a cart, rattling down the lane to the mill. Soon they were back, and I saw them ride away on the road to London. They must have brought the body and dropped it off on the road, so that there could be no association with the mill.'

'Why?' I said.

Roger cast me a short look. 'I doubt Hal would like everyone to know that his woman had been sold to men like the priest.'

'What then?' Sir Richard said.

'I was still standing there when that foul-mannered man – the miller – came lurching out. I didn't mean to do anything, but he barged into me, and I was . . . I suppose I was already angry and upset, and when he called me names and insulted my parents, I could only see little Jen and her sweet, kind face screwed up as her father raped her, or sold her to his friends, or . . . I don't know. Something just snapped in my mind, and I stabbed him, just the once, and he turned away and lurched back into the inn.'

'And then?' Sir Richard said.

'I was about to go to the church when I heard a rumbling noise. When I went to the mill's road, I saw Nyck, Dorothy and her oldest boy with a wheelbarrow. They had the miller on it, and it was then that I realized I had killed a second man that night.' He covered his face suddenly, his shoulders moving with silent sobs.

'Continue.'

He pulled his hands away and stared blankly at the cross on the altar. 'I don't know why, but I followed them all the way down that lane to the mill. They lifted the miller's body and quietly set him inside, and then came away in great haste. I hid in among the trees until they were past me, and then I realized that I had placed Jen and Hal in great danger. I couldn't leave them suspected of murder. The idea was intolerable. If anyone was to find the miller's body sitting in his home, people would be bound to assume Jen was guilty. Or Hal. Either way, it was unfair. So I found an old shovel in the mill's shed and dug a shallow grave. I went as deep as I could, but the ground was very difficult, and I am not built for hard labour. And I returned and dragged the miller's body out to the grave and buried him as decently as I could.'

'So you slew my brother and then the miller, too,' Sir Richard said.

'I am sorry, sir. Yes.'

'You have set in train a distressing series of events, and you took away from me my only brother,' Sir Richard said. He sighed heavily and wiped a huge hand over his features. 'Will you sit up with these two and hold vigil for their souls? Will you beg forgiveness for your murders every day?'

'Yes. I must atone.'

'Aye. Mustn't we all,' Sir Richard said. He sounded weary. 'You have work to do, Master Roger. Best get to it.'

'Will you not have him arrested?' Atwood said as we walked from the church.

Sir Richard stared past him, back towards the church. His eyes rose, following the squat tower, and continued up to the sky. 'Have him arrested? I am only a Crowner, when all is said and done. An officer of the law would be better to arrest him. Perhaps a keeper of the King's peace, or a bailiff. But I was forgetting: he's a sexton – he falls under the ecclesiastical law. Which would be best, I wonder? But me? Friends, I came here full of fury and fire, determined to punish the man who killed me brother, but I have learned that Peter was only a man. And one who would take advantage of others. Tryin' it on with a woman like Sarah – that was forgivable. She was of an age to know her own mind, and if she was willin', maybe they could have made a happy enough pair. But accepting Jen, when he knew she wasn't willing, and that she was forced into it by her father – worse, he knew she was keen to escape. She had come here to the church to let him know what her father was doing to her, using her and selling her – she told him in the confessional. He betrayed her trust by going to her father, and compounded that by paying to share her.'

'But Roger killed him. He killed the miller – and your brother!' Atwood protested.

'Aye, and perhaps it was for the best. He stopped me brother from molestin' other women, or pursuin' Jen further. And when he saw that his actions could have dropped Jen or others

into trouble, he sought to defend them. He did what he thought
– what most people would think – was right.'

'A murderer.'

'A homicide, yes. But then I killed today. So did Jack here,
and Humfrie. We are also homicides. We killed to defend
others, and stop worse injustice . . . which is what Roger did,
too. So should we punish him for doin' what we did as well?'

Atwood shook his head, bemused. I confess, I was myself
surprised. I had expected the knight to take a far more rigorous
approach to Roger. I asked him later, and he looked somewhat
shamefaced and muttered something about having killed men
himself, and not being capable of standing in judgement of
others. But then he stared off into the middle distance and
said something which sounded quite deep.

'Ye know, if I had wanted to help me brother, I could have
come and spoken to him, rather than waiting till he was dead.
Perhaps if he had known I was about, that I cared about him,
maybe I would have been able to do more. Perhaps allowed
him to stay with his wife and children, so he could have curbed
his worse instincts and not assaulted Jen and other women in
the area. He died for his assaults on women. Perhaps that is
my fault. My inaction helped ensure his murder. If I'd been
here, if he'd kept Dorothy at his side, perhaps given up the
priesthood, and I'd supported him, maybe he wouldn't be dead
now. So perhaps I helped kill him by doing nothin'. That's a
thought, isn't it?'

EIGHT

We stayed at the village for another day after the little battle at the inn. Dorothy and Nyck seemed wary of us, and when we saw Roger, he averted his gaze as we walked past, as if he expected to be seized at any moment. Sir Richard, for his part, spent his time either telling outrageous stories and drinking or sitting and staring into the middle distance.

Sir Richard finally seemed to shake off his strange mood in the middle of the morning of that day. He rose and strode out. Humfrie and I joined him as he marched up the lane towards the church. Inside, Roger was bent over the two corpses, deep in prayer. Atwood was sweeping the floor, showing more enthusiasm, I noticed, than he had ever displayed while cleaning my house. He looked up as we entered, and leaned on his besom while he studied us. 'Jack, it is good to see you.'

'Is it?' I asked. I was past caring.

Sir Richard scratched at his nose. 'So you haven't found it yet?'

'Found what, Coroner?' he said.

'I know all about the treasure, Master Atwood.'

Atwood glared at me then, as though I had told the knight. 'I am not happy to be forced to share it three ways. This could cost you your share, Jack.'

'I doubt you were content to share it two ways,' I said coldly.

'Jack, you should trust your friends more. I was there all the time, looking after you.'

'You were looking after me?'

'Wherever you went, I was behind you. I didn't want to see you hurt. So once I made it obvious to some fellows that you were investigating Peter's death, I watched your back. On the way to the mill, on the way to Sarah's house, on the way to . . .'

I gaped. 'You told people I was . . . You could have had me killed!'

'No. I was there every step. You were perfectly safe.'

'It doesn't matter,' said Sir Richard. 'It is not going to be shared.'

'You mean it does exist?' I said. I had been growing increasingly doubtful.

'Oh, it exists, certainly,' the knight said.

'You have looked in there?' I said to Atwood, pointing to the box at the wall.

'Of course. That was the first place I looked,' Dick Atwood said sourly. 'It only contains religious clothing, some books, some items for services. Nothing in the way of gold.'

'But do you know what sort of treasure the box contained?' Sir Richard said.

'Treasure is treasure,' Dick said.

'In some ways,' Sir Richard said.

'What does that mean?'

In answer, I nodded to Humfrie. He led the way to the tower's door and showed us the alcove he had discovered, where a box had lain. 'You haven't cleaned this. Look: you can see clearly the outline of a box.'

He was right, the outline was still there.

Dick grew excited. 'You mean this could be the box's size?'

'Yes. But you may not like what you discover,' Sir Richard said.

'I will be happy with my share,' Dick said.

'Come with me,' Sir Richard said.

Sir Richard led us down the path and into the village, and from there, to my surprise, out on the lane towards Sarah's house. All the way the knight spoke in a reflective tone that was so quiet that it only made the nearer trees tremble gently.

'The trouble is, I imagine, a priest arriving here with a box filled with gold – well, a box like that would be an appalling weight, wouldn't it? And a lowly priest sent here from his old parish could not carry much with him. A massy box of treasure would hardly be likely, would it? If it was small enough to carry, it would not be filled with much gold. A man couldn't carry much gold very far. A small amount, perhaps, but not a great trunk load like that chest in the church.'

'So you are saying that because he was a priest, he thought a matter of a few coins would be an enormous treasure? I suppose that is true enough.'

'It is. But many priests would consider some other things to be even more valuable,' Sir Richard said. 'And Peter was very pious, no matter what he did to the female members of his congregation.'

'Not the priests I know,' Dick said. 'They consider gold to be gold. Riches are riches.'

We were at the gate to Sarah's house now and entered her garden. Dick looked about him with disdain. 'Why are we here?'

'Because this woman was one whom Roger trusted,' Sir Richard said. 'And he asked her to look after his treasure.'

Dick Atwood cast a suspicious eye at him on hearing that, but he made no objections as we entered the house.

Sarah was waiting for us. Ben had been despatched with a message before we left the inn to speak with Dick Atwood, and now she stood stirring a pot over the fire. 'Ah, you are already here? That is good.'

'You have the box, mistress?' Sir Richard said, once the usual pleasantries had been exchanged.

'Yes.'

'It was given to you by Roger of Ilford?'

'Yes.'

Dick Atwood's eyes were almost on stalks as she confirmed this. He glanced at me with a wolfish grin. I could tell that he was excited. 'May we see it?'

She gave him a curious look. In it were mingled amusement and some contempt. 'If you wish.'

Walking to the back of the chamber, she reached for a light-coloured box. There were tracks and trails in the wood, and I guessed it was oak. It was the same dimensions as the mark in the church's alcove, but it was no great height, and was not set about with bands of steel as a strongbox would be. I could feel Dick Atwood's confusion mount as she brought it to us, rubbing the lid where some mark had marred the surface.

'Here it is,' she said.

Dick took it from her. A simple hinged hook of metal fitted over a metal button. He slid the hook from the button, and lifted the lid. The inside of the box was beautifully lined in green velvet, and nestling softly on the cloth was a leather-bound book.

'It's a list of all the books that the abbey owned at Ilford,' she said. 'The father abbot was very proud of his library. When his monastery was to be dissolved under the new religion, he felt that it must at some time be reversed.'

'A book?' Dick Atwood said. He looked shattered by the revelation.

'Yes,' Sarah said. 'He caused all the books to be listed carefully, so that when King Henry died, the abbey could acquire all his books once more. So each book is listed, and who took it. He felt that they must all be returned when the abbey was renewed. Of course, the poor man never saw that. He gave it to Peter, and Peter told Roger about it back at Ilford. When Roger came here, he found the box again. After Peter's death, he brought it to me and asked me to look after it, knowing my religion.'

'But . . . there was gold. A great treasure, I was told,' Dick said.

She took it from him again, holding it gently in her hands and smiling at him. Then she replaced the book in the box and closed the lid. 'The abbot felt that this was indeed a great treasure. There is much learning in those books. It's just sad that the abbot did not live long enough to see the Queen on the throne, bringing renewed hope to all of the Catholic faith. In time, with God's grace, the abbey might be rebuilt, and then this will guide the new abbot in his quest for the books that were once his.'

'There's no gold?' Dick Atwood said hollowly.

Sir Richard shrugged. 'King Henry didn't give abbots time to hide all their gold and jewels. He had auditors list everything that was in each abbey's possession, down to the weight of lead on the roofs, so that when he closed the abbey, he had a full inventory. He did the same with all the abbeys and monasteries in the kingdom. There could never be a great treasure hidden from the King. And nothing so vast that a mere country priest could easily carry it from his parish, having kept it concealed for many years, and bring it all the way here, with never a single person noticing his wealth, or being suspicious at the great weight of some of his belongings. Did he come here with four or five chests like a baron on procession? No! He was a priest. He arrived with a pack over his shoulders, and little more.'

Dick's mouth opened, and I was delighted to see that no words came to him. I gazed at him enquiringly, wondering whether anything might emanate, but nothing was said. He cast a look of deep pain at the box containing the ledger, then turned and left.

He looked a broken man. It was a delight to see him so low.

'Would you like a bowl of pottage?' Sarah asked us.

And that was the end of the tale. That afternoon, I left the village of St Botolph's, hoping never to see it again. The sun was trying fitfully to burst out through the clouds that loured overhead, but after we had ridden a scant mile, the rain began.

Humfrie pulled his cowl over his head. 'That was an interesting diversion,' he said.

I said nothing. The horses themselves were walking on with their heads down as though in agreement with my own feelings.

London was a riot of noise when we arrived. I had not noticed in recent months just how raucous the people were. Sellers of all wares bellowing their offerings, trying to outdo those nearest, and the whores trying to hide from the pelting rain by standing in doorways and offering themselves to passers-by. I don't know why they bothered. They would have no trade on a day like that. They would be better off sitting before a fire and offering themselves to the drinkers in a tavern.

There was one standing in my own doorway, when we had left the horses at the stables and walked the short distance to my house. I sent her off with a threat to call a bailiff, and she scampered away with a curse hurled over her shoulder at me. But then I opened my door, to be accosted by a monster.

I had stepped inside and was pulling off my gloves when the beast launched itself at me. I gave a cry and stumbled backwards, but my foot caught on something, and I was sent over. Instantly, the brute was at my throat, so I thought, yelping and making an unholy row. I had to fend it away with my arms and try to slap it with my gloves, but that seemed only to send it into further paroxysms of viciousness.

After many long minutes, I heard Raphe hurtle down the corridor. I could hear Humfrie laughing uproariously at my undignified entrance, and then Raphe had his 'Hector' by the scruff and pulled him away, wriggling and panting. I climbed to my feet and was incapable of speech, wiping the slobber from my face and throat.

'He likes you, master,' Raphe said hopefully.

'The vile brute tried to bite my throat! He attempted to savage me!'

'Nay,' Humfrie said, trying to control his own amusement. 'He was welcoming you to your home.'

'Well, I can live without his welcomes!' I said. 'Keep the thing away from me, or I'll have it thrown from the house!'

But as I looked at it, the monster did seem to be struggling to get to me less for reasons of aggressiveness and more for an opportunity to demonstrate his affection. Perhaps he would be a companion; my needs of a guard were lessened now that Arch and Hamon were gone.

I walked through to my hall and pulled off my dripping cloak and hat, telling Raphe to bring wine and spices so Humfrie and I could share a pot or two of something warming. Humfrie sat on a bench near the fire, which, fortunately, Raphe had not forgotten to light that morning, and I took my seat. When Raphe came in, so did Hector, but this time, when he tried to climb into my lap, Raphe gave a loud 'No!' and the creature subsided, casting a wary look up at him. He did appear to be able to learn obedience, then.

We left the jug beside the fire with the spices in it.

'I thought Atwood would faint away when he saw what his vaunted "treasure" was,' I chuckled.

'He was barely able to walk,' Humfrie said with a smile.

'Do you think Sir Richard really will contrive to leave Roger without seeing him captured?'

'I think Sir Richard is an interesting man who is learning

to consider his own actions carefully,' Humfrie said with quiet contemplation. 'I believe he will try to support Dorothy and her children more.'

The knight had said as much as we parted. He wanted to ensure that the children and Dorothy were helped. Perhaps, he thought, he could arrange for apprenticeships for the older boys, and perhaps some service for Ben. However, Dorothy would have her own say in such matters, it was plain. And Nyck had done much to ease her life and protect her and her children, so it was reasonable to think that he would continue to have a role in their futures.

'What of Jen and Hal?' he said. 'Will you be seeing them again?'

I shivered. 'When the pair of them robbed me of everything? If I never see them again, I will be content. I hope that the mutt there will be able to warn us of any attempt to rob me again, but I am not hopeful.'

'Still, at least you are free of Arch and Hamon,' he said.

'Yes. I wonder what will happen to all those who owe them money?'

'They will be free of Arch and Hamon's greed.'

'But they used to wait near the gambling dens and offer men money so they could return to gamble some more.'

'No doubt someone will take over that business.'

I guessed what he meant. 'You?'

'Someone must see to their customers, I suppose.'

'So you will take on their system of loans?'

'Not in the same manner, no. But if someone wants a short-term loan, and I think they are a secure person to lend money to, I suppose perhaps it would make sense to offer them terms. But no one works for nothing, obviously.' He held out his hand, and I realized he wanted his money.

'Oh, yes, of course,' I said. 'I owe you for the days you were working with me. That will be—'

To my surprise, he held up his hand to silence me. 'No. Two guineas.'

'That was if you were to stay with me for two weeks!'

'No, Master Jack, it was for the removal of two felons trying to rob or kill you.'

'Well, you didn't!'

He shrugged. 'I had to fight three. I slew one. You managed to kill another, but that was an accident. I think that is fair effort for so little reward.'

'But two guineas is a fortune!'

'Think how you would feel if those snippers had come closer to your nose or your ballocks.'

'This is robbery!'

'No, it is an investment. After all, you wouldn't want an assassin to be disappointed in you.'

There was an edge to his voice. Suddenly, I realized that he was quite right. I wouldn't want him to be upset by me.

I paid him.